"Wit, murder, and ~~~~~~~~~~~~~~~~ **a.
I LOVE THIS NEW** ~~~~~~~~~~~~~~~~~~~~~~~ **."**
—Nancy Pick~~~~~~~~~~~~~~~~~~

Murder Between the Covers

"Wry sense of humor, appealing, realistic characters, and a briskly moving plot."　　　　　—*South Florida Sun-Sentinel*

Shop till You Drop

"Elaine Viets has come up with all the ingredients for an irresistible mystery. . . . I'm looking forward to the next installment in her new Dead-End Job series."
—Jane Heller, national bestselling author of *Lucky Stars*

"Fans of Janet Evanovich and Parnell Hall will appreciate Viets's humor."　　　　　—*South Florida Sun-Sentinel*

"Elaine Viets's debut is a live wire. It's Janet Evanovich meets *The Fugitive* as Helen Hawthorne takes Florida by storm. Shop no further—this is the one."
—Tim Dorsey, author of *The Stingray Shuffle*

"I loved this book. With a stubborn and intelligent heroine, a wonderful South Florida setting, and a cast of more-or-less lethal bimbos, *Shop till You Drop* provides tons of fun. Six-toed cats, expensive clothes, sexy guys on motorcycles—this book has it all."
—Charlaine Harris, author of *Club Dead* and
Poppy Done to Death

"Fresh, funny, and fiendishly constructed, *Shop till You Drop* gleefully skewers cosmetic surgery, ultraexclusive clothing boutiques, cheating ex-husbands, and the Florida dating game as attractive newcomer Helen Hawthorne takes on the first of her deliciously awful dead-end jobs and finds herself emeshed in drugs, embezzlement, and murder. A bright start to an exciting new series. This one is hard to beat."
—Parnell Hall, author of The Puzzle Lady
crossword puzzle mysteries

Dying to Call You

A DEAD-END JOB MYSTERY

Elaine Viets

A SIGNET BOOK

SIGNET
Published by New American Library, a division of
Penguin Group (USA) Inc., 375 Hudson Street,
New York, New York 10014, USA
Penguin Group (Canada), 10 Alcorn Avenue, Toronto,
Ontario M4V 3B2, Canada (a division of Pearson Penguin Canada Inc.)
Penguin Books Ltd., 80 Strand, London WC2R 0RL, England
Penguin Ireland, 25 St. Stephen's Green, Dublin 2,
Ireland (a division of Penguin Books Ltd.)
Penguin Group (Australia), 250 Camberwell Road, Camberwell, Victoria 3124,
Australia (a division of Pearson Australia Group Pty Ltd.)
Penguin Books India Pvt. Ltd., 11 Community Centre, Panchsheel Park,
New Delhi - 110 017, India
Penguin Group (NZ), Cnr Airborne and Rosedale Roads, Albany,
Auckland 1310, New Zealand (a division of Pearson New Zealand Ltd.)
Penguin Books (South Africa) (Pty.) Ltd., 24 Sturdee Avenue,
Rosebank, Johannesburg 2196, South Africa

Penguin Books Ltd., Registered Offices:
80 Strand, London WC2R 0RL, England

First published by Signet, an imprint of New American Library,
a division of Penguin Group (USA) Inc.

First Printing, October 2004
10 9 8 7 6 5 4 3 2 1

*To all the people I called who were in the shower,
at supper or asleep: I'm really sorry.
I hope you'll forgive me when you read
this book about telemarketing.*

Acknowledgments

The boiler room in this book resembles none of the telemarketing companies I've worked for, except in this way: Most telemarketers have rotten jobs. Hang up on them gently, please.

As always, I want to thank my husband, Don Crinklaw, for his extraordinary help and patience. My agent, David Hendin, is still the best.

Special thanks to my editor, Kara Cesare, who devoted long hours to editing and guiding this project, her assistant, Rose Hilliard, and to the Signet copy editor and production staff.

Many people helped with this book. I hope I didn't leave anyone out.

Thanks to Captain Brian Chalk for his help with the boat chase scene, and to Charles A. Intriago, president of Alert Global Media, Inc., and the Money Laundering Alert newsletter.

Thanks to Joanne Sinchuk and John Spera at south Florida's largest mystery bookstore, Murder on the Beach, in Delray Beach, Florida.

Thanks also to Valerie Cannata, Colby Cox, Jinny Gender, Karen Grace, Kay Gordy, and Janet Smith.

Rita Scott does indeed make cat toys packed with the most powerful catnip in kittendom. They have sent my cats into frenzies of ecstasy. Read all about them at www.cats-high.us.

Special thanks to the law enforcement men and women who answered countless questions on weapons, police interrogations, and emergency procedures. Rick McMahan, ATF special agent; the Broward County sheriff's office, and the United States Coast Guard. Thanks to Robin Burcell, author of *Cold Case*. Particular thanks to Detective RC White, Fort Lauderdale Police Department (retired). Any mistakes are mine, not theirs.

Jerry Sanford, author of *Miami Heat* and federal prosecutor for the northern district of Florida, answered many complicated legal questions.

Thanks to the librarians at the Broward County library and the St. Louis public library who researched my questions, no matter how strange, and always answered with a straight face.

Thanks to public relations expert Jack Klobnak, and to my friend Carole Wantz, who takes such joy in books and bookselling.

Special thanks to librarian Anne Watts, the person who lives with Thumbs. Thumbs is a real cat and a real polydactyl.

Chapter 1

"Hi, Mrs. Grimes. This is Helen with—"

"Not interested." *Click.*

"Hi, Mr. Lester, this is Helen with Tank Titan Septic System Cleaner. We make—"

"I told you people to take my name off this list." *Click.*

"Hi, Mr. Hardy, this is Helen with Tank Titan Septic System Cleaner. We make a septic-tank cleaner for your home system that is guaranteed to help reduce large chunks, odors and wet spots . . ."

"You just woke me up, bitch. Call here again and I'll kill you." *Click.*

"Have a good day, sir," Helen said, as he hung up on her.

It was ten o'clock in the morning. Helen Hawthorne had made more than a hundred calls all over the country in two hours, waking up people in Connecticut, irritating them in Iowa, ticking them off in Texas.

She hadn't sold anything so far today. She was desperate. So was everyone else in the telemarketing boiler room. Desperation was ground into the foul wrinkled carpet. It clung to the dirty computer screens. It soaked into the scuffed white walls.

How did scuff marks get eight feet up on the walls? Helen wondered.

"Let's hear you selling, people," Vito the manager said, as he prowled the aisles, making sure everyone was calling. "Loud and proud."

There was nothing proud about this job, although it was loud. All sixty telemarketers were shouting their sales spiel into the phones.

Suddenly, Helen's computer went blank. It crashed again, making it the third time in a week.

Vita screamed like a wounded animal. "Goddamn it, I'm paying thousands to these computer geeks, and these worthless machines still don't work. How can I make money when nobody's calling? Don't sit on your heinies, people. Everyone in the break room for a pep talk."

Vito was always giving pep talks, so the boiler room would meet the quotas set by the New York headquarters. Helen had seen some of the quota makers when they visited the Fort Lauderdale office. They looked like elegant reptiles.

Getting sixty telemarketers into an eight-by-ten break room was like cramming college kids into a Volkswagen. Her coworkers fell mostly into three groups: Hopeful but poorly educated young Hispanics and African-Americans. Middle-class, middle-aged whites down on their luck. Plus a sprinkling of felons and junkies. Helen was on the run from the court and her ex-husband, so she knew what group she belonged in. At least she did not look twitchy and tattooed.

Helen suspected Vito, the manager, had been in trouble with the law. During one pep talk, he'd said, "I know this place looks like a shithole, but you sell a product that works, a product you can be proud of. If you didn't, the ATF guys would come busting through that door, and you'd be down on the floor with guns to your heads."

Helen was pretty sure the Bureau of Alcohol, Tobacco, Firearms and Explosives didn't investigate boiler-room fraud, but she figured Vito knew what a government gun to your head felt like.

Vito was an energetic package of round, pink muscle. His arms looked like thick rolls of bologna. His fingers were sausages. His head was round and pink. Even his black hair looked muscular.

He paced back and forth, then pointed at a young woman with skin like brown satin. "Taniqua, why aren't you selling today?"

"My computer be acting strange," she said. "It keep calling New York. They be talking about some kinda terror alert. They scared. Not my fault I ain't selling."

"It is your fault," Vito said. "So what if there's an orange alert? I know people are worried about terrorism, but the twin towers have tumbled and you still have to flush your toilet. Life goes on.

"Richie, why didn't you sell anything this morning?"

"Because people got mad and hung up on me. One guy was ninety-seven and said he didn't need a seven-year supply."

"So sell him the three-year supply," Vito said. "People live to be a hundred all the time."

A kid from the computer room, who looked like a mouse with a moustache, stuck his head in the door and said, "Computers are up."

"Quit wasting time," Vito said to the telemarketers. "Everybody back to work. I need sales, people. First one to sell gets a free trip to Meyer Lansky's grave."

Helen's computer started dialing State Center, Iowa.

"Hi, Mr. Harmon," Helen began. She made it past the crucial first paragraph. She steamed through the section about "one of your neighbors in State Center gave me your name as a homeowner with a septic tank." He still didn't stop her.

She told him that Tank Titan contained natural bacteria "that will break down and liquefy. And liquidity is just as important in septic tanks as it is in banks, right, Mr. Harmon?"

"Why, yes," he said. He was still with her.

She told him the product was simple and easy to use. "Just flush a package down your commode once a month." He let her keep talking. She was on her way to a sale.

She made her final pitch: "We guarantee complete satisfaction with your septic-tank system for seven years, Mr. Harmon, or you'll get one hundred percent of your money back. Does that sound fair to you, Mr. Harmon?"

"Why, yes it does," he said, in his soft country accent. "What's this gonna cost me?"

"Right now, we are offering an eighty-four-pack supply that will last you seven years for only two hundred ninety-nine dollars. That's less than twelve cents a day for septic peace of mind."

There was a long silence. Helen feared she'd lost him and the sale. Then he said, "I guess I do need this product. I've kinda let things go since my wife died. We were married thirty-seven years. She died last March."

"I'm sorry, Mr. Harmon," Helen said.

"I miss her each and every day. I dream about her at night and then I wake up and the bed is empty, and I know she's never going to be beside me again."

Helen had to get him back on track. "I am sorry, Mr. Harmon," she said again. She started reading from her pitch. "But I am sure our product will bring you complete satisfaction."

Ouch. That was a bad choice of words. She expected him to slam down the phone, but he didn't. "What is your address so I can send it out to you?" she said.

The lonely man ordered the full seven-year supply, probably just to hear a woman talk to him, even if she was discussing raw sewage.

Helen recorded her sale on the big board on the scuffed wall. Then she wrote down the address on scrap paper for her records. She'd get a ten-dollar commission, but Helen felt like one of the larger chunks in Mr. Harmon's septic tank. Too many telemarketing sales were made to the old and the lonely.

To feel better, she became Telemarketing Goddess. It was a dangerous game. Helen could only risk playing it for ten minutes at a time.

After each call, telemarketers hit one of eight choices on

their computers: NOT INTERESTED. ANSWERING MACHINE. SALE. HAS TANK TITAN. WRONG NUMBER. CALL BACK. DOESN'T SPEAK ENGLISH. REMOVE FROM LIST.

"REMOVE FROM LIST" were the three words telemarketing companies dreaded. It meant that person could never be called again. If the company disobeyed the command, it could be fined major money. Vito threw out a different amount each pep talk. Sometimes the fine was ten thousand dollars, other times it was twenty-five thousand. He warned that consumers could record their remove requests and collect in court if their orders were ignored.

But if the person didn't say those three little words, they were fair game. Helen was supposed to remove rude people from the list even without the magic words. Tank Titan didn't want any more enemies. But she ignored that rule when she was Telemarketing Goddess.

The computer was now dialing Montana, catching septic-tank owners in the morning before they went to work.

Helen launched into her spiel. An angry man interrupted her with, "You got a lot of balls calling here at eight in the morning."

"Sorry, sir," Helen said.

He started clubbing her with ugly, unprintable names, but Helen listened with a smile. He'd never said the three magic words. When he slammed down the phone, Helen hit the CALL BACK button. Septic-tank calls would pursue him from eight in the morning till nine at night.

A woman with a soft voice answered the next call. Helen could hear the lung-busting cry of a newborn. The woman struggled to listen to Helen over the howling baby. "I'm really sorry, but I'm kind of busy right now," she said.

"That's OK." Helen removed the woman from the list without being asked and sent her to telemarketing heaven. She'd never be bothered again.

Helen was rolling with her sales pitch on the next call, well into her fourth sentence. "One of your neighbors in Missoula, Mr. Dixs, gave me your name as a homeowner with a septic tank."

A voice like an ax blade cut her off. "A neighbor, huh? I don't have any neighbors, you lying bitch," he snarled and hung up.

Helen sent Mr. Dixs to telemarketing hell. Two more nasty men joined him. Thanks to Helen, they'd all get up to seven septic tank calls a day.

A weary mother with two sick kids (Helen heard one barfing) went to heaven. So did a sad, polite man who sounded like a movie cowboy. When he said simply, "Ma'am, I'm out of work," Helen gave him a break and rescued him from further calls.

Helen woke up a sick woman and atoned for her sin by sending her to heaven. If people were having a worse day than she was, Helen took them off the list. They never knew what she did. She enjoyed her secret power: punishing the outrageously rude and helping the downtrodden with a small kindness.

Nine calls, nine minutes. Her time was almost up. She could only play Goddess once more.

"Hi, Mr. Richards, this is Helen with Tank Titan Septic System Cleaner. We make—"

"Mr. Richards?" the man said scornfully. "You're retarded. What are you, stupid? Mr. Richards doesn't live here, moron."

"Thank you, sir," Helen said, and happily sent him to hell.

Two sales later, her shift was over. Vito looked at her sales figures and said, "I'm going to reward you, Helen. Tonight, you work the survey side."

Vito was playing telemarketing God. He sent her to telemarketing heaven.

Helen walked out of the building and blinked at the harsh South Florida light. In the windowless boiler room, she'd had no idea it was a sunny November day. When she'd lived in St. Louis, she'd dreaded November, the gray month that brought the first ice and snow. But winter in Florida was gorgeous. Red impatiens bloomed in planters. Purple passionflowers rioted on garden walls. Palm trees rustled like taffeta skirts.

As she walked home, she tried to clear her head of the nearly three hundred phone calls that had pounded her ears in the last five hours. Tank Titan telemarketers worked a brutal schedule: The first shift was eight A.M. to one P.M. The boiler room closed in the afternoon, when many people weren't home. Then the telemarketers came back to work from five to ten P.M. Each shift was five hours straight, with only one five-minute break each hour.

Helen worked ten-hour days, taking nearly six hundred calls each day.

For that, she was paid five dollars and fifteen cents an hour, plus a ten-dollar commission on each sale. Three commissions per shift were good. She'd worked there four weeks and made at least five hundred dollars a week. She sometimes earned more, but Vito helped himself to about fifty bucks of her commission each week. That was his reward for paying her in cash. Helen did not want her name in any company computers. She'd be too easy to trace.

She walked home quickly, stretching her sore arms, neck and back, reveling in the warm sun. Survey work was like a vacation after the slamming boiler room calls. She'd make ten to twenty calls an hour, instead of sixty. It was a reward for the top sellers. The well-spoken top sellers. Telemarketers like Taniqua, who started her spiel with, "I wanna ax you a queshun" could make a hundred sales a day, and they'd never get survey duty at a snotty place like Girdner Surveys.

But Helen had a college degree. Helen had once made one hundred thousand dollars a year in a St. Louis corporation. Then she'd come home early on a balmy day like this and found her husband Rob with her next-door neighbor, Sandy. They were buck naked on the sun-drenched deck. Sandy was wrapped around her husband like an Ace bandage.

Helen had picked up a crowbar lying nearby and felt the satisfying *crunch!* That *crunch* changed her life. Now she was on the run, reduced to dead-end jobs. She felt safe in these awful jobs. No one from her old life would look for her in a boiler room.

This job was a fifteen-minute walk from the Coronado Tropic Apartments, where she lived. Helen loved the swooping Art Deco curves of the old white and turquoise building. On her days off, she sat out by the pool, drinking wine and watching the purple bougainvillea blossoms float on the water.

Her landlady, Margery Flax, must have heard her walking by. She opened her door and called, "Come join me for lunch by the pool."

Helen was happy to forego the scrambled eggs she'd planned to eat. Especially when she saw the spinach salad on the picnic table. It had fat slices of chicken and avocado and lots of crumbled blue cheese. There were hot pumpernickel rolls and chocolate-covered strawberries.

Margery was opening a bottle of wine that had a real cork. She always wore purple, but today's shorts outfit looked positively royal. Helen's landlady was seventy-six, with a face as wrinkled as a shar-pei puppy. She also had some of the best legs in Lauderdale. Today, she showed them off in jaunty purple suede mules.

"What's the occasion for a real bottle of wine, not a box?" Helen said.

"I've finally rented 2C, so we're celebrating," Margery said. "I swear that apartment had a weird magnet. It's attracted one wacko after another."

Helen wasn't going to argue with her. The last tenant was a psychic named Madame Muffy. The one before that was still in jail.

"So who's the new person?"

"Persons. A nice normal retired couple from New Jersey. Fred and Ethel Mertz."

"Like on *I Love Lucy*?"

Margery looked at her blankly.

Helen said, "Lucy's sidekick was Ethel Mertz. She was married to Fred."

"Before my time." Margery poured Helen a generous glass of wine.

"Not too much wine," Helen said. "I leave for work again at four-thirty."

"You still have that worthless job? No, I shouldn't have to ask. I can see you do. You look beat. Those coast-to-coast insults are taking their toll on you, Helen. Why do you work there?"

"For the money." Helen took a bite of her salad. She hoped Margery would start eating and get off this subject.

"An attractive, hardworking woman like you should have no trouble getting a decent job. Why don't you let your friend Sarah give you some good leads? She has lots of corporate contacts."

Because I can't be in a corporate computer, Helen thought.

"I make twice as much here as my last job. It's good money," she said.

"No," Margery said. "It's bad money, and you'll pay a high price for it."

Helen suddenly lost her appetite. She didn't want this conversation. She didn't like to think about her old life, or some of the things she did in this new job. She didn't want to think, period. She was too tired.

She put down her fork. "Margery, I'm dead tired. I really need a nap before I go back to work. Lunch was lovely. Let me help you clear up and I'll go inside."

"I'll do that," Margery said. "Go get your sleep. Take your salad with you. You can eat it later."

Helen was greeted at her door by her gray and white cat. Thumbs looked like a stuffed toy, until you saw his outsized front paws. He had the biggest feet Helen had ever seen on a feline. He was a polydactyl cat, with six toes on each paw. She absently scratched his ears while she surveyed her two-room furnished apartment. It was like a fifties exhibit. Helen loved the turquoise couch with the triangle pattern, the lamps shaped like nuclear reactors, the boomerang coffee table. The Barcalounger was the best. Helen didn't dare sit down in it this afternoon. She'd never get up if she did. She put her salad in the fridge and stretched out on her bed for just a moment.

Helen woke up at four-forty-five and ran all the way to work. She didn't want to be late for survey duty.

Girdner Inc. was a company with a split personality. The Girdner Sales boiler room was on the first floor of the office building. Dirty, dingy, hidden from sight in the back of the building, its staff sold septic-tank cleaner from Maine to California.

On the top floor was their showcase, Girdner Surveys. They conducted slick surveys for suits at the national ad agencies. Girdner Surveys looked like an expensive lawyer's office. A rain forest had been cleared to provide its mahogany paneling. The carpet was expensively subdued, some color between blue and gray. It was like walking through a soft smoky fog. The dignified receptionist could have been a dean at an exclusive women's college.

Helen thought there was something weird about the dual operations. Why was the survey side fit for corporate kings, while the boiler room was the most awful office squalor? Couldn't Girdner afford fresh paint and carpeting for the boiler room? Couldn't they at least clean the place?

Vito, the boiler-room manager, was never seen in the elite Girdner Surveys. Neither were most of his telemarketing employees. The Hispanics and young blacks in their tight tank tops and outrageous platform shoes, the junkies, felons and bikers, were not allowed through the mahogany doors.

Boiler-room refugees like Helen came in the side entrance and were hidden away in a phone room. That door was kept shut. She was below-stairs help, well-spoken enough for survey work, but never seen by the high-priced clients.

Girdner Surveys was presided over by a preppie named Penelope. In her early thirties, Penelope's beige hair, skin and suits were forgettable. What Helen remembered was her stiff, rigid manner. She reminded Helen of those dolls with the bendable joints. Penelope talked through clenched teeth. Helen thought her other orifices were probably clenched, too.

Penelope did not give pep talks to the phone staff like Vito. She hated talking to them. When she was forced to communicate with the lower orders, she sat behind her desk, gripping her chair arms and staring straight ahead.

Mostly she issued orders to the phone-room supervisor, Nellie, a lively blonde who had more personality in her little finger than Penelope had in her whole body. Nellie, fat and fifty, had a voice so alluring that men proposed marriage when she called them.

"OK, ladies, it's just the three of us tonight," Nellie said. "We're recruiting from the A-list, which does not stand for asshole, no matter how abusive these guys get. These are the richest names in Miami-Dade, Palm Beach and Broward Counties. We'll pay good money—two hundred bucks if they'll participate in a martini study. Just remember, two hundred bucks is pocket change to these people."

Berletta, the other woman working the phones, groaned. "The richer they are, the meaner they are," she said in her beautiful Bahamian accent.

It was true. Surveys for beauty products, candy and beer paid only forty or fifty dollars. But most blue-collar subjects needed the money. They were polite.

"Cheer up," Nellie said. "You could be calling doctors."

Doctors were paid the most—up to three hundred dollars per survey. Arrogant and greedy, they acted as if they were stepping off their thrones to participate.

"You know the drill," Nellie said. "Be polite. Be persuasive. We need to sign up thirty people, ages twenty-five to forty, who make more than one hundred thousand a year and drink martinis made with Silver Spur vodka. The computer database is sorted and ready. Start dialing."

Girdner's computers had incredible information on their survey subjects. Tidbits mentioned in a casual phone conversation with a survey recruiter found their way into the database.

The computer told Helen who took Prozac, lived with a boyfriend, split with their mate or suffered from bipolar disorder. She knew who just had a baby—a newborn opportunity for diaper and formula surveys. Helen could see which women used tampons or pads, information used for personal-care product surveys. She knew who had hysterectomies, disqualifying them for those same surveys.

For nearly an hour, she labored through voice mail, answering machines, "he's not home" and "don't call me at dinner" without one bite. Not even a nibble. She was getting discouraged.

She looked at the information on the next prospect: "Age 40. Occupation: Financier. Annual income: More than five hundred thousand. College educated. Smokes Dunhills. Drives a Land Rover and a vintage Porsche 911. Owns a Cigarette boat. No pets. Uses MCI long-distance service. Drinks martinis made with Silver Spur vodka more than three times a week."

There was one other comment, this one by a survey recruiter: "Good talker in focus groups but has a bad temper on phone. Can be mean."

Mean or not, he had the right demographics for this survey. Helen took a deep breath, dialed and said, "May I please speak to Mr. Henry Asporth?"

"This is Hank." The man had a rich voice to go with all that money.

"Hi, this is Helen and I'm with the—"

"What? Sweetie, wait a minute." Sweetie. Helen ground her teeth. She'd rather he was mean than call her sweetie.

Asporth had put the phone down. Helen would wait thirty seconds before she hung up on him. An old anti-telemarketer trick was to put down the phone and never come back.

Helen heard someone say, "Hey! Wait a minute." A woman. She sounded young. She seemed surprised and a little scared. Then Helen heard a man and a woman arguing, but it sounded far away. It probably was. A house like Hank's was measured in acres, not square feet.

"What do you mean, 'What am I doing in here?'" The woman's voice was higher and clearer than the man's.

The man's voice was a low, angry rumble, but Helen couldn't pick up any words.

The woman sounded defiant, but there was a taunting, teasing quality to her voice. She seemed to have the upper hand. "You want it? Well, then you better give me what I want. Otherwise, you'll never get your hands on it. You'll be sorry. I can put you away for a long time. You've been a very bad boy, Hank. You're just lucky I like bad boys. I've waited long enough. I want an answer, and I want it tonight."

Helen heard the man's voice again, low and angry, but still impossible to decipher. Even without the words, Helen felt its cutting edge.

"I'm not lying," the woman insisted, her voice rising.

Then the woman's voice changed. Now she was afraid. "What are you doing here? Get away from me. No!" More voices, talking over each other. The man, angry. The woman, sounding more frightened. Her high, light voice was easier to understand. His was a low rumble. And was that a third person? Helen couldn't tell. They were too far away.

Helen heard a loud clunking noise, like something heavy was overturned. Then the woman said something that didn't make sense. It sounded like, "It's the coffee—" Her words were stretched into a short, explosive scream.

But there was no misunderstanding her next frantic words: "What are you doing? No! No! Hank!" Her scream was cut off.

Helen had never heard anything as terrifying as the next sound. It was an awful guttural choking noise. It sounded like someone was fighting for air. Helen had her hand protectively on her own throat, as if the strangler might grab her through the phone.

"Hello?" Helen said, her voice a frightened croak.

Dead air. Then a click.

Someone had hung up the phone.

Chapter 2

"Oh, my God," Helen yelled to the other survey takers. "Someone's being killed. I heard it. He's killing her right now. What do I do?"

"Call 911," said her supervisor, Nellie. "Now." She put down her phone and came over to stand by Helen. The big blonde's presence was solid and reassuring. Nellie was one of those people who became calmer in a crisis. Berletta, the other woman working in the survey room, stopped calling but said nothing. She was there if Helen needed her.

Helen's fingers moved slowly, as if she was dialing under water.

"Wait. Nellie, what if I'm wrong? What if he really didn't kill her? What if I didn't hear what I think I heard? What if I'm sending the police to an innocent man?"

"Then the cops will leave, no harm done. But ask yourself this: What if you really did hear someone killing a woman, and you did nothing? Could you sleep at night?"

"No, of course not. It's just that . . ."

"Helen, what was your first thought when you heard those sounds?" Nellie said. "Your first thought—not your second."

"A woman was being killed."

"Then listen to your instincts. Make the call."

Helen's fingers felt cold and unwieldy, a dead woman's

fingers. Her brain was racing: Nellie believed her, but what if the cops didn't? What if—?

"911. Do you need police, fire or medical?"

"Police." Helen had trouble getting out that one word. The others came in a gasping rush, as if she'd been running for miles. "I just called a house. I heard a woman being hurt. No, killed. I heard her die. They were having a fight and she was screaming and he killed her." At least I think so. Helen silently smothered her doubts.

The 911 operator said, "Where is help needed?"

Helen found her businesslike tone soothing. Just the facts, ma'am. We can deal with this, no matter how bad it seems. Helen read the address on her computer screen. "It's 1751 Seamont. On the Intracoastal Waterway. Hurry, but I think it's too late."

"What city?"

"Brideport," Helen said.

"What was the phone number of the person you were calling?"

Helen read it from the computer screen.

"What is your name and telephone number?"

"Helen Hawthorne." She gave the Girdner number.

"Where are you calling from?" The litany of questions was comforting. The 911 operator's voice was soothing as poppy syrup.

"Girdner Surveys," Helen said. "It's near Broward Boulevard and U.S. 1. I'm a telemarketer there. I was calling the Asporth house when I heard someone murder this woman."

"And the name of the person you were calling?"

"Henry Asporth. He answered the phone. He said his name was Hank. Then he put the phone down and I heard him arguing with a woman. She sounded young, but I don't know who she was. She screamed, but it was cut off. I think he strangled her or broke her neck. He killed her. I heard it."

"For my own clarification, you did not hear shots," the operator said. "You heard the male subject strangle the female?"

"Yes," Helen said. "I didn't hear a gun. I think he killed her with his bare hands. It was horrible. Then he hung up the phone."

"How much time has gone by since you hung up?"

"I don't know," Helen said. "A couple of minutes. Maybe five at the most. Nellie—she's my supervisor—she told me to call. It hasn't been real long. And I didn't hang up the phone. He did."

"Did he sound like an older male or a younger male?"

"Old. No, young. But not too young. He was grown up."

"Did it sound like there was another male present?"

"I didn't hear another man. Just Hank Asporth and the woman he strangled." And maybe another woman, Helen thought. But before she could say it, the operator said, "What makes you think that he strangled her?"

"I heard him! It was this awful choking noise."

"Was she choking on food?" the 911 operator said.

"No, it wasn't choking like that. She was fighting, trying to stay alive, and then she made this terrible sound."

"What sound?"

Helen couldn't describe the sound and she couldn't forget it.

"A dying sound," Helen said. "She was murdered and I heard it."

All her doubts went away. At least for the moment. After Helen repeated everything Hank had said again, the 911 operator told her the police and paramedics had been dispatched and that the police would contact her later. Helen put down the receiver. It felt like it weighed twenty pounds in her hand.

"Are you OK?" Nellie asked.

"I'm fine," Helen said.

"You don't look fine," Berletta said. "Not unless you're wearing flour for makeup. Let me get you some water."

Penelope had strict rules about telemarketers being seen but not heard. "You can't go out now," Helen said. "There are clients here. If you're caught roaming the halls, you'll be fired."

"If they want to fire me for acting like a human being, shame on them," Berletta said.

Helen started to get up, but Nellie pushed her down. "Sit. You look like particular hell. I'll lie for Berletta if I have to."

"It's too big a risk," Helen said. "Berletta needs this job."

Berletta had a ten-year-old daughter with cerebral palsy. Her free days were spent fighting with the insurance companies for disallowed medicine and treatments. Her evenings were spent at Girdner, trying to pay off medical bills that had climbed to six figures.

"Don't worry, I'm packing protection," Berletta said. She picked up a clipboard. "This is a trick my husband learned in the army. If you walk around with a clipboard, nobody questions you."

Helen laughed. The laugh turned into a shrill giggle that she had trouble stopping.

"Do you want to go home?" Nellie said to Helen. "I'll write you an excuse."

"I'm fine," Helen said. She could feel tears clogging her throat, but she fought them back.

"How about some chocolate therapy?" Nellie said. "Sugar and caffeine are good for shock. The almonds will give you protein." She pulled out a gold-wrapped chocolate bar.

"Ah, the healing powers of Godiva," Helen said. She ate the chocolate. Berletta returned unscathed with a bottle of water and a damp paper towel. Helen gulped the cold water, then wiped her face with the towel and took a deep breath.

"Enough," she said. "I'm going back to work."

"You're one tough woman," Nellie said.

"It's all the abuse I take as a telemarketer."

The hourly insults, sexual slurs and questions about her parentage had toughened her up. She could work. She would work. She had a quota to fill, or she'd never get survey duty again.

Helen didn't want to think about what she had unleashed.

If the cops really did find a dead woman, they might look into Helen's past. She'd changed her name, but she was still on the run. Any halfway smart cop could figure it out.

The cops would find no credit cards, no bank account, no phone in her name. They'd realize she was using a false name in about thirty seconds. She'd be on her way back to St. Louis. Helen wondered if she'd have to wear handcuffs the whole trip.

She went back to the computer, and called the next person, a thirty-two-year-old stockbroker named Ashley Lipston. "May I speak to Ms. Lipston?" Helen's voice sounded like it came from a newly opened tomb.

"I can't hear you. Speak up."

"I'm doing a sturbay, I mean, a survey for Spilver Sur—"

Ms. Lipston slammed down the phone.

Helen stumbled through her next presentation, too. Then she started signing up Silver Spur martini drinkers, finding a strange relief in doing her job.

A shaky hour and a half later, two Brideport police officers came to Girdner Surveys. The night receptionist, who looked like Helen's third-grade teacher, Sister Wilhelmina, brought them back to the phone room.

"These police officers are here to see you," she said.

The receptionist gave Helen a disapproving look, as if she'd just earned six demerits. Helen wondered if any clients had seen the cops.

Nellie and Berletta put down their phones and frankly eavesdropped.

The two officers were as clean and new as their uniforms. One was dark, compact and muscular—a farm boy with a nose like a new potato. The other was a blond woman with short, untidy hair. The shirttail of her uniform blouse was creeping out of her waistband and her collar was crooked. Helen had an urge to straighten it.

"There was no murder, ma'am," the boy officer said. "We wanted to set your mind at ease. What you heard was a movie. The guy was watching it when we got there."

Hot shame flooded Helen. She remembered the woman's teasing tone at first: "You've been a very bad boy, Hank. You're just lucky I like bad boys." That did sound like a line from a movie.

She was a fool. A public fool. She would lose her job. All because she'd overreacted and called the police. But then she remembered that desperate, guttural choking noise. That was no movie sound effect. She'd heard a woman die. She was sure of it. . . . Almost sure.

"He killed a woman," she said. "It wasn't a movie. She said his name, Hank. Twice. Explain that."

"You heard wrong." Officer Untidy tucked in her shirttail. "You said you couldn't hear what the man said, just the woman."

"I heard a woman being murdered." It came out stronger than she felt.

"No, ma'am," Officer Untidy said. She had a coffee stain on her shirt. "We found no sign of anyone else living there. We found no women's personal effects. No female clothes, shoes or makeup."

"He's very rich. Maybe you didn't look hard enough," Helen said.

Berletta sat at her desk, frozen. Nellie gave a warning cough.

Good move, Helen thought. Insult the police. That will make them change their minds.

The boy cop, the muscular one, moved forward in a way that seemed threatening. But Helen realized every move this young tank made would seem that way. "Ma'am, I will put that remark down to stress, because of the situation. We didn't take Mr. Asporth's word for it. We had reasonable suspicion to search the house and the garage without a warrant. The yard could be seen from public view, so we had cause to search that, too. Mr. Asporth also gave us permission."

"How much time was there between my call and your response?" Helen interrupted.

"We responded in a timely manner," he said, which was no answer at all.

"Inside the house we looked in the closets and under the beds. We checked his storage containers and his walk-in freezer. We even checked the bait freezer on his boat. A guy hid his wife in one of those a couple of years ago."

When you were still in diapers, Helen thought. I've got sweaters older than these two. When did they graduate from the police academy—yesterday?

The boy cop frowned, as if he could read her thoughts.

Office Untidy started talking. "We found nothing. There was no sign of a struggle. There was no blood. The neighbors heard no unusual noises. The vehicles in the garage were registered in his name. He wasn't hiding her car in there."

"Did you look in his cars?"

"He opened them for us. They were empty." Officer Untidy was wrestling with her shirttail—and losing.

"You made an honest mistake, ma'am," the boy officer said. "You did your duty as a citizen and called us. You reported what you thought was a murder. We checked it out and found nothing."

Helen couldn't bear the condescension in his voice. This young twerp thought she was a hysterical woman.

"It wasn't a mistake." Helen sounded really hysterical now. "I heard him murder a woman."

"I wouldn't say that too loud if I were you," the boy officer said. "He could sue you for your last nickel."

Chapter 3

"Ten. Twenty. Thirty."

Helen was counting crumpled ten dollar bills. The money had been stuffed inside her teddy bear, Chocolate.

"Two hundred. Two ten. Two twenty."

She pulled more stuffing out of the bear. The pile of wrinkled tens grew higher. Helen breathed in the dirty perfume of used money. Last night, she'd heard a woman being murdered. Then two cops treated her like a nutcase. It was a trying evening. But this morning, Helen had her hands on something reassuring: money. She knew she'd be fired in a few hours. But if her bear Chocolate was as fat as Helen hoped, she could tell Girdner to go to hell.

"Two ninety. Three hundred. Three ten."

Telemarketing was wretched work, but Helen made more at it than at any other dead-end job she'd ever worked. She had an odd, embarrassing knack for selling septic-tank cleaner. The money was piling up. Helen couldn't have a bank account or even a safe-deposit box. Those would make her too easy to trace. Instead, she stashed her money in a place she thought un-bear-ably clever.

"Three seventy. Three eighty. Three ninety."

The money pile had grown to a fat mound. Helen had not had so much cash since she worked for that St. Louis corporation. Actually, she hadn't had much cash then, although she made a hundred thousand plus. She spent her salary on designer suits for a job that bored her, massages to ease the work tension, and Ralph Lauren window treatments (when you spent that much, you did not call them curtains) for a house designed to impress other people.

"Four ten. Four twenty. Four thirty."

She threw away more money on Rob, her rat of a husband. He'd looked for work for years, but never found a job. Rob needed a Rolex to get to job interviews on time, a new SUV to get there in style, and a state-of-the-art sound system to soothe his shattered nerves when he was rejected—again. But Rob was no mooch. He was building a new deck, wasn't he?

"Six forty. Six fifty. Six sixty."

When Helen remembered what happened on the deck, she started counting faster, spilling bills every which way. One hot summer day, Helen decided not to be such a corporate grind. For the first time in seventeen married years, she left work early. She would surprise her husband, handsome and sweaty in the sun. They would make passionate love on the new deck furniture, then swim naked in the pool.

Her husband had had the exact same thought. Helen found him sweaty and naked with their next-door neighbor, Sandy.

"Eight seventy. Eight eighty. Eight ninety."

Bills leaped like spawning salmon as Helen recounted her humiliation that awful afternoon. She'd picked up a crowbar on the deck and started swinging. When she finished, she'd smashed her old life completely. Now she was on the run in South Florida, a female version of *The Fugitive,* condemned to nowhere jobs that paid in cash under the table.

"Nine twenty. Nine thirty. Nine forty."

Helen pulled out one last ten-spot wedged inside Chocolate's paw. Nine hundred fifty dollars. She shoved the money back in the bear and patted his swollen belly.

Rich Chocolate, indeed. But she had another money cushion. She unzipped the couch pillows and started counting. She had seven hundred dollars stuffed in the turquoise throw pillows. Twelve hundred fifteen dollars in the black couch pillows. Seven thousand and something in the old Samsonite suitcase in the closet. She could survive for months on her stash while she looked for another job. She was going to be fired, but people at her level didn't need references.

Helen wished she could get last night's sounds out of her head. That gurgling scream played in an endless loop. But the police said she'd imagined it. Hot humiliation overwhelmed her. The police had been inside Hank Asporth's house. They'd seen no overturned furniture. No sign of a woman, dead or alive. They told Helen she'd heard a movie. But no movie victim had ever screamed like that. She couldn't shake the feeling that she was right.

She was also sure she was right when she followed her first instinct. Look where that got her. Out of work.

She was ready to face the firing squad.

Helen clocked in at seven fifty-eight A.M. on what she knew would be her last day in the boiler room.

Taniqua was spraying her phone with Lysol. She said she hated when the night shift used her desk and left their trash on it. Taniqua had style. She looked like she walked off a New York runway in her red silk crop top, tiny skirt and sexy four-inch satin heels with rhinestone buckles. She's young, pretty and ready to party, Helen thought, and she's stuck here.

Nick, skinny and jittery, came in carrying his usual breakfast of orange soda and jelly doughnuts. Marina's toddler, Ramon, was trying to put a hairy pink piece of chewed gum in his mouth. His mother snatched it from his chubby hand, and Ramon burst into loud sobs. Marina swung the howling child onto her hip with an easy motion. The woman has the balance of a tightrope artist, Helen thought, lifting that kid when she's wearing tight jeans and skinny heels. Ramon cried and clutched his mother's long dark hair while she soothed him into silence.

The computers came on at precisely 8:01. This morning, they were dialing New Hampshire. Helen glanced at her screen. "Hello, Mr. Harcourt. This is Helen with Tank Titan . . ."

Mr. Harcourt had just finished cussing her for waking him when she was called into Vito's office.

Vito looked more like a sausage than ever, with a tight red shirt for a casing. He was not his usual chipper self.

"They want to see you upstairs," he said. "I hear you called the cops on a survey client and accused him of murdering some broad. Helen, did you have to pick a rich one on the A-list? You're a good seller. I'd like to keep you. But I hired you. It's my heinie in the wringer, too."

Helen didn't say anything. It wasn't Vito's fault. For all she knew, the New York lizards would come down and fire him or break his legs or whatever those scary guys considered corporate discipline.

Helen rode up the elevator up to Girdner Surveys, feeling like she was ascending into heaven for final judgement. She would be cast out into boiler-room hell soon enough. When the doors opened, Helen was once again startled by the contrast between the boiler room's dirt and the survey side's elegance.

Melva, the dignified day receptionist, said, "You're supposed to go to Penelope's office. Some lawyer's been in there since seven thirty. And Helen . . . good luck."

"I'll need it," Helen said.

She knocked and went in. Penelope was sitting more rigidly than usual, like an Egyptian stone statue. She did not invite Helen to sit down. Helen stood there like a kitchen maid who'd dropped the best teapot, while Penelope talked about her. Penelope's buttoned-up suit had a tight bow at the throat, as if she needed to hold in her rage.

If I get to tell her to go to hell, it just might be worth it, Helen thought.

A sleek, plump man in blue pinstripes was sitting across from Penelope. This must be the lawyer. Penelope indicated Helen with a nod of her head. "This woman used this office to create an incident last night. It was unforgivable, but Mr. Asporth has graciously decided to overlook it. You're sure you don't want her fired?" Penelope acted like a queen, casually offering to execute a worthless slave.

"Mr. Asporth has specifically requested that she not be fired," the lawyer said. "It is his express wish that she return to her job as a—what is it?" He looked at his notes. "Oh, yes, a survey taker."

Smart man, Helen thought. Mr. Asporth is afraid if I'm fired, I'll make a stink and have plenty of time to do it.

"But if she discusses this incident with anyone, including the authorities, we'll be forced to take action against your company. After all, she is an employee of Girdner Surveys and its parent company as well."

I don't have any money, Helen thought. But Girdner was loaded. Asporth knew what he was doing.

The lawyer rose, fat with confidence, and left without a goodbye.

Helen was still standing. Penelope turned furious eyes on her and said in a hissing whisper, "You heard him. You'll keep your job, but not because I want you to. If I hear you've been talking to anyone, you're out on the street. I'll make sure you never work in Broward County again."

Helen breathed a sigh. By some miracle, she still had her job. She went back down to the boiler room and told Vito.

"Good," he grunted. "Sit down and start selling."

Helen tried to concentrate on her sales pitch, but she couldn't. The scene in the office had been humiliating. Her hands itched for that crowbar. She longed to smash Penelope's computer. And that was just the beginning. But she tamped down her rage. She still had her job.

She had something else, too. Hank Asporth's actions had just confirmed that he'd murdered that woman. An innocent man would demand she be fired, not send a slippery lawyer to shut her up—and make sure she kept her job. An out-of-work Helen would have time to stir up trouble. She would trust her instincts once again and hope she didn't get herself into trouble. But she knew better.

Maybe Helen couldn't talk about the murder here at work, but she could do some background checking. She had to sell so she could get survey duty again and look at those computer files.

"I gotta get a sale," jittery Nick said. He had the computer next to hers. "I really want to keep this job."

"Me, too," Helen said.

"But you're selling," Nick said, biting into his fifth jelly doughnut of the day. "I saw your numbers on the board yesterday. I haven't had a sale in two weeks. If I don't sell anything soon, I'm gone."

He was right, and they both knew it. Nick was a junkie trying to go straight. He'd been on the street, then moved into a halfway house. Now he was living in a rented trailer. He was touchingly proud of that. But the less he sold, the more twitchy he grew. Now Nick could hardly sit still long enough to sell anything. Helen suspected he was back on drugs.

"I've got to work, Nick," she said.

Helen tried to sell all morning. But the more she pushed her potential clients, the more phones were slammed down. She was cursed, insulted and propositioned. The computers were calling Kentucky and Tennessee in areas where the gene pool needed some chlorine.

"Hi, Mr. Moser, this is Helen with Tank Titan. We make a septic-tank cleaner that is guaranteed to help reduce large chunks, odors and wet spots."

"Wet spots?" Mr. Moser had a Gomer Pyle accent. "Wet spots are a big problem for me, honey. Got them all over my mattress. You wanna come over and—"

Helen hung up and hit REMOVE FROM LIST so no other telemarketer would be subjected to him.

No one was selling that morning. There wasn't a single sale posted on the board. All around her, she heard the rustle of candy wrappers and chip bags. Telemarketers ate through their stress. Jittery Nick ate yet another jelly doughnut and popped the top on his third can of orange soda. Marina, the Latina single mother, was scarfing Snickers. She couldn't afford day care. Ramon, her dark-eyed toddler, played at her feet on the dirty carpet, a truck in one hand and a melting candy bar in the other.

Taniqua was popping Pringles. Helen noticed a slight bulge above her red skirt. When Helen first met Taniqua, she'd had a model's flat stomach. Now, like nearly everyone else in the boiler room, she'd packed on pounds. Helen had put on five pounds in two weeks, which was why she struggled to ignore the call of the salt-and-vinegar chips in her desk drawer.

"I don't hear you talking," Vito said. He walked the aisles with a fat black monitor phone, listening in on conversations, trying to get the staff to say the right stuff and sell. Finally, even he gave up.

"Break time!" Vito said. "Everyone clock out and come into my office."

The telemarketers groaned. They would have to listen to a Vito lecture at their own expense. Sixty telemarketers piled into Vito's plywood-paneled office. The crowd pushed Helen forward until she was sitting on the edge of Vito's dusty desk. Vito marched up and down behind it, a rotund general trying to rally his dispirited troops.

"You!" he said, pointing at Taniqua. "Why didn't you make your last sale?"

"When I say she ought to buy it from me, she say she want to think about it," Taniqua said in a soft voice.

"And you said?"

"I say she should buy it."

"But she didn't, did she? Here's what you should have said, 'What's there to think about? It's like putting oil in your car every three thousand miles. It's more expensive not to do it than to do it.' Then she would have bought it.

"You! Richie! What about your last call?"

"Some old lady said, 'I'm not interested' and hung up."

"And you said?"

Richie shrugged, too discouraged to answer.

"You should have said, 'Not interested? Not interested in saving over seven thousand dollars in repairs?'"

"You gotta fight for those sales, people. You got to use psychology. How many of you heard, 'I have to ask my wife'?"

Most of the room raised their hands.

"Don't let any guy use that excuse. Here's what you say: 'Does your wife ask you when she buys fifty bucks worth of lingerie? Be a man. Make your own decisions.'

"Make him feel like he doesn't have anything between his legs unless he buys that septic-tank cleaner. That's psychology. Selling is aggressiveness. It's a tug-of-war. The last one to let go is the loser. And I don't employ losers."

With each word, Vito punched the air with thick pink fingers like hot dogs. He'd attack someone's manhood to make a sale, but Helen didn't work that way. Watching him shout, pace and punch made her more tired. She looked down at Vito's desk, and saw the boiler-room employee roster for the week. Helen looked at the ninety names on the list. She only recognized sixty of them. That's because there were only sixty desks in the phone room. Vito's list had thirty phantom employees. What was he doing?

"What am I doing? I'm trying to get you to sell. Right, Helen?"

She looked up, startled and guilty. "Right, Vito," she said.

When in doubt, always agree with the boss. Her eyes shifted back to the bloated roster. She checked the names again. No doubt about it. Vito had listed thirty people who didn't exist.

"End of lecture," he said. The effort left him red-faced, with sweat rings on his shirt. "Go get me some sales."

Helen couldn't sell beer at a frat party today. It was hopeless. She would not get upstairs to do survey work tonight, and she had to. How else could she search for more information about Hank Asporth? What if she went into a sales slump and got fired? She'd seen it happen before. She might never get up to the survey section again.

One minute to go, and no sales. The computer shut down. Helen packed up her purse in defeat and headed for the time clock. Vito blocked her way. "You're working survey duty tonight. If it was up to me, you'd be here. But the suits requested you."

Helen knew the suits didn't request her. She was working survey duty at the express wish of Henry Asporth's lawyer. Thank you, Mr. Asporth, she thought. I'll use that time to nail you.

Helen did not see Margery when she came home for lunch. She missed her landlady. She saw too little of her these days. She missed her friend Peggy, too, and their companionable evenings sitting by the Coronado pool drinking wine. Now she spent too many evenings in the boiler room trying to make more money. For the hundredth time, she asked herself if this job was worth it. She still didn't have an answer. She opened a can of tuna and dumped it on a slightly stale bun. Thumbs, her cat, made a dramatic leap for her plate.

"Down, boy," she said. He sat sulkily on the floor. Some lunch. She had to fight the cat for her food.

After a nap that left her groggy and muzzy-headed, Helen returned that evening to the hushed, expensive offices of Girdner Surveys.

"You're still here?" Nellie asked. The night supervisor seemed surprised and relieved.

"Against all odds," Helen said. "Penelope's not happy about it. I don't think I'd better waste any more time talking."

Helen picked up the phone, so it looked like she was working. She typed in Henry Asporth's number and stared at the computer screen, looking for some way to get to him. She reread his information and took notes: Name and address. Phone. Cell phone. Vehicles. Income. Age. Hobbies. Pets. Some unknown telemarketer had left a warning about his rotten temper. Interesting.

Wait. What was this? "Lives with #948782." That note made sure the telemarketer didn't pitch the same place twice.

Helen typed #948782. The entry was for Laredo Manson, a twenty-two-year-old woman with a year of junior college and an annual income of less than twenty thousand dollars.

Laredo did not smoke. She drank wine, liquor and beer. Her occupation was "actress/waitress."

Reading between the lines, Helen saw a much younger woman living with an older, richer man. Virtue went cheap in Florida, when job choices were hauling plates, cleaning houses or working the phones.

Was Laredo the woman Hank killed? Twenty-two years old is so young.

Helen dialed Laredo's second number. An answering machine said, "Hi, this is Laredo. You know the drill: Leave a message." The voice was young, sweet and slightly country, with the hint of a giggle.

"This is Helen Hawthorne at Girdner Surveys. Please call me. I'm worried—"

A woman picked up the phone.

"Laredo?" Helen said, relief flooding her. She hadn't heard a murder after all. The woman was safe. Hank Asporth was just a generous man who didn't want to see her fired.

"Hello? Who's this? Laredo's not here. I'm her sister, Savannah."

"Oh," Helen said, disappointed. "I . . . I was just checking to see if she's OK."

"She hasn't been home in a week. Do you know where she is?" Savannah was older, maybe Helen's age. She had a deeper voice than her sister, tinged with a bit of country.

"I think she's in trouble," Helen said.

"What kind of trouble?" the voice demanded.

Helen didn't know what to say. Should she tell the woman what she heard?

"Tell me. I have the right to know."

"I think I heard her being killed. But no one believes me." As soon as Helen said those words, she wanted to take them back. She should have broken the news gently. She was talking to the woman's sister. What was wrong with her?

She expected Savannah to scream, cry or deny. Instead the woman said, "I knew it. I felt it in my bones."

Chapter 4

"I think we better get together," Savannah said.

Helen realized she'd been holding her breath. "I thought you'd call the cops on me, the way I blurted that out."

"I've got a good feel for people," Savannah said. "I hear a lot of things besides words when they talk. I think you want to help me. Where do you live?"

"Right off Las Olas," Helen said. "How about the Floridian?"

"Sure, it's my favorite grease spot."

They agreed to meet there a little after ten P.M., when Helen got off work.

A distracted Helen signed up two more people for the martini survey, but she couldn't keep her mind on her work—or her eyes off the clock. Nellie, her supervisor, must have noticed, but she said nothing.

The black hands crawled around the clock face like they were crippled. After half an eternity, it was ten o'clock. Helen walked up Las Olas with long, impatient strides, slowed by tourists fluttering around the chichi stores like moths around patio lights.

"Isn't that cute!" she heard over and over. Helen wondered how everything from a spike heel to a cat statue could be cute.

The Floridian had resisted the yuppification of Las Olas. There was no valet parking. The waitresses took no sass off anyone. The cashier took no checks or credit cards. In fact, a blond couple in impeccable unwrinkled linen was arguing with her now. Helen stood just inside the door and watched the drama.

"But we don't carry cash," the blond woman said.

"We got an ATM right here," the cashier said, pointing to a pint-size money machine across from the cash register.

"Our credit cards don't work in that one," the blond man said, as if that settled it. He had the smooth face of someone who always got his way. A tiny wrinkle now marred the woman's forehead. She glanced warily at the kitchen, as though afraid she might have to put her pale, perfect hands in dishwater.

"There's a bigger ATM at the convenience store across the street," the cashier said.

"OK, we'll be right back," the blond man said.

"You're not going anywhere until you pay."

"But I have to get the cash. Here—I'll leave you my watch." He started to remove a watch that cost as much as a small car.

"This isn't a pawn shop," the cashier said.

"How about my driver's license?"

"How about your wife?" the cashier said.

"My wife?"

The blond woman looked frightened now. Was she going to be sold into white slavery for a waffle?

"You leave your wife here until you get back with the money."

"I'll be back soon, honey, I promise." The blond man looked amused. His wife did not.

"You'd better," she said. She picked up a free paper from a rack by the door and pretended to read, her cheeks flaming with embarrassment.

"Your money or your wife. I like that," said the woman standing next to Helen. Her white-blond hair was long, straight, and parted in the middle. Her black cowboy boots were scuffed and her jeans were worn at the knees. Her voice had a country lilt that Helen recognized right away.

"I'm Savannah Power."

Helen stood six feet in her sandals, but Savannah was tall enough to look her in the eye. She shook Helen's hand with a strong, callused grip. Savannah was about forty. Hard times were etched in her pale, freckled face and lean body.

"That guy didn't mind leaving his wife hostage in a hash house," Helen said.

"You could leave me here any time," Savannah said. She was wearing a light, flowery perfume. Underneath it, Helen caught a curious sharp smell—bleach or some kind of household cleaner.

"Sit anywhere," said a passing waitress, loaded with plates.

They found a table under a sign that read, DON'T STEAL . . . THE GOVERNMENT DOESN'T LIKE COMPETITION.

On a street known for serious snobbery, The Floridian had a sense of humor. The menu offered a "fat-cat breakfast" of steak, eggs and Dom Perignon for two for $229.99. It also had a "not-so-fat-cat breakfast—same as above with a bottle of our finest el cheapo champagne" for $49.99.

Helen felt suddenly lonely. She wished she could laugh with a man and order cheap champagne for breakfast. But she'd sworn off men after her last disastrous romance.

"What can I get you?" the waitress said.

"Eggs, grits and a Bud," Savannah said.

"You want a glass with that?"

"Bottle's fine," Savannah said.

A straightforward woman, Helen thought. She ordered coffee, ham and eggs.

"Savannah Power. Interesting name," Helen said, when the waitress left.

"My momma had a rough time when she had me. She gave birth at home. She saw this name on her bedside dresser: Savannah Power. She kept concentrating on it to get her through the pain. She thought it was a message. It was. It was a shut-off notice from the light company, but Momma didn't know that then. Anyway, Savannah Power's my name.

"We're all named after cities. My middle sister is Atlanta Power. Momma lived there next. She was in Texas when Laredo was born. She's the baby."

"Laredo has a different last name," Helen said.

"Different daddy," Savannah said. "Lester Power took off by then, and Momma hitched up with Woodbridge Manson."

"Just the three girls?" Helen said.

"Yes, and that's a good thing. With her third husband, Momma moved to Wood River, Illinois, which wasn't a proper name for anyone. Atlanta lives in California now. I only see her every couple of years. But I'm real close to Laredo."

Helen felt like she was in a Who's on First routine. She was glad when the waitress returned with the butter-soaked platters of food.

"Why do you think something happened to your sister?" Helen said, between bites.

"She disappeared a week ago. We share a double-wide. I got home from work and her things were gone. Every last stitch. Even my new red heels, which she'd borrowed. Laredo loved red shoes, but she would never take my best heels. And she'd never leave without telling me. She knows I'd worry. She would have left a note, at least."

Savannah rummaged in a floppy leather purse the size of a saddlebag. "Here's a picture. Look at her. Does that look like a girl who'd just up and leave?"

She produced a washed-out snapshot of a curvy young woman with a street urchin's grin and a mane of honey-colored hair, thicker and curlier than Savannah's. She wore a white tank top, tight white shorts and red heels, and posed in a parody of a pinup. Laredo knew just how pretty she was. She stood in front of a sagging green mobile home with a straggly palm tree. Laredo was laughing, vibrant, out of place in those hangdog surroundings.

Helen thought she looked exactly like someone who'd run away. She certainly would.

"That's where we live," Savannah said. "Would you pass me the salt? I called the police and filed a missing person report. They weren't real interested, her being an adult and all. But they went and talked to a waitress who worked with her at Gator Bill's."

"The restaurant owned by Bill Shannigan, the Gators football star?" Helen said.

"The very one. Right here on Las Olas. Laredo was a waitress there. Wore the cutest cheerleader costume. That was gone, too. This waitress, name of Debbie, told the police my sister was bored and wanted to hit the road. Said Laredo had talked about packing up everything and driving off into the sunset. Oh, I forgot, her car's gone, too."

"What kind of car?" Helen said. She'd eaten her way through a slab of ham and two eggs. She started on the butter-soaked toast.

"Little yellow Honda Civic. But that isn't like her to up and leave. Besides, Laredo had a part in a real Shakespeare play. The director's called twice looking for her. Laredo worked hard to get that part. She thought it was her big break. She'd be at the rehearsal come hell or high water."

Savannah sounded more like a mother than a sister. Another reason for a young woman to suddenly leave home.

"Was she restless?" Helen said.

"She said she didn't want to wind up like me: trailer trash working a bunch of lousy jobs, stuck with a mountain of debt."

Helen winced. "That must have hurt."

Savannah shrugged. "She was young. She didn't mean it." Again, she was the protective momma.

"Laredo said she was going to make it big. She would live in a mansion, marry a rich man, wear pretty clothes and be part of Lauderdale society."

"Did she say how she was going to do this?"

"No, that's how young girls talk. I figured that's why she

took that part with the theater. She was hoping to make it as an actress. There's a lot of movie roles here in South Florida, if an actress can get the right showcase. A Shakespeare play would have been a big step forward."

Maybe, but Helen thought Laredo's talk of a big score sounded like trouble. Her plate seemed to be empty. She must have eaten the whole mound of food. Savannah had a few bites of grits and eggs, but she let the waitress remove her nearly full plate.

Savannah took a long drink of beer. "I know something's wrong. I told the police that, but no one believed me. I got this feeling Laredo's dead. Then you called. It was the call I'd been dreading, but it was a relief, you know?" She started peeling the label off her beer bottle.

"But I don't know," Helen said. "All I know is I think I heard a woman strangled. The police disagree. They say it was a movie. But that was no movie. It was about the worst sound . . ." Helen stopped. "I'm sorry. I keep forgetting she was your sister."

"No, go ahead," Savannah said. "Don't spare me the details. What makes me crazy is everybody saying nothing is wrong. Just tell me what happened."

"Your sister knew a guy named Henry Asporth, right?"

"He hung around the restaurant," Savannah said. "Hank liked to flirt with the waitresses. There were a lot of guys like that. Men with more money than sense, trying to forget middle age was creeping up on them. Laredo went out with him for a while." She pulled away another strip of label.

"Our survey files say she lived with him," Helen said.

"She stayed over weekends sometimes, but she never moved in. That was more wishful thinking. She did that survey thing as a joke. She came home laughing about it. Hank was talking business with the boys one night, and Laredo was bored. Some survey taker called and asked boo-coo questions. Laredo made up a bunch of stuff about how she lived with Hank in that big house and was an actress. She was always pretending to be somebody else, even when she was a little kid."

Helen heard Laredo's teasing voice again, like a forties movie star: "You've been a very bad boy, Hank. You're just lucky I like bad boys."

Another strip was gone. Savannah's beer bottle was half-naked now.

"Laredo wanted Hank to marry her, but that was never going to happen. Hank never treated her right. She finally walked out on him. Had to, for her own self-respect. I was proud she did that. Takes courage for a girl to walk away from a man with money.

"Laredo told me all about it, why she finally pulled the plug. She was over at his house. She was all ready for a little lovin' when he got a business call on his cell phone. He answered it. He kept talking on the phone while they were doing it. He finished up, still talking on the phone. He got out of bed and went into the living room. Didn't say a word to her."

"What a pig," Helen said.

"Oh, yeah. He woulda been a prize swine at the state fair. Hank's call lasted for hours. Laredo could see him in the other room pacing around bare-naked, with the lights on so the neighbors could see him."

Savannah hit a tough patch of label, but kept picking at it.

"Laredo said she read a magazine, then played around on his computer. She liked video poker. Hank never did come back to bed," she said. "She was good and pissed. When he finally returned, Hank said he'd be tied up all night and sent her home in a cab. Laredo told me she never went out with him again. Said no man was going to treat her like that."

Pick. Pick. The label was stubborn. But so was Savannah.

"Your sister told you all that?" Helen trusted her sister, Kathy, more than anyone in the world. But there were some hairy escapades in her past that even Kathy didn't know about.

"Laredo knew I wouldn't judge her. I know she kept stuff

from me, but she told me most of her adventures. She was so mad at ol' Hank, she had to tell somebody. I thought she might put sugar in his gas tank or something." *Pick. Pick.*

"Did she have any particular plan for revenge?" Helen said.

"Not really. She said when she finished with him, he'd be sorry. She said he'd be begging her to marry him. She was going to be one of the fine ladies of Lauderdale." The last of the label gave way, and Savannah had a little pile of crinkled paper on the table.

"But that was Laredo, all talk and dreams. I couldn't see how she was going to make Hank marry her—she wasn't pregnant, she wasn't going out with him and she made fun of him. She said he was always looking in the mirror and combing his hair to cover his bald spot. He was getting those hair plug things. Once she said he was making so much money that he could afford the best defense lawyers."

"What did she mean by that?"

"She didn't say. It was just a casual remark. They were definitely finished." Savannah took a final drink. The beer bottle was empty, inside and out.

"Then why was she at his house the other night?"

"I don't know," Savannah said. "I don't for the life of me. All I know is she's gone and I haven't heard from her in a week."

"I heard her say 'It's the coffee.' Does coffee mean anything special to Laredo?" Helen said.

"Well, she had to have a cup first thing in the morning," Savannah said.

"Listen, Savannah, do you really think it was your sister I heard? Maybe it was someone else who got . . . who . . ."

"I know it's her. But I figured you'd ask that question. That's why I brought this."

She dug around in the floppy purse again. This time, she pulled out a dented cassette recorder and a tangle of wires and sponge that were headphones.

"I thought it might help if you could hear her voice. She

was working on her lines for that Shakespeare play. She'd tape them. Helped her memorize them. She was going to play Lady Macduff."

"She was in *Macbeth*?" Helen said.

"Yes. She had a big scene where she . . ." Savannah stopped, and her pale face went even whiter. She took a deep breath. ". . . Where she got murdered. Laredo told me the play was bad luck. You couldn't even say the name in the theater. They called it 'the Scottish play.' Laredo slipped and said 'Macbeth' during the audition and they made her go out-side, turn around three times and ask permission to come back in because it was such bad luck. Laredo laughed, but she did it. She really wanted that part. I helped her with the script. I read the other parts, the murderers and the son."

Savannah turned on the clunky old tape recorder and pushed a button. "I've got it at the right place."

Helen put on the headphone. The sound was tinny and it was hard to hear over the clatter of plates and restaurant con-versation. She took a sip of coffee, hoping the caffeine would help her concentrate.

Helen recognized Savannah's voice. "Okay, Lady Laredo, are you ready?"

There was a giggle like the one on the answering ma-chine. Unfortunately, the woman Helen had heard on the phone wasn't giggling.

Then another voice, younger and lighter: Laredo. "I've been practicing my screams. I think I'm getting good at them. Erin told me it's like being an opera singer. You've got to open your lungs. Let me take a last drink of water and let's do it."

Savannah was talking again: "I'm reading the parts of the murderers and the son. You're doing Lady Macduff, right?"

"Right." Helen guessed that's what Laredo said. "Born to be Wild" was playing on the restaurant sound system. Step-penwolf's wail drowned out the words.

Savannah started reading in a stilted monotone. "First murderer: 'Where is your husband?' "

Laredo spoke next. Helen could hear the fear and defiance

as she said, "I hope, in no place so unsanctified where such as thou may find him."

Damn. Steppenwolf was running over Laredo's words. Helen couldn't tell if she recognized the voice. She wished Laredo would say more. Instead, she heard Savannah's flat voice: "Thou liest, thou shag-eared villain!"

With absolutely no change of tone Savannah said the murderer's part: "What, you egg! Young fry of treachery! *Stab! Stab!*"

Savannah read the son's dying declaration like a grade schooler with a primer: "He has killed me, Mother. Run away, I pray you."

Finally, Laredo's voice again. Her emotion overwhelmed the tape recorder's tinny little speaker: "Murder!" she cried. "Murder!" There was an unearthly scream.

Helen knocked over her coffee. "It's her," she said. "That's the woman on the phone."

"I knew it," Savannah said with satisfaction, as she mopped up Helen's spilled coffee. "Now tell me what you know about my sister's death."

Helen told her everything. Savannah did not cry. Her sorrow seemed beyond tears.

"Have you seen this Hank Asporth?" Helen said. "Was he big and strong enough to hurt her?"

"My sister was just a little bit of a thing. It would be easy. She didn't even weigh a hundred pounds." Helen noticed Savannah was talking about her sister as if she was dead.

"The police think I heard a movie," Helen said. "But I heard her say 'Hank,' twice, and then I heard her scream— like the scream on the tape only more real. I know that was no movie. But the cops searched the place and found no body, no blood, no sign of a struggle, no sign of a woman. The only cars in the garage were registered to Asporth. They don't believe she was killed. I know she was."

"I do, too," Savannah said. "I knew the moment he did it. It felt like someone reached in and ripped out my heart.

"I want the man who did this to her. I want him dead."

Chapter 5

A cold wind hit Helen in the face when she left The Floridian. The temperature was supposed to drop down to sixty degrees tonight. She hunched her shoulders against the sharp breeze.

A bare-chested guy in shorts and sandals staggered past her, his arm around a tipsy brunette in a strapless dress. Tourists. The cold didn't bother them. You could always tell. Sixty felt warm after the brutal winters of New York, New Jersey and Quebec. In St. Louis, where Helen used to live, sixty would have been a spring day. But she had been in Florida for more than a year. Her blood had thinned.

Another gust of wind sent a beer bottle rolling down the street. She shivered, glad she was almost home. It felt warmer around the pool at the Coronado Tropic Apartments. The swooping cream-white curves of the old building blocked the winter wind. The lights on the purple bougainvillea gave the pool a warm glow. The box of cheap wine gave the party around the pool its own glow.

"Hi, there," Peggy said.

"Awwk," said Pete, Peggy's parrot.

Both Peggy and Pete were exotic-looking, with elegant beaks. Officially, the Coronado had a no-pets policy. Etiquette required that Helen ignore Pete when their landlady,

Margery, was around. He patrolled Peggy's shoulder restlessly, until she gave him a pretzel to settle him down.

"Pull up a chaise longue," Margery said. Her purple shorts set was the same color as the night shadows. The darkness had smoothed out the wrinkles on her sun-damaged face, and Helen caught a glimpse of a younger woman.

She studied Helen with shrewd old eyes. "You look terrible. What happened?"

"I heard a murder last night." Helen told them the story over a generous glass of wine.

"You're not sure it was a murder," Margery said. "You're not even sure the woman was dead."

"She's dead," Helen said. "Nobody sounds like that and lives."

"Well, you've found the sister," Peggy said. "That's a relief. Your part is done. She can turn it over to the police."

"No, it's not," Helen said. "Laredo's missing. The police won't investigate it. They think she took off. I need to prove to myself she's dead. I heard a woman die. Do you know how horrible that is? Don't you get it?"

She could see Peggy frowning in disapproval. She could feel Margery doing the same thing. She started talking before they could object. "Tomorrow, I'm going to Gator Bill's restaurant to see that waitress, Debbie. Savannah's talking with the neighbors in Hank Asporth's area to see if they noticed her sister's car. She's also going to follow Hank around and see where he goes."

"Sounds like you got the hard part," Peggy said. "And the expensive part. Even if you just have a drink at Gator Bill's, it will cost you twenty bucks."

Pete gave a disapproving squawk.

"Savannah's taking a day off work to follow Hank. That will cost her a lot more than twenty bucks."

"Are the cops hassling you about this?" Margery said.

"No. As far as they're concerned, nobody was murdered. I'm just a crazy woman who made a hysterical call. They checked it out and saw nothing. Case closed."

"Then why can't you let it go?" Margery asked. "You don't know this Laredo woman. She sounds like someone who'd leave town for no reason. She's a waitress living in a double-wide. She doesn't have any roots."

"I heard a woman die," Helen said. "I didn't make it up. And I don't walk away from murder."

"Hush," Margery said, looking toward the parking lot. "Here come the new neighbors in 2C, Fred and Ethel Mertz. I don't want these nice, down-to-earth folks to hear you talk about murder."

Ethel was about sixty. She had a chunky body, tightly permed gray hair, and a T-shirt with prancing cats on it. The back of the T-shirt showed the cats' butts. Helen figured that was as down-to-earth as you could get.

Fred was wearing a baseball cap that said, I'M RETIRED—DON'T ASK ME TO DO ANYTHING, and a T-shirt that didn't quite cover his expanding belly. Helen stared at his massive gut. The flesh was firm and smooth, like a prize gourd. The rest of him was lumpy, as if he'd been constructed of modeling clay. He had a jowly face with a knoblike nose. More lumps for chins, arms and knobby knees.

Fred and Ethel declined Peggy's offer of a glass of wine. "We don't believe in strong drink," Ethel said. "We're high on life."

"Awwk," Pete said.

Helen felt the same way. "What are you retired from, Fred?"

"I sold pre-owned cars." Of course. Helen should have recognized that insincere smile. "Ethel worked for the IRS for thirty-eight years. What do you do?"

"I work for Girdner Sales," Helen said.

"Never heard of them," Fred said, as if that counted against the company. "What do they do?"

"We're a telemarketing firm."

"A telemarketer?" Fred said. "You know what I tell telemarketers? 'Why don't you give me your home number, honey, so I can call *you* at eight in the morning?' "

He looked pleased with himself, as if he'd said something clever. Helen heard that routine twenty times a day.

"I hang up on them. Hard," Ethel said. "I want their ears ringing like my phone."

Helen wondered why people felt compelled to tell her the ugly things they did to telemarketers. She didn't tell Fred what she wanted to do to used-car salesmen—especially the one who sold her that hunk of junk she drove to Florida. Nor did she tell Ethel that she thought most IRS agents weren't smart enough to crunch numbers in the private sector, and that's why they had government jobs. She kept her mouth politely shut. But telemarketers were such pariahs, even used-car salesmen didn't have to be polite to them.

"What do you do when a telemarketer wakes you up?" Fred asked.

"I don't have a phone," Helen said.

"Huh," Ethel said. "You bother people all day, but no one can bother you."

Helen was not about to tell Ethel the reason she didn't have a phone. "Nice meeting you," she lied. "It's getting late. I'd better head home."

"Me, too," Peggy said.

Helen felt mean and petty. Five minutes with the new neighbors, and she hated them. Fred and Ethel had attacked her job and her integrity. They didn't even know her. Was that what nice, down-to-earth people did? She'd been living in South Florida so long, she didn't know.

On the way to her room, Helen walked through the perpetual marijuana fog outside of Phil the invisible pothead's apartment. In some ways, he was the perfect neighbor. He was quiet and considerate. He was supposed to be a Clapton fan, although he never bothered her with loud music. But he drove her crazy. She'd never seen him in the year she'd lived at the Coronado, not even when he'd saved her life. There had been a fire in her apartment and Phil had pulled her free. All she saw then was his CLAPTON IS GOD T-shirt, and felt his powerful hands pulling her out of the smoke and flames.

She'd give a lot to know what he looked like.

Gator Bill's was the tackiest restaurant in South Florida—and that was no small claim. As she stepped inside, Helen was nearly blinded by the decor. The walls were slashed with strips of orange and blue neon, the Gators' colors. The neon blinked on and off, making Helen's eyes cross.

The lobby fountain had a ferocious twenty-foot blue gator with orange teeth. Brightly painted wood fruit and vegetables spilled from its open jaws, cornucopia style. It looked as if the gator was barfing bushels of corn, carrots, strawberries and oranges. Helen wondered if this said something about the food.

Gators were everywhere. Small gators slithered up the walls. Large gators lurked under plastic palm trees. Gator tracks crossed the ceiling.

Orange televisions hung in every corner. When there were no live Gators games, taped games featured Gator Bill's exploits. In between, there were tapes of Mr. Two Bits leading his famous Gator cheer: "Two bits, four bits, six bits, a dollar. Gator fans, stand up and holler." Naturally, all the Gator fans in the restaurant did that every time he went into his chant.

No opportunity to honor the Gators was overlooked. Even the bathroom was Gator country. When Helen closed the orange stall door, she saw "Go, Gators!" on the inside door.

The rest room had an attendant, a dignified older African-American woman in an orange uniform. She had the usual tray of hair spray, mouthwash and perfume. But instead of hand towels, the attendant took two pulls on the towel dispenser and handed Helen a strip of brown paper. Helen tipped her a dollar. This woman had an even worse job than she did.

Helen found the hostess stand, which was shaped like the state of Florida. It was crawling with blue gators.

"Is Debbie working tonight?"

"Sure is," the perky hostess said. She was dressed as a Gators cheerleader. "I can seat you in her section."

She showed Helen to a tiny table under a huge stuffed alligator. It was so lifelike, Helen felt like gator bait. The hostess handed her a leather-bound menu the size of a law book, decorated with heavy gold tassels.

"Can I bring you some Gator Bites while you wait?" she said.

Helen stared at the gleaming gator teeth over her head. "Er, no thanks."

She read the menu, which featured wildly overpriced meat. Thirty bucks for prime rib. Fifty for filet mignon. Five bucks for a baked potato. She'd rather starve. She might, if Debbie didn't show up soon.

Then she saw the middle-aged man at the next table put down his salad fork and stare. His teenaged son blushed until his ears turned red. A waitress in a cheerleader uniform was putting steaks on their table. Her platinum blond hair fell below her waist. Her white bosom nearly popped out of her orange top. The older guy almost had a coronary.

This must be Debbie. Helen didn't think she was drop-dead gorgeous. Debbie's features were small and regular but without character. Helen doubted the men noticed. They could not take their eyes off her gorgeous platinum hair, which was rippling past her cheerleader's skirt. That gleaming silver waterfall caught every man's eye.

Helen expected Debbie would ignore a mere woman, but she was fast and efficient. She took Helen's order for the crab-cake appetizer and a small salad. In less than fifteen minutes, she plunked down the plates.

"Anything else I can get you?"

"Debbie, do you know another waitress who works here? Her name is Laredo."

"Laredo, sure. But she's not here anymore. She took off a week or so ago. Got restless, packed up her car and headed out. That's what I'd like to do." Debbie's smile did not reach her pale blue eyes.

"Do you know where she went? I owe her some money."

"No, she took off real sudden." Debbie flipped her shimmering hair away from her face and every man in sight practically sat up and begged. Helen was not so easily distracted. She noticed Debbie would not look her in the eye.

"That's odd," Helen said. "I didn't think she'd leave town without her money."

"Well, she did," Debbie said sharply, her good nature gone. "Anything else I can bring you?"

"The check," Helen said.

Interesting, she thought. Debbie's attitude did a one-eighty when her story was questioned.

Helen counted out half a day's pay for her meal and went to the bar. The bartender's name tag said TAMMY. She was another eye-catching blonde surrounded by a gaggle of gaga males. Tammy's hair was shorter and brassier than Debbie's, but her bosom was bigger. Helen knew it was unfair to judge a woman by those attributes, but Tammy didn't seem to have any others.

When a fat, red-faced man got up to go to the john, Helen took his seat. She figured she was doing him a favor, saving his liver. She ordered a club soda. Tammy brought her a tall glass garnished with lime.

"I'm trying to find Laredo," Helen said. "I need to give her some money. Do you know where I can reach her?"

"Took off for greener pastures, the way I heard it." Tammy poured something blue into a blender, added ice, and switched it on. Over the noise she shouted, "I don't think she'll need your money."

"Did she strike it rich?"

Tammy poured the drink into a margarita glass, added a plastic gator and an orange slice, and set it on a tray for a server. She started washing glasses while she talked.

"All I know is she was flashing lots of cash before she left, and it was more than tip money. One night, she came in and wanted change for five one-hundred-dollar bills. The next night, she had another five hundred. Then it was a thousand. That was cash, too."

"Where'd she get that kind of money?"

"Some charity gig. She wanted me to work it, but I said no thanks. I'm not giving up a job with health insurance, no matter how much it pays in cash under the table. But Laredo was too young to worry about medical bills."

"Laredo never mentioned anything like that," Helen said. "Are they hiring? I could always use some extra money." That was the truth, at least. Helen might need another job soon, with stone-faced Penelope looking for an excuse to fire her.

"Well, she left me some cards. I've got one here somewhere. I've sent a couple girls there." Tammy dried her hands on a blue towel, then picked through a pile of papers by the cash register.

"Here it is. You're supposed to call and ask for Steve. It's OK to mention my name."

She handed Helen a business card. It was plain white, with stark black numbers. No name, no address. There was nothing on it but a phone number.

Helen thought the number looked naked and slightly sinister.

Chapter 6

It took three calls before Helen found Savannah. That meant three dashes to the lobby pay phone on her breaks, although you could hardly call them that. Helen got five minutes each hour. When she finally got Savannah, Helen was so rushed, she sounded like a telegram: "I found something. I'm off at one."

"Me, too," Savannah said.

She'd never noticed it before, but Savannah drawled her words. It took precious time. Helen had to clock back in in two minutes.

"Sounds like we better meet," Savannah said, drawing out each word with irritating slowness. "I don't have the time or money for lunch. How about we find a bench on Las Olas about one fifteen?"

"Fine." Helen hung up and clocked in with thirty seconds to spare.

There wasn't a bench free on the entire street. Whole families and entire offices roosted on them all. The best bet was one bench occupied by a white-haired man primly eating a tuna sandwich, but he didn't look like he'd be moving soon.

Savannah sat down on the other end of the bench. The man glared at her and rustled his lunch bag. Savannah said loudly, "Helen, my period is really awful this month. There's so much blood—that nasty black stuff—and I . . ."

The white-haired man picked up his sandwich and fled. Helen was caught between horror and admiration. Today, Savannah looked like a dignified matron in a fussy ruffled dress and pink high heels. But she'd chased off a grown man with a few words.

"I hated to do that, but I only have ten minutes." Savannah pulled two soda cans out of her floppy purse. "Want a Vanilla Coke?"

Helen found two slightly melted chocolate energy bars in her purse. "Chocolate, caffeine and sugar. All the major food groups are covered."

"I don't know. The energy bar's a little healthy," Savannah said. "It might throw off my system."

The two munched and sipped, while Helen talked about Debbie the waitress and her dramatic mood change.

"Here's what burns my buns," Savannah said. "You figured out Debbie was lying—but the cops didn't."

"Were they male cops?" Helen said.

"Yep. Cute young doughnut chompers."

"There's your answer," Helen said. "Debbie gives most men an instant lobotomy."

"I've got good news and bad news," Savannah said. "Which do you want first?"

"Let's get the bad over with," Helen said.

"Hank busted me. I followed him nearly four hours yesterday. He ran errands—the dry cleaner, the bank, the gas station and this fancy salon for a haircut. Then he stopped at Publix. I pulled into the side entrance where I could watch him go in and out, thinking I was real clever. Next thing I know, he's standing by my car. Snuck right up on me, and I didn't even know it till I smelled his cologne.

"He said, 'Why are you following me in that junk heap?' Hank's a scary dude, Helen. Huge, too. And he's got this one big old eyebrow all the way across his forehead. You'd think he'd get that fixed. They could've cut it in two when they did his hair."

"Savannah," Helen said. "What happened?"

"Nothing. I hemmed and hawed and said I wasn't following him, it was just a coincidence.

"He said, 'One more coincidence and I'll call the cops and have you arrested for stalking.' I think he meant it."

"We're stuck," Helen said. "I can't follow him. If he busts me, I'll lose my job and get sued. Besides, I don't have a car. We'll have to find some other way to get him. Give me the good news. I could use it."

"I found out something interesting. It wasn't easy. Brideport doesn't allow solicitors. I thought of collecting for a charity door-to-door, but those rich old buzzards would have called the police the minute I rang their bells. So I made me up some flyers."

She reached in her purse and handed one to Helen.

"SAVANNAH'S SUPER-CLEAN SERVICE," it began. *"Excellent references. Will do windows and hands-and-knees scrubbing your housekeeper won't touch. Cheap."*

"Is that what you do for a living? Clean houses?" I'm getting lazy, Helen thought. I never bothered asking her occupation, but it would explain the bleach odor under the flowery perfume.

"It's one of my jobs. I have three. I'm an office manager by day. I work at a convenience store on State Road 7 four nights a week. In my spare time, I clean houses." She said that last line with a straight face.

"Jeez, Savannah. What happened?"

"A bad divorce and some medical bills that weren't covered by insurance." Savannah shrugged. She was not looking for sympathy.

"A dozen flyers from Kinko's got me all over Brideport. Nobody turns away a cleaning woman, even if they have a housekeeper. In fact, some rich folks hire me to keep their housekeepers happy. What are these energy bars, anyway? They're not bad."

"Pria bars," Helen said. "I live on them." She'd been trying to eat them instead of the salt-and-vinegar chips. Instead,
she ate both. She'd gained another two pounds.

"Most of that stuff tastes like chocolate-covered ceiling
insulation." Savannah looked at her watch and said, "I have
to get back to work. I talked with the neighbors on either side
of Hank Asporth. One was a lovely saleslady, Ms. Patterson.
She sells medical equipment and travels all the time. Must
make boo-coo bucks.

"We got along real well. Ms. Patterson hired me to do her
heavy cleaning. I told her I saw the police cars at her neighbor's house the other night, and I wasn't sure it was safe to
work in Brideport. She assured me it was a secure neighborhood. She wasn't home at the time, but Mr. Asporth told her
the police were called for a false alarm."

"He would," Helen said.

"Mr. McArthur, the old man on the other side, was eighty-
two and almost deaf. He was also lonely and liked to talk. We
sat in his kitchen and drank coffee and ate butter cookies. He
didn't hear a thing that night, which was no surprise. I had to
practically yell at him the whole time. Hank Asporth has a lot
of girls at his house, but Mr. McArthur never heard any wild
parties. The old man sounded kind of disappointed. His
house could use a good cleaning, but he didn't hire me.

"There's only one neighbor across the street, Mrs.
Kercher. She lives on a big five-acre spread. She didn't hear
anything, but she saw something. A little yellow Honda was
parked in Ms. Patterson's drive for several hours that
evening. That's the medical saleslady's driveway—the one
who was out of town.

"My sister drove an old yellow Honda." Drove.

"What does Ms. Patterson drive?"

"A new black BMW," Savannah said. "Her housekeeper
has an old brown Ford. It was the first and last time Mrs.
Kercher saw that yellow car. Too bad she didn't see who
drove it.

"I think it was Laredo's car. You can't park on the street

in Brideport. Before the police showed up, Hank Asporth moved Laredo's car to the driveway next door. Nice old Hank takes in his neighbor's mail. He knew the saleslady wouldn't be back that night."

"Do you really think he'd have time to move a car and clean up any sign of a struggle before the police came?"

"That's the hitch. It doesn't seem likely, does it?" Savannah said. "Do you think he had help?"

"If he did, the police didn't mention another person. Wouldn't Hank have produced him as a witness? You know, 'Officer, George and I were watching the movie all afternoon.' Did Mrs. Kercher say she saw another car in Hank's driveway?"

"No. I asked her. The only car she remembers was the yellow Honda in the drive next door. But what was Laredo's car doing there?"

"Maybe your sister parked it over there so Hank wouldn't see her coming," Helen said.

"Why would she do that?"

Savannah had created more questions and found no answers. "I'm going to scrub floors at Ms. Patterson's and see if I can find out anything more."

"I'll call Steve and see if I can get that charity bartender's gig," Helen said.

"At least we're making money while we're detecting." Savannah dumped her soda can in the trash. "Back to work."

Helen called Steve from a pay phone. He wasn't there. "Call back after eleven tonight," a woman said. She slammed down the phone.

Helen's life seemed to be nothing but phone abuse, personally and professionally. In the boiler room, she hadn't made a sale all morning. She longed for the quiet of survey duty. But Vito had put his foot down: "No sales, no surveys." Tonight, she was working the boiler room.

The jittery Nick was not sitting next to her. He did not show up for work. Helen wondered how much longer he would last. Shellie, a bouncy blond cheerleader type, took his seat. Helen found her more irritating than the junkie.

Shellie oozed enthusiasm, squealing with delight when she said, "Yes, sir, Tank Titan is guaranteed to help reduce large chunks, odors and wet spots."

Helen felt a mean, secret satisfaction when she heard Shellie say, "Ewww. That's disgusting." She dropped the phone like it was covered with slime.

"What did he want?" Helen said.

"A blow job. Vito's got to take that line about wet spots out of the sales pitch."

Helen was taking her own lumps. A Texas woman screamed, "It's eight fifteen at night. We're getting ready to settle into bed. We're tired. We don't appreciate calls this late."

They packed it in early, deep in the heart of Texas.

Bill, the next caller, was rested and ready. Helen was halfway through her spiel when he said, "You have a good product there, Helen, but I have a better one. Have you ever thought of exploring the Amway opportunity? I could sponsor you. I'm an IBO—independent business owner, and—"

"Uh, thanks, Bill. I gotta go. My doorbell's ringing," Helen said. The words came automatically. It was what she always said to telemarketers, back when she had a phone.

Helen didn't think the night would ever end. But it finally did. At ten twenty, she was sitting out by the Coronado pool with Peggy and Margery. The lights on the turquoise water were as romantic as ever. The palm trees whispered night secrets. But Helen did not enjoy her evenings there anymore. Fred and Ethel, the new tenants in 2C, infested her enchanted place. Even the most harmless conversation triggered one of their diatribes.

Tonight, they were smugly swigging root beer. Helen, Margery and Peggy were drinking cheap white wine. Pete was sitting on Peggy's shoulder with his head under his wing. He couldn't stand Fred and Ethel, either.

Conversation was a struggle. There were long, uncomfortable silences. Peggy broke one by saying, "I think the starter's going on my car. I'm going to need a new one."

"That's what you get for driving a foreign car," Fred said. "You pay for that foreign prestige. Nothing beats American-made. That's what I always say."

Helen didn't see much prestige in Peggy's green Kia, but she couldn't say that without hurting Peggy's feelings.

"American-made isn't what it used to be," Ethel said. Her eyes were small and hard as BBs. "You ask me, it's the American workers. They want too much money for too little work."

No one asked her. The conversation lay there like a dead fish.

Margery, who usually had an opinion on everything, puffed quietly on her Marlboro. Peggy said nothing. Even Pete stayed silent.

Helen studied Ethel's tightly permed hair. How did you get a style like that, she wondered? Did you go into a beauty shop and say, "I want to look like a complete frump?"

"Our son, Fred Jr., is coming for a visit," Ethel said. "He's single. He's a good Christian man, Helen. Doesn't smoke or drink and fears the Lord."

"Uh, thanks, but I'm dating someone."

"What's his name?" Ethel said. It was a demand and a challenge.

"Phil," Helen said. "Lives nearby. You must have seen him."

Peggy choked on her wine. "I think I'll turn in." Pete woke up and screeched his approval.

"We're tuckered out, too," Fred said. "Think we'll head inside." He patted his gourdlike gut as if it were a baby. Ethel followed respectfully behind him.

When Helen heard their apartment door slam she said, "How can you stand them?"

"It doesn't hurt to spend some time with normal people," Margery said.

"Normal does not have to mean boring," Helen said.

She left her landlady sitting alone in the darkness. It was soothing to walk through Phil's perpetual pot fog to her own apartment. She breathed in the sharp, oily sensimilla smell. Phil was too laid-back to criticize his neighbors. He was too invisible to bother them. Fred and Ethel could take a leaf from his book. A spiky green leaf.

Thumbs, her six-toed cat, greeted her at the door. Helen scratched his gray ears until he purred. Then she found some change. It was getting harder to find a pay phone. They all seemed to be occupied by kids making drug deals or Canadians too cheap to use their hotel phones.

It was eleven thirty when she finally called Steve. He answered on the first ring.

"I hear you're looking for servers for charity parties," Helen said.

"Where'd you find out about us?" His voice was abrupt and demanding. Helen wondered if it was his New York accent, or if the guy was just rude.

"Tammy at Gator Bill's gave me your card," she said.

"Tammy has a good eye for talent," Steve said, sounding friendlier.

How could Tammy spot a talent for bartending by watching Helen drink club soda?

"Ever tend bar before?" Steve said.

"Yes," Helen lied.

"It's not hard. We'll put you on a portable bar outside by the pool. It will be just your wine, beer, liquor and your soft drinks. Your blender drinks and specialty martinis will be at the main bar. You won't have to do those."

Helen relaxed. Even she could open a beer.

"You'll be working with your movers and shakers. We got your doctors, your lawyers, your school board members, people like that. They live in your better areas, like Bridgeport. They bankroll your worthy causes. Saturday night, it's the Langley School in Lauderdale."

That was worthy indeed. Langley was one of the richest schools in the area.

"Can you work then?"

Helen could. There was no telemarketing on Saturday night.

"Wear a white shirt and black pants. You'll work the first party. You'll get two hundred dollars for three hours. There's another party after that for the heavy hitters. If we like you, we'll ask you to work the second party next time. That pays five hundred. Cash. You keep your tips, of course."

This was some bartending gig. It paid almost a week's wages to pour wine and beer. That was way too much money, especially for South Florida.

So what exactly did Steve want her to do? Bartending couldn't be all that was expected of her.

Chapter 7

Helen did not have a car, but she treated herself to a water taxi for her well-paying bartending job Saturday night. Fort Lauderdale had more than two hundred miles of canals. For five dollars, she could ride all day on a water taxi. It made regular stops on a route like a bus.

The little yellow boat met her at the dock behind the Riverside Hotel on Las Olas. The setting sun stained the sky a brilliant flamingo and turned the water a delicate pink, like the inside of a seashell.

Fort Lauderdale floated on oceans of money. Billionaires' yachts had their own helicopter landing pads. Casino ships took seagoing suckers on cruises to nowhere. Cruise ships pampered the overprivileged.

Tonight, Helen felt a kinship with the moneyed boaters. In any other city, I'd be sitting in a bus in rush-hour traffic, eating exhaust, Helen thought. In Fort Lauderdale, I'm riding to work like a Venetian doge.

And working in a palace. Mindy and Melton Mowbrys' mansion was in the obscenely rich part of Brideport, where houses were the size of shopping malls. Their owners were perpetually in the papers. One Sunday, they'd be praised in the society pages. The next Sunday, they'd be indicted on the front page.

The Mowbry mansion was bristling with towers and bursting with bay windows, slathered with pink stucco and encrusted with red barrel tile. The architecture looked like Mizner on magic mushrooms. The massive wood and wrought iron double doors belonged on a Spanish cathedral. Helen knew she could not walk through the front door. She went around back to the service entrance, a mean little area with a cheap screen door. She could hear someone screaming in the steamy kitchen.

"I'm looking for Steve," she said to a man in a white chef's coat carrying a silver coffee urn.

"Follow the shrieks," he said in a weary voice.

Steve was dressing down two waiters. The reprimand sounded worse in his harsh New York accent. "I don't want to ever see that again, understand?"

The waiters nodded, too scared to speak, and backed out of the room.

Steve was small and dark and needed a shave. He pointed to Helen and said, "You! Don't stand there like a potted plant. Are you the new bartender?"

"Yes," she said.

"Speak up," he said. "Are you a woman or a mouse?"

"I'm somebody here to work, not take abuse," she said.

Steve broke into a smile. "Good-looking and sassy. I like that. You'll do."

He planted her at a service bar by the swimming pool. It was landscaped to look like a jungle pool with a waterfall. Ferns and pink orchids grew along the waterfall. Thick pink clouds of frilly blossoms bloomed alongside the paths. Pink-flowered vines dripped from the trees.

Long serving tables were covered with crisp pink cloths and lavish hors d'oeuvres. Huge bouquets of pink roses were being carried outside. Candles were lit. An ice sculpture dripped. A busboy brought Helen a tub of ice. She checked out the booze. No box wine here. The Mowbrys served only the finest wine and liquor.

The first guests trickled in half an hour later. By eight, the party was in full swing, and Helen was pouring drinks one after another. This was a thirsty crowd.

Brideport parties had people of breeding. In fact, it was all they talked about. As she scrambled for ice and bottles, Helen heard a white-haired man in a yachting jacket say, "We really need better birth-control programs at the schools for the great unwashed. Those people have too many children. Indiscriminate breeding, I tell you. They all grow up to be Democrats." The man said "Democrat" the way others might say "child molester."

Helen thought his three double scotches made him talk that way.

But a face-lifted brunette in red sparkles had had only one white wine when she said, "How can we encourage people like us to have more children? I know they're terribly expensive, but people of our class must understand their duty. Otherwise, we're going to be overtaken by the wrong sort."

Her balding companion nodded sagely and downed another neat bourbon.

A hatchet-faced man with dyed black hair ordered two red wines and told the man next to him, "There must be some way to sterilize Chelsea Clinton, so the Clinton genes are not passed on."

Helen nearly dropped a full bottle of club soda at that one, but caught it before she was spotted as a Democrat sympathizer.

Otherwise, it was a typical, dull charity party. Helen had attended too many when she'd been in corporate life. The women were mostly blond and thin. The men were mostly overweight and over fifty. A bored photographer from the local paper snapped pictures of the partygoers and said they would run in a week or two. The fundraising chair gave a long speech thanking everyone, "including our gracious host, Dr. Mowbry and his beautiful wife, Mindy." Whatever kind of doctoring Mowbry did, it must have paid well. There was lots of booze, decent hors d'oeuvres and a mediocre band that played tired old songs like "I Left My Heart in San Francisco." Helen wondered why rich people liked stodgy music.

The men flirted with her and asked if she was staying for the second party. Helen said, "Not this time." Some seemed genuinely disappointed.

Helen thought that was odd. No one noticed the servers at parties. The women were suitably cold, but she saw few of them at her bar. The men mostly did drinks duty. That was fine with Helen. These guys handed out five- and ten-dollar tips like business cards. One short, chubby old man with a white toothbrush mustache gave her a twenty, "So you'll be sure to remember me at the second party."

"Oh, I couldn't forget you, sir," Helens said, stuffing the money in her pants pocket. Not in that getup. The old guy was wearing a tux with a shamrock bow tie and cummerbund.

The bar opposite hers, manned by a blonde named Kristi, was even busier than Helen's. Kristi offered the same drink choices as Helen, but the men lined up as if she was giving away vintage champagne. Her line was twice as long as Helen's.

Kristi had a face like a doll's, and it was just as expressionless. Her dyed blond hair was puffed up. So were her chest and lips. The enhanced hair, lips and breasts looked obvious and artificial to Helen. The guys didn't seem to care. Kristi was a silicone siren. Men longed to throw themselves on her rocky breasts.

Helen had never been to a party with such generous tippers. The rich usually hung onto every nickel. When another busty blonde came around with a tray of mini-quiches, six men slipped her bills. The chubby old man gave her a fat wad and said again, "So you'll be sure to remember me at the second party."

Poor old fellow must have a real ego problem. Probably felt he was nothing without his money, Helen thought.

While the fundraising chair gave her speech, the booze

traffic slacked off. That's when Debbie, the long-haired wait-ress from Gator Bill's, showed up at Helen's service bar.

"Hi," Helen said. "I didn't know you worked here, too."

Debbie pulled her silk curtain of hair forward to hide her face and said in a low, angry voice, "What the hell are you doing here?"

"I'm trying to find Laredo."

"I told you, she left town," Debbie said. She tilted her head and her amazing hair fell back off her face. Helen looked into those pale blue eyes. They were hard as marble. Were they also shadowed with fear?

"I don't believe you," Helen said.

"Then believe this. You don't know what you're getting into. If you have any sense you'll get out fast."

A few heads turned their way. Some men stared. Debbie smiled fetchingly in their direction and left, her white-blond hair rippling down to her waist.

Helen wondered what could be threatening at this party for middle-aged rich people? By ten o'clock, many of the guests had said goodnight and drifted away.

Helen's shift was over at eleven. Steve came by her sta-tion and said, "Don't bother to clean up. Kristi's going to take over here."

Steve counted out her pay in cash. "You did a nice job," he said. "I heard a lot of good comments about you tonight. Call me again for another gig."

Helen liked the feel of two hundred dollars in her hand. She had another one-fifty in tips. There was no downside to this job, except that her feet hurt. But for three hundred fifty bucks, she could stand that.

She walked out the grimy back entrance in a green glow. Already she was dreaming about spending her bartending money. Maybe she could finally get her car fixed. The rust-ing heap needed eight hundred dollars in repairs, but she could make that in three weekends. Look at the money she had right in her hands. She ought to put it in her purse. It wasn't safe walking around with that much cash, even in Brideport.

Helen stopped dead. She didn't have her purse. She'd left it in the service bar.

Helen felt like a complete fool. Well, at least no one would notice another bartender at the party. She could get her purse and get out again. She ran the block back to the Mowbry mansion. No one saw her slide into the dismal back entrance and along the kitchen hall to the pool. There was no one at her service bar under the palm tree. Helen pulled her purse out of a cubbyhole in the bar. Fresh tubs of ice and glasses had been put out. New lemons and limes had been cut.

It was a long trip home on a lot of water. Helen stopped in the closest bathroom. The Mowbrys' place seemed to have about twelve on the first floor. It had no lock, but Helen figured a shut door was enough. She was washing her hands when a man opened the door. She'd seen him at her bar before. A scotch on the rocks who saw himself as a player, with too-tanned skin, too-white teeth and too much gold jewelry.

"Excuse me," she said.

"You're excused." He exposed the teeth. "I saw you earlier tonight. You must be new. Wanna get it on?"

"Do I *what*? I don't even know you. Get out of here."

"Hey, why are you so upset? You're here for the second party, aren't you?"

"No, I'm not. I came back because I forgot my purse."

"Oops, sorry." He oozed out the door.

Oops? What was going on at the second party? Helen slid along behind the ferns and frothy pink flowers for a look. At first, she had trouble believing what she saw. A topless Kristi now stood behind Helen's bar, her giant white breasts like mounds of snow.

The same waitresses were walking around with the same canapés, but now the women were topless. Helen thought the half-naked servers looked bizarre instead of sexy. They also looked cold. Some had goose bumps bigger than their nipples.

But it wasn't just the servers who were half-naked.

The blond women guests had shed their dresses and were parading rail-thin bodies in expensive thong underwear. Helen did not want to estimate what those La Perla panties cost per square inch.

The men, alas, were in an equal state of undress. Florida's male movers and shakers wobbled like Jell-O in a hurricane. When they weren't grabbing canapés, they had their hands on the waitresses' breasts.

The chubby old man in the green cummerbund now had on only his shamrock boxers. The busty blond server was on her knees before him. Her tray of mini-quiches was abandoned on a stone bench.

All around on chairs, couches and tables, people were entwined in positions Helen had never seen in the want ads.

It was a charity swingers party.

Chapter 8

Helen expected to feel shocked. Actually, she was rather proud.

Trust South Florida to find a way to liven up one of the deadliest events in the social calendar. Naked fat men and skinny women weren't her thing, but an orgy was an interesting way to raise money for charity.

As she boarded the waiting water taxi, Helen wondered what other charities the swingers had sponsored: Single mothers? A sperm-donor bank? A school for delinquents?

The possibilities were endless. The advantages were obvious. There were no speeches at an orgy, and nobody wanted their name read out loud for any reason. Of course, the thank-you notes might be a problem. "Dear Mr. Harrison-Smythe: Thank you for your contribution to the fifth annual charity ball. . . ."

The water taxi hit the wake of a passing yacht and Helen got a face full of cold, dirty water. Ugh. Her hair was soaked. It was what she needed to shock her back to reality. This wasn't funny. Laredo had been a waitress at the swingers' party shortly before she disappeared. She'd asked Tammy, the Gator Bill's bartender, for change for five one-hundred-dollar bills. Five hundred dollars was the amount Helen had been offered to work the second party. Now she knew why

the party paid so much. She'd have to do more than serve
drinks.

How was she going to tell Savannah her little sister was a
topless waitress—and maybe worse?

Helen remembered the blond server kneeling before that
silly old man in the shamrock shorts, and his wad of tip
money. She hoped Savannah would never find out. But Savannah wasn't stupid. She'd know pretty young women
didn't get that kind of money for being good little girls.

Cold water from her drenched hair slowly dripped on her
shirt. Her teeth chattered, and she shivered in the cool night
breeze. The water taxi was open as a veranda. She wished
she'd brought a jacket.

Poor Savannah. Her baby sister was murdered, and now
her memory was being killed, too. Helen saw once more the
pinup photo of the flirty little blonde. Laredo looked so
eager, so willing to do anything to get out of that drab trailer
park. Her sweet desperation would attract rich old men the
way honey draws bees—or WASPs.

Important people went to those parties. Fort Lauderdale's
money men and women frolicked in their overpriced underwear. They were served a sea of alcohol, and at the second
party, possibly drugs. People let their guard down in those
situations.

Had Laredo seen or heard something that got her killed?
Some illegal business deal, some improper political alliance?
Had she tried to blackmail someone? Just being seen at that
second party was enough to ruin most of those guests. Soc-
cer moms or city councilmen, no one would want their
names connected to that charity affair.

Helen was bone cold by the time the water taxi bumped
against the dock behind Las Olas. Her shirt stuck to her like
she'd been in a wet T-shirt contest. The short walk home did
nothing to warm her. No one was sitting out by the pool at
the Coronado on this chilly night. The only sign of life was
Phil's cloud of pot smoke. The man was a perpetual party of
one.

Back in her apartment, Helen took out her money again and counted it on the bed. Her cat, Thumbs, jumped up and rolled around in the pile of bills, making the money crackle. Yesterday, she would have joined him, laughing at her good fortune. Now she lifted her cat off the bed, quickly bundled up the cash, and stuffed it in a couch pillow. It was blood money. She wanted it out of her sight.

Helen slept badly that night. Thumbs complained loudly at her restlessness. Most nights, he slept peacefully at the foot of her bed. But not tonight. Once she rolled over abruptly and sent him spinning off the bed. Then she dropped into a twitchy sleep and kicked the poor cat. He nipped her heel.

At six A.M., she gave up, got up, made coffee and bought a newspaper. She was glad it was Sunday, her day off. She took the paper back to bed. Thumbs burrowed playfully under the pages and tore into the funnies. He was enjoying the paper.

Helen could not read or fall back asleep. She tried to clean house, but she couldn't keep her mind on it. At nine A.M., she could put it off no longer: She found a pay phone and called Savannah Power.

As the phone rang, Helen prayed she wouldn't be home. But Savannah picked up on the third ring. Helen told her about last night, leaving out only the old man in the shamrock shorts. It was a smart move. Savannah didn't make the connection that Laredo might have been passing around more than the canapés.

"Your Saturday night was more interesting than mine," Savannah said. "My boyfriend came over and we watched TV until we fell asleep. Must be getting old. Ten years ago, we would have torn each other's clothes off."

Helen didn't want to go there. She felt distinctly nunlike after stumbling into that orgy last night.

"You know what gets me?" Helen said. "Debbie made a special trip over to my bar to warn me off. She sounded angry. But I think she was also afraid. That woman knows something. We'd better have a talk with her, and not at Gator Bill's, either."

"No place like home," Savannah said.

"Do you know where she lives?" Helen said.

"No, but the Gator Bill's servers get off at eleven on Sunday nights. That's when I used to pick up Laredo. Most of them are too tired to party on Sunday. We can probably follow Debbie straight to her home. I'll pick you up about ten forty-five tonight."

Savannah's old brown beater showed up at the Coronado right on time, its engine knocking loud enough to wake everyone in the complex. No wonder Hank Asporth had spotted Savannah tailing him, Helen thought. She wondered why it took him four hours.

The car lurched out of the parking lot. "The Tank has a little cold-start problem," Savannah said, "but it's a great car."

Helen was afraid they wouldn't let the noisy, battered Tank near the Gator Bill's lot, but the attendant knew Savannah and waved her in.

"How's that cute little sister of yours?" he said. "I haven't seen her around. Latched onto something better?"

"She's in a much better place," Savannah said, and for a minute Helen thought she was going to cry. But Savannah set her lean, freckled jaw and drove to the back of the lot.

Debbie was one of the last servers to come out the kitchen door. She was wearing her cheerleader's uniform and talking to a Hispanic chef. The young man was so dazzled he could hardly get out a tongue-tied "Goodnight."

"That's her," Helen said.

"Practicing her womanly wiles on that poor young man," Savannah said. "Look what she's doing to him. You can tell she hasn't the slightest interest in him. Woman's got a definite mean streak."

Debbie walked across the parking lot, round bottom twitching, long hair switching. She unlocked a purple Neon that looked like a rolling jelly bean, and pulled out onto Las

Olas. They tailed her in the shaking, lurching Tank. Helen wondered why Debbie didn't notice them.

About five miles later, the purple Neon abruptly swung into an apartment complex. It was a square white shoebox set in an asphalt parking lot. They saw Debbie pull into a spot marked "203." When the lights came on in a second-floor apartment, Helen and Savannah got out of the car and tiptoed up the stairs.

"Let me get us inside," Savannah whispered. "That little witch is going to talk or else."

She sounded so menacing, Helen was afraid. "You aren't going to do anything foolish, are you? You don't have a gun?"

"I hate guns. I promise you, no guns." Savannah patted her big black leather purse. Then she knocked on the door and said loudly, "Landlord! Open up! We're having problems with electrical fires in the ceiling. We need to check your kitchen."

Helen stepped back out of sight. She could hear someone unlocking the door. Debbie opened it slightly and said, "I'm OK. My smoke alarm hasn't gone off."

Savannah pushed her way inside the beige apartment. Helen followed. When Debbie saw her, she said, "You! What are you doing here? I'm calling the cops." She picked up a cell phone from the hall table.

"Go ahead," Savannah said. "Then you can tell them where my sister is."

"I don't know your sister," Debbie said, but her voice wavered. Her long hair hung limp. She knew no amount of flirtatious flipping would beguile these two women. Debbie put down the cell phone and backed into the dining room.

Savannah followed with long, lean strides.

"My name is Savannah Power. Laredo is my sister. She's missing and you're going to tell me where she is." Savannah took a bright yellow can from her purse.

"Is that pepper spray?" Debbie's voice was a squeak. She held a dining-room chair in front of her.

"No," Savannah said. "When I use this on you, you'll

wish it was. It's oven cleaner. You wanna lie? I'll give you lye. Start talking."

"But that could blind me!" Debbie backed up and hit the wall. Savannah grabbed the chair and threw it aside with one hand.

"I think it will help you see more clearly." Savannah shook the can. Helen thought she'd never heard such a threatening sound.

"I . . . Um . . ." Debbie tried to slide sideways along the wall. Savannah blocked her move and put her finger on the spray nozzle. Debbie let out a frightened yip, then the words tumbled out. "They paid me to say she left town. They said they'd hurt me if I didn't lie. I don't know where she is."

"Who paid you?" Savannah demanded.

"I can't tell you. I'm afraid of them."

"Better be more afraid of me, missy."

"They'll hurt me. They'll hurt me bad."

"So will I," Savannah's voice was so low, Helen could hardly hear her. Her finger twitched on the spray nozzle. Debbie tried to move, but she was trapped in a corner. Savannah shook the can again and held it in front of Debbie's eyes.

"Please," Debbie begged. "Please, don't shoot. It was some friend of Steve's. A guy who goes to some of the special charity parties. Name's Hank."

"Hank who?" Helen said.

"I don't know his last name."

"How much did he pay you?"

"A thousand dollars," Debbie said, her voice rising in panic. "But I didn't do anything."

"You lied to the police," Savannah said. "Because you lied, they won't investigate why Laredo is missing. I'm waiting for my sister to come back, but I don't think that's going to happen. You don't either, do you, Debbie?"

"No! Yes! I don't know."

"What happened to my sister?"

"I don't know. She worked the back room at the Mow-brys' parties. I didn't. I wouldn't even go back there, I was so afraid. There was some kinky stuff going on. I stayed away from it, even though they paid extra."

"What kind of kinky stuff?"

Debbie didn't answer. Helen wondered what was kinky in South Florida: Small pets? Large lizards? Little children?

"Tell me," Savannah said. Helen had never heard such menace in two words.

Debbie tried to break out of the corner, but Savannah pinned Debbie's face between her elbows and held the spray nozzle an inch from her right eye. Debbie clamped her eyelid shut. Helen could see the eyeball moving underneath, spastic with fear.

"Something to do with d-d-dead people." Debbie had developed a stutter. "They called themselves the Six Feet Unders. Like the TV show. They'd make jokes about it. Said it was their 'grave undertaking.' They paid a lot of money to go in that room. It was their big fundraiser. I don't know anything else. I never went back there. I was too scared."

"Who did?" Savannah said.

"K-Kristi. It was Kristi. She was always there after midnight."

"Does she work at Gator Bill's?"

"N-no. I don't know where she works, except those parties at the M-M-Mowbry mansion. I don't know where she lives, either."

"Then you're going to get us her address, right?"

Debbie nodded. "We're working a party together at the Mowbrys' tomorrow night. I'll call you with it."

"I'll call you. And you better not tell her why you want that address. You better not mention anything about us at all. Understand?" Savannah shook the can of oven cleaner. That sound again, that poisonous rattle.

"You may think Hank is a bigger threat than I am, but you haven't seen me when I'm really crazy. Got it?"

Debbie nodded again, too frightened to speak.

Savannah backed away from her, and Debbie slid down the wall.

Chapter 9

I'm going crazy, Helen thought, as she made her shaky way down Debbie's steps. First, I heard a woman die, but the police wouldn't believe me. Now, I'm hanging around with an insane redneck, forcing my way into apartments. What's next?

"Kristi's next," Savannah said, marching past her down the stairs. "She's going to tell me what she knows about Laredo."

"What are you going to do?" Helen said. "Squirt her with Windex until she comes clean? I can't believe you were going to shoot that woman in the face with lye."

They were arguing in whispers in Debbie's parking lot so they wouldn't wake the neighbors.

"Hey, I promised you I wouldn't use a gun, and I didn't. I'm trained in the use of household products."

"You threatened to blind a woman, and I stood there and let you. If Debbie complains to the police, I could be arrested." Then the cops would find out I was on the run, Helen thought, and send me back to St. Louis.

"She's not going to complain," Savannah said. "She doesn't want them to know she lied about Laredo."

Helen relaxed a bit. Savannah was right about that, at least.

"OK, but I'm not getting in that car until you hand over that oven cleaner. You're a menace with that stuff."

Some threat, Helen thought. Savannah has the car keys. I could wind up walking home.

"Oh, all right." Savannah surrendered her weapon. Helen dumped it in her purse before she changed her mind and grabbed it back, then opened the Tank's dented door and sat down heavily. A seat spring stuck her in the rump.

"I knew that murdering Hank Asporth was behind this," Savannah said. "We've got to get to him."

Helen said nothing. She didn't want to talk anymore about Hank Asporth. She just wanted to know that Laredo was dead, so she could get on with her life. Great. Now I sound like some sort of self-help book: *Browbeat Your Way to Closure.*

The two women rode in silence while the Tank bucked and rumbled past karate schools, XXX-rated topless joints, cheap bars and check-cashing stores. It was not a landscape to inspire optimism.

My life is a mess, Helen thought. My job is a nightmare. People hate me from coast to coast. I've been cussed in sixteen languages. I don't enjoy my evenings by the Coronado pool anymore, thanks to Fred and Ethel. I don't have time to see my friend Sarah. I've gained almost ten pounds eating potato chips and Pria bars.

The private litany of failure continued until Savannah pulled in front of the Coronado. She put the Tank in PARK and set off a symphony of squeaks and rattles. "You'll call me when you get off work tomorrow night, right? So we can talk about our next step?"

"There is no next step," Helen shouted over the engine noise. "Not when you want to maim people."

"It won't happen again," Savannah said. "I admit my temper got the best of me. But I wouldn't have hurt Debbie. Really."

Helen had seen the murderous look in Savannah's eye.

"Please," Savannah said. "My baby sister's lying some-where in an unmarked grave. I've got to find her."

A light came on in a second-story apartment. The Tank had awakened Fred and Ethel. Helen would never hear the end of it.

"I'll think about it." Helen wanted to slam the Tank's door for emphasis, but it refused to catch. Savannah had to lean across the seat to close it, which spoiled the drama.

The Coronado's turquoise pool shimmered invitingly, but the chaise longues were empty. Helen was disappointed. It was warm tonight, and she'd hoped that Margery and Peggy might be out by the pool. Especially when she saw the lights in Fred and Ethel's apartment.

A single ficus leaf dropped into the pool and drifted aim-lessly. Helen felt just as lost. She missed Peggy and Margery, but it was more than that. She longed for someone to love, even though she'd been badly hurt.

Right. You really need another man, she told herself. You can sure pick 'em. So far, in Florida she'd dated a cheap-skate, a con artist, a married man who said he was single and a guy so possessive he gave her a bracelet of bruises for talk-ing to another man. No chance of her falling for anyone as long as she worked in the boiler room. The only men she saw all day were her crude boss, Vito, and Nick the junkie.

She sniffed the night air and caught the thick, heavy scent of marijuana. Oh, yeah, there was Phil the invisible pothead. Just what she needed after dating drunks, crooks and deadbeats—a druggie. She wondered what he looked like. Even when he saved her life, there was only the slogan on his T-shirt, floating in the air like a dream message: "Clapton Is God." She still remembered the feel of his hands, strong and sure, as he pulled her from the deadly fire.

Was Phil straight or gay, single or married? She didn't know. He seemed complete in his chemically altered world. He didn't need any woman.

The smell of Phil's weed was extra thick tonight. It re-minded her of the rock concerts she used to go to in St.

Louis. That made her feel old. It had been eons since she'd held up a lit Bic and gotten silly.

When she opened her front door, Thumbs was waiting for her, rubbing against her legs and purring his greeting. Usually her cuddly cat made her feel better. Not tonight.

I'm an old maid living alone with my cat, Helen thought. And I'm only forty-two years old.

The next morning Helen was back in the boiler room. Discouragement—or maybe it was dirt—settled on her as she walked through the grimy door. Her phone stank of cigarette smoke. She wished she had Taniqua's Lysol to wipe it down.

In ten minutes, the computers would come on, and she would start waking up East Coast home owners. But now, sick and tardy telemarketers were calling Vito with their excuses.

She could hear Vito was yelling into the phone, "Your hand is all swollen and hurts? So what do you want me to do? Kiss it? If you're not coming in, I need a doctor's note."

The phone rang again. "You promised me you weren't going to do this shit again," Vito screamed. "You want the day off? Take the rest of the week off—at your expense. No, don't come in. You screw up one more time and you're fired."

Vito slammed down the phone and said, "Seven fifty-five and the fuckups are calling."

The phone rang again. Vito picked it up and shrieked, "If you're not here at eight A.M. you're fired. Fired. Get it? Oh, hi, Mr. Cavarelli."

Suddenly Vito's voice was soft and respectful. "You'll be in this week? Yes, sir. No, sir. No, we didn't make our quota last week. We'll make it this week for sure. I'm trying to fire the junkies and bring in quality people, but it takes time, Mr. Cavarelli."

"I'm one of the junkies," Nick said.

He was eating his usual breakfast of jelly doughnuts and orange soda. Despite his sugary diet, Nick was a skeleton. He talked in nervous bursts. "Finally got out of the halfway house. I'm sharing a trailer now. My own place. First time in years. I used to live on the street. I've come a long way. I don't want to lose my home, but if I don't sell something today I will."

"You'll make a sale," Helen said. But she knew Nick was doomed. This morning, he couldn't sit still long enough to sell. He'd flit to his computer and make a call, then buzz around, bothering everyone. He looked like a big dragonfly in his bright yellow shirt.

"Nick, sit down and sell," she hissed.

"I will, but I gotta get a sody," he said, and zipped up front to the machine. Next she saw him crawling on the filthy carpet with Marina's little boy, Ramon, playing with his dump truck, promising to get him a candy bar.

Nick had an unerring instinct for bothering the wrong person. He tried to borrow a quarter for the candy machine from Mabel, the boiler room's longest survivor. She'd been there an astonishing five years. She was a large, placid woman who used a headset so she could knit while she called. Mabel seemed friendly, but Helen noticed that she watched everyone. Helen heard her reporting their minor infractions to Vito at the end of the shift. The Madame Defarge of the phone room would complain about Nick panhandling for sure.

Nick sat down at his computer and made a call, then threw down his phone and said, "They hate me. Everybody hates me. I can't get any sleep. My roommate was drunk and he kept me awake all night. How am I going to sell if I can't sleep?"

"I'm sorry, Nick," Helen said. "I've got to get back to work."

By twelve thirty, Helen had been insulted one hundred and twenty-six times, propositioned twice, and hung up on sixty-three times. Some woman in Oklahoma blew a police whistle into her phone. Helen's ear was still ringing from that. She put the whistle woman on CALL BACK. She'd be pursued by septic tank calls till her last breath.

Helen managed to make two sales, one in Maine and another in Kentucky. It wasn't enough to get her into survey heaven, but at least her job was safe for the day.

Nick had not sold anything. Helen was not surprised. When he did sit down at his phone, he argued with the callers. She heard him saying, "Listen, lady. I'm trying to tell you something. I can save you thousands in septic-tank bills. Lady, please don't say that."

He hung up his phone in despair. "It's over. I didn't sell anything again. That lady just told me to fuck myself and die. I can't take all this hate with no sleep." He put his forehead down on his sticky desk. It was five minutes to one.

"Nick!" Vito called. Nick sat up with a trapped, panicked look. He knew the end was coming. He hunched his skinny shoulders and went up front. Vito's firings were always done in public.

"Nick, you haven't had a sale in two weeks. You're out of here."

"Please, Vito," Nick said. "Give me one more day."

"I can't waste space on losers. And I can't have you bothering the help. You're out."

"I'll lose my home," Nick pleaded.

"I gotta have sellers. Get lost."

Nick left. She saw him sitting next to the smokers' trash can at the entrance, weeping. He didn't notice he was sitting in a pile of cigarette butts. Helen averted her eyes and walked past him, then wondered if she should go back and give him some money. Would it be an insult, reducing him once more to a homeless beggar?

In their world, money was never an insult, Helen decided. She found twenty-two dollars in her purse, and gave it all to Nick. "Here, buddy. Dinner's on me."

He would be panhandling soon enough.

At the Coronado that afternoon, Margery was drinking a screwdriver by the pool.

"I thought you'd be high on life," Helen said.

"OK, I admit it. Fred and Ethel are getting on my nerves, too," Margery said. "But they pay the rent, they aren't weird, and they aren't conning anyone—unlike some of my previous tenants."

"I'm beginning to miss the con man," Helen said. "At least he never lectured me on the joys of clean living. How long are they staying?"

"For the season, at least. They signed a lease through March."

March seemed a long time away, especially when Fred and Ethel came bouncing through the gate, looking preternaturally chipper.

"We had a lovely lunch on Las Olas," Ethel said. Helen could just imagine what the exclusive Las Olas restaurants made of her gold tennis shoes and I LOVE FLORIDA sweats printed with maps. The state looked even bigger stretched across Ethel's rear end.

"It was lovely till some bum asked us for money," Fred said.

"I told him to get a job," Ethel said. "I don't know why those people won't work."

Helen saw Nick sitting by the trash can, crying for his lost job and soon-to-be-lost home.

"Because you people hung up on him." Helen stormed off, slamming the gate. She heard Ethel say, "What set *her* off?"

I can't take any more misery, Helen thought, as she wandered aimlessly around her neighborhood. The walk did not comfort her. The neighborhood was disappearing. The exuberant Art Deco apartments and affordable cottages were being torn down for overpriced condos. Soon only the rich would live here.

Porta-Potties and construction Dumpsters camped on every block. A construction worker whistled at her, and Helen glared at him. He was the enemy, the destroyer. She shouldn't complain about Fred and Ethel. If her landlady couldn't keep their unit rented, the Coronado might be torn down, too. Then where would she live? In a soulless shoebox like Debbie.

Everything she cared about seemed to be slipping away. She couldn't stop the construction, but she could keep in touch with her friends.

Helen rummaged in her purse for change, and then for Sarah's phone number. She found a pay phone on Las Olas. "Hi, Sarah," she said. "I haven't talked to you in way too long. Want to meet for lunch sometime this week?"

"Anything wrong with today?" Sarah said. "When do you have to be back at work?"

"Not till five."

"Good. Do you like crab?"

"Love it," Helen said.

"I'll pick you up in twenty minutes."

Helen ran back to her apartment. The pool was once more deserted. Helen was glad she didn't have to face Margery after her outburst. She fed Thumbs and changed into her good black pantsuit, which was only a little tight from the potato chip binges.

Chocolate, her stuffed bear, was nice and fat. She reached inside for a fistful of money and caught a flicker out of the corner of her eye. Someone had passed her window. She hadn't shut the blinds. She tiptoed to the window hoping she would finally see her neighbor Phil, but no one was there. The man was maddening.

Sarah pulled up in her Range Rover right on time, and Helen settled into its unaccustomed luxury. Her friend had played the stock market, parlaying a small inheritance into major money, thanks to Krispy Kreme doughnut stock. Now she indulged a taste for pretty clothes and jewelry. Today, she wore a silver and shell pink necklace that highlighted her rosy skin and dark hair.

"Nice jewelry," Helen said.

"It's a modern Navajo design," Sarah said.

The Range Rover was soon in the desolate wilderness by the Lauderdale airport. "Where are you taking me?" Helen said, looking uneasily at the acres of empty scrub, abandoned boatyards and rusting trailer parks. Sarah was wearing a small fortune around her neck.

"Ever been to the Rustic Inn Crabhouse?"

"Never heard of it. But if you say it's good, it must be." Sarah was a woman of size, free of the modern mania for dieting. She liked to eat well.

The Rustic Inn lived up to its name. It was a series of long, low buildings sprawled along a canal. They looked like they'd been tossed there. Inside, the decor was early beer sign with offbeat touches: a Victorian bronze of a boy holding a crab, art-glass windows, a monster lobster claw over the bar. The claw was as long as an average lobster. Helen wondered what the outrageous crustacean had weighed.

She breathed in the air, a heady mixture of butter and garlic. Then she heard the pounding. It sounded like the building was infested with carpenters. The tables were covered with newspapers and set with wooden mallets. The customers wore bibs, and were happily pounding crab legs and cracking claws.

A waitress tied bibs on Helen and Sarah, and brought out their crab samplers: long golden crab legs, garlicky little blue crabs, pink Jonah crabs and half a lobster with clam stuffing, all swimming in butter.

Helen picked up her mallet and hit a thick Jonah crab claw. Nothing happened.

"You're too polite," Sarah said. "You've got to whack it hard, like this." She dealt her crab claw a crushing blow.

Helen swung her mallet harder. The claw cracked slightly. She thought of Nick and Vito, and Fred and Ethel, and hit the claw with a resounding thwack. It split wide open. This meal was downright therapeutic.

"A little frustrated, are we?" Sarah said. "Want to tell me about it?"

Helen did, starting with the night she heard Laredo die. When she finished, Sarah said, "Savannah sounds like a loose cannon. You're lucky you weren't arrested at Debbie's.

Now that the sister's on the scene, why don't you back away?"

"I heard a murder. I can't," Helen said.

"Of course you can," Sarah said, sucking the meat out of a crab leg.

"Savannah's all alone. I have to help her."

"Savannah can take care of herself."

"She only looks tough," Helen said. "She could disappear tomorrow and who would look for her? She's one of the disposable people. I guess you'd call her trailer trash, but she's braver than anyone I know. I don't know how she keeps working those awful jobs."

"Are you doing this for her—or you?" Sarah said. It was amazing how shrewd she looked covered in butter sauce.

Helen picked crab bits out of a smashed leg, while she searched for an answer. "I hate to see a rich guy like Hank Asporth get away with murder. He's a skirt-chasing, martini-drinking user. He's never worked a day in his life."

"Like your ex?" Sarah said.

Another direct hit, Helen thought, and pounded a crab leg to inedible mush.

"You can tell all that about Hank Asporth from a computer survey and one very strange phone conversation?" Sarah said.

"Yes," said Helen. She walloped a crab claw. "I know he's a rich bully because he sent his lawyer to shut me up."

"But he didn't succeed," Sarah said. "You kept going. You found the sister. You've done your part—more than your part. You have a way out of this, but you won't take it."

Helen swung her mallet again. The only sound was the crunch of buttered crab.

"Helen, why are you being so stubborn?"

"Because I'm sick of rich people trying to push me around. Rich people who never did anything to deserve their money, while Savannah and I work our fingers to the bone and get nowhere."

"You could get somewhere," Sarah said, "if you'd let me

get you a decent job. I'm worried about you, Helen. You're mixed up in a murder. It's because you're working that ugly job. People call you terrible names all day. How can you stand it?"

"I'm making twice what I made at the bookstore," Helen said.

"You're paying too high a price. Let me find you a good job. I know lots of people—"

Helen cut her off. She couldn't be in a corporate computer and she couldn't tell Sarah why. "I have a job. I'm through with corporate life. I'm never wearing a suit and pantyhose again."

"But you have no life. You work morning and night, two five-hour shifts with a four-hour break in the afternoon. When's the last time you kicked back and had white wine with Peggy by the pool?"

"Weeks ago, but that's not because of my job. Margery rented 2C to this awful couple, Fred and Ethel Mertz."

"Nobody's named that."

"They are. They're so smug. They give sermons. Peggy and I can't stand them. When they show up, we go inside."

"They sound horrible." Sarah must have seen she was getting nowhere trying to change Helen's mind. She changed the subject instead. "How's your crab?"

"Spectacular," Helen said. "The butter, the garlic, the parsley potatoes. This is heaven on earth."

After a brief interlude of pounding and picking crab meat, Sarah returned to her theme. "You can't date anyone with the hours you work. And you won't meet a nice man in that boiler room."

Helen had been telling herself the same thing, but she didn't want to hear it from Sarah. "Don't need men when there are buttered crab claws."

"Helen, be serious."

"Sarah, you used to say my problem was I dated too many men. You were right. I made some bad choices. Now you complain I don't date enough. I'm learning to live without men. I'm sick of men. Men have brought me nothing but misery."

Her friend looked sad. "I'm sorry. I shouldn't have said anything. You're still not over the man who betrayed you."

"Which one?" Helen said, and hit a crab so hard it exploded like a bomb.

Chapter 10

A black Mercedes with smoked-glass windows slid into the boiler room's parking lot, silent as a shark. It looked ominous. It also looked out of place. The power car sat among the beat-up staff clunkers like a prince in a housing project.

Was someone from the New York office here to squeeze higher quotas out of the overworked staff?

Helen ducked behind an old lime green Dodge and watched. The man who got out was not an elegant New York lizard, but she recognized his type. He was an executive from his high-priced haircut to his shined shoes.

At her old job in St. Louis, when she made six figures, Helen wouldn't have given him a second look. But he was so unusual here, she studied him. His hair was a meticulously cut and shining black. He was beautifully shaved. Most boiler-room men had *Miami Vice* stubble. Even the clean-shaven ones missed little patches, as if they were too hung-over to handle razors.

This man had the sleek, well-fed look of someone who dined on expense-account lunches. His shirt was professionally pressed and white enough to snowblind. His gray suit pants broke perfectly on his shoe tops. There was one odd note. He wasn't wearing a suit jacket or tie. His type was rarely out of uniform, even in South Florida's heat.

She followed him into the boiler room. He went straight to Vito's office. Helen clocked in for the evening shift.

Someone had left a full ashtray on top of her computer, bristling with lipsticked butts. A half-empty Big Gulp was leaking on her desk. Where did that come from? She dumped the mess in the trash and wiped up the sticky soda. She tried not to look at Nick's sad, empty chair. Sitting next to the jangled junkie had been an ordeal, but she still felt sorry for him.

"Hi," said a cheerful male voice, and a soft, manicured hand was stuck in her face. "I'm Jack Lace, your new seat mate."

The executive with the smoked-glass Mercedes sat down in Nick's chair. She'd bet his pampered bottom had never touched anything but leather office chairs before it landed on Nick's ripped seat.

"You're working here?" Helen couldn't hide her surprise.

"Absolutely," he said. "A new day, a new challenge, that's what I always say."

"But you don't look like . . . I mean you're so . . ."

"I used to be a broker," he said.

"Oh. Nine-eleven do you in?"

"Something like that," Jack said. "But sales are sales. If I can sell stocks, I can sell septic-tank cleaner. Right now, both are in the toilet."

He laughed at his own joke. Helen noticed he wore no wedding ring. He must have seen her staring at his hand. "I'm divorced," he said. "It's the main reason I'm here."

"Bad?" Helen asked.

"The worst," Jack said.

"Another veteran of the marriage wars," she said. "Well, we've got plenty of them. See Zelda over there—the tiny woman in the big red sweater? She's always cold, poor thing. Husband divorced her after thirty-five years. Didn't give her a nickel. She's sixty-one, with no work skills outside the home."

"Um, yes. Well, I'm sure there are two sides to every story. Are you married?"

"Not anymore," Helen said.

"Good," Jack said.

The computers beeped on. "We're calling Connecticut this evening," Helen said. "It's fairly decent. New Hampshire and Vermont are harder sells."

"All right, people, let's get our heinies in gear," Vito bawled, ending their conversation. Helen's evening went strange from the first call.

"Hi, Jody. I'm Helen with Tank Titan and—"

Jody was weeping. "Me and my boyfriend are breaking up. I'm moving out. I caught him with the lady next door. Walked right in on them. I never knew they were making it. I feel like such a fool. He said he was lonely."

"Well, well," Helen said. "I'll fix it so he's never lonely for a telemarketer."

"You do that, honey," Jody said. "And thank you."

Helen hit CALL BACK. Women had to stick together.

"Loud and proud people, let's hear you loud and proud," Vito yelled, but Helen had nothing to be proud about. A tired mother, her voice trembling at the breaking point, was next. "I'm trying to get four kids to bed," she said.

Four kids? At least I'm not in that trap, Helen thought.

While she worked, Vito stalked the aisles, plump and pink as a prize pig, listening to their sales pitches on his black monitor phone, telling them what to say to make a sale.

Helen thought she was doing well with an Indianapolis woman. Then the woman said, "I don't know. My septic-tank man told me to never put anything in my tank."

She was about to hang up, but Vito materialized at her desk with his black phone, whispering lies in her ear like a swinish Satan.

"Of course he did, ma'am," Vito said softly. "Your septic-tank man would lose his job if you used Tank Titan. Buy our product and you'll never have to pump your septic tank again. We guarantee it. Otherwise, we'll refund every penny of the cost of our product."

But not the repair costs, Helen thought.

Vito poked her back with a meaty finger, and she parroted his words. The woman bought a five-year supply. Helen wished she hadn't.

"You made the sale," Vito said. "Great way to end the night." He turned to Jack. "And how did you do on your first night?"

"I sold six," Jack said, with the proud air of a retriever that brought home something smelly.

"Phenomenal," Vito said. "You're a natural."

He was. Helen rarely made more than four sales on one shift, and she was good.

"Congratulations," she said when the computers shut down.

"Thanks," Jack said. "Like I said, sales is sales. Listen, would you like to go for coffee or a drink?"

Helen started to say, "I don't know you." But she did. Helen had worked with men like Jack Lace for almost twenty years. She thought of Sarah's luncheon lecture about her love life, and worse, of another night alone with her cat.

"Yes," she said. "I'd like that very much." She was glad she was still wearing her good black pantsuit from her lunch with Sarah.

"What about your car?" Jack said.

"A friend dropped me off at work," Helen said. She couldn't admit she didn't even have a clunker.

"Good," Jack said. "We'll take mine."

Jack's car no longer looked threatening, shining in the moonlight. It looked rich and comforting. For the second time that day, Helen sank into luxurious leather seats and listened to the hum of a well-tuned engine.

"I thought we'd go to the Pier Top Lounge."

"Jack, can you afford that?" Helen knew from bitter experience that it took time to realize you no longer had money. Soon, he would have to sell this extravagant car. He'd never be able to afford the upkeep.

"Hey, I'm the top seller in the boiler room."

Jack was a fast, aggressive driver, weaving in and out of

traffic, cutting people off, refusing to give anyone a break. They were at the Pier Sixty-Six resort in ten minutes. Jack pulled into valet parking, another outlandish expense.

I won't say anything, Helen thought. He'll learn the same way I did. A few missed meals and he'll figure out he needs to budget.

Jack handed over the keys to the valet and reached into the backseat for his suit jacket and a Ralph Lauren tie. Now he looked complete. Even at ten thirty at night, he had no beard shadow. How did he do that?

It was fun to take a hushed elevator to the penthouse. The Pier Top was a revolving bar with a panoramic view of Fort Lauderdale. Helen had forgotten the simple, overpriced pleasures of sitting in a lounge chair and drinking cosmopolitans. They kept the conversation impersonal at first, discussing the view and their work. Then Helen asked, "Do you live in Lauderdale?"

"I do now," he said, "in a crappy apartment near I-95. I used to live in a big house in Coral Springs. My wife got it. She got my Range Rover, too. And both kids. Like the song says, she got the gold mine, I got the shaft."

"You must miss your children," Helen said.

"I do. But she's turned them against me. It's like they aren't even my kids anymore."

"I'm sorry," Helen said. "My marriage was a mess, but at least there weren't any kids."

"I'm not going to sit around feeling sorry for myself," Jack said, and stood up. He held out his hand. "Come on, let's go out on the observation deck."

They were alone on the windswept deck. The Pier Top was seventeen stories above the city, a skyscraper by Lauderdale standards. Helen felt queasy. She backed away from the edge, wondering if anyone had ever jumped off the deck.

"Beautiful, isn't it?" Jack said.

It was. She forgot her fear, caught by the glittering view: the sweeping glory of the Seventeenth Street Causeway, the splendor of the cruise ships. The sparkling tourist hotels and the outrageous mansions. And the black, shining water that made all this wealth possible.

Helen shivered. It was cold up here, so high above the city. All this beauty, and no one to share it with. She wondered if she would ever find someone to love, or if she would die alone. There are worse things for a woman than being alone, she reminded herself. But that thought didn't warm her.

Jack took off his suit coat and put it around her shoulders. It smelled of some manly cologne, with a hint of citrus. He put his arms around her and pulled her close. He felt warm and strong. He felt right.

This was happening awfully fast, she thought. But she'd watched Jack today. He was decisive. He knew what he wanted—and he wanted her. She was flattered. She was forty-two, but she made this man act like an eager young lover.

"Helen, I promise you, the telemarketing is only temporary," he said. "I'll be back on top of the world soon and you'll be with me."

He believes it. She liked his promises, even if they could never come true. He seemed hopeful. That's what her life was missing. Hope. The promise of something better.

Then Jack kissed her. The city sparkled below, just for her.

It was after midnight when Helen wove her way to her apartment, giggly from kisses and cosmopolitans. The night had been perfect. There was a slight awkwardness when Jack had wanted to come back to her place. But she'd said, "Not tonight," and he'd obeyed.

Then he'd kissed her so hard she'd almost changed her mind. But she wasn't that drunk. She'd had too many wrong men. She wasn't going to hop into bed with this one. Not right away, anyway.

She passed Phil's door and inhaled deeply. "I'm higher

than you are." She was startled that she'd said it out loud.
She unlocked her door and nearly fell inside.

"Hi, cat. Did you miss me?" Thumbs sniffed her with disapproval.

"Don't look that way. I deserve a good time. I'll tell you
all about it. Just let me sit down a minute." She flopped into
the turquoise Barcalounger.

She woke up at six A.M. She'd slept in her pantsuit. It was
covered with wrinkles and cat hair. Her mouth felt like it was
stuffed with fur. Thumbs had slept on her chest, judging by
the large patch of cat hair on her suit. The ten-pound tom was
gently patting her face with his huge six-toed paw.

"I'm sorry, boy," she said. "I know it's breakfast time."

She stood up. The room had a funhouse tilt. Her stomach
lurched like Savannah's Tank. Savannah. She forgot to call
Savannah last night.

I didn't really promise I would, she thought. Not a firm
promise. But she remembered what Savannah had said, "My
baby sister's lying somewhere in an unmarked grave. I've
got to find her."

And what had she been doing? Drinking cosmopolitans in
a penthouse, like some subtropical Marie Antoinette.

Helen stumbled into the bathroom. She didn't have the
courage to look in the mirror. She ate an inch of toothpaste
straight from the tube. Coffee. She needed coffee. It tasted
funny, but Helen didn't think that was from her Crest breakfast. It was going to be a long day.

She clocked in at seven fifty-nine and sat down at her
desk. There was a half-eaten slice of pizza draped over her
phone like a pepperoni tea cozy. It left a trail of orange grease
on her desk. Her stomach flip-flopped when she dropped it in
the trash.

"Good morning," Jack said. He was smiling. She hated
cheerful people in the morning. Once again, he was beautifully shaved. His skin was a healthy pink, his eyes clear, his
shirt crisp. It was unnatural.

"Thank you for a lovely evening," he said, and handed her a single red rose.

"Oh," Helen said. It was all she could manage. The rose looked so velvety dark and perfect in this boil of a boiler room. It made the scuffed walls and shabby carpet look worse.

"It's lovely," she said, as the computers flipped on.

"OK, people. Get your heinies in gear," Vito screamed. "We're starting with Vermont this morning."

"Hi, Mrs. Cratchley," Helen said. "I'm Helen with Tank Titan—"

Mrs. Cratchley said, "Well, isn't that lovely?"

Helen stopped in surprise. She wasn't used to kind words.

"And how long have you been a telemarketer, dear?"

"Several months now. I sell a product that . . ." Helen tried to get back on track.

"It must be difficult, a single woman like yourself," Mrs. Cratchley said. "You are single, aren't you?"

"Yes, ma'am," Helen said. "And Tank Titan is the single most popular—"

"I thought so," Mrs. C said. "My daughter Rita's single, too. She has to support herself and my grandson, Jerrod. That poor girl works so hard. We never get to sit down and visit any more. Jerrod is four now, and he's . . ."

Help! Helen thought. I'm trapped by a nice person. Nasty, I can handle. I don't know what to do with nice.

"And then Jerrod said to me, 'Granny'—he calls me Granny—"

"Mrs. Cratchley," Helen said, "I'd love to chat with you, but my boss is here and I have to go."

"I understand, dear," Mrs. Cratchley said. "You call anytime."

Helen's next call let loose with a string of profanities that nearly wilted her rose. She felt better. She was used to that.

When she got her five-minute break an hour later, Jack was still on the phone, happily peddling septic-tank cleaner.

Helen dug a plastic soda bottle out of the trash can and walked back to the battleship gray bathroom.

She was filling the bottle with water for her rose when Taniqua came out of a plywood stall. A boiler-room diet of junk food was slyly putting pounds on her slender figure. Taniqua definitely filled out her powder-blue halter top and tight low-rise pants. Helen wondered what brought this beauty to this beastly place.

"That rose from the new guy?" Taniqua said.

"We went out for drinks last night. He brought me this. Wasn't that sweet?"

"He nothing but trouble."

"He's romantic."

"Huh," Taniqua said. "A love rose. Oldest trick in the man's book. Get those at the 7-Eleven for a buck. That makes you a dollar ho."

"Taniqua! What's he done to you?"

"He be a bailiff boy."

"A what?"

"You find out soon enough. Just don't be trusting no bailiff boy."

Taniqua slammed the bathroom door.

Chapter 11

Helen's morning started with a hangover. It ended with a mutiny.

Mr. Cavarelli slithered in at ten o'clock. He was one of the elegant reptiles from the New York office. His eyes were flat and yellow. Even his suit was a lizardlike greenish brown. He wore alligator shoes, which Helen thought was no way to treat a relative. She wondered if his silk-clad feet were covered with scales.

Mr. Cavarelli kept his upper lip curled as he walked through the boiler room. He glided into Vito's office like a hungry predator and silently slid the door shut.

Helen did not see Vito for the rest of the morning. He didn't even come out to monitor the telemarketers. Maybe Mr. Cavarelli had disemboweled him and was snacking on his entrails.

Helen made four sales in quick succession. She sold better when Vito wasn't looking over her shoulder.

Vito did not emerge until the end of the shift. He looked mauled. His smooth pink skin was blotchy white. His shirt tail hung out. He seemed nervous. Well, who wouldn't be, after three hours with Mr. Cavarelli? It probably felt like the intake interview from hell.

Vito plastered on a sick smile and started passing out

commission-check envelopes. Helen could never figure out the commission pay schedule. It seemed to be based on sun signs and the position of the moon.

Taniqua eagerly tore into her envelope. "What's *this* shit? They be paying me for fifteen sales. I had seventeen. I got my list right here."

Her "proof" was a tattered piece of paper with a hand-written list of names, addresses and dates. No supervisor had signed it. No supervisor would. Records were conveniently vague at Girdner Sales. Taniqua had no hope of getting that missing money.

"Goddamn crooks," Zelda said, hugging her red sweater closer to her tiny body. "I didn't get my commission on four sales."

"They ripped me off." That was from Bob, a huge tattooed biker.

And me, Helen thought. Her envelope was a little thicker than the others. I can't complain, because I get my money in cash. Vito helps himself to a commission on my commission.

Panhead Pete, another biker, said, "Hey, I been cheated, too. I'm short three sales. I want my fuckin' money."

He crushed his check in a hairy paw, which made the death's head on his bicep grin wider. Pete was a mountain of lard with a beer-keg belly. He loomed over Vito, who started sweating.

Mr. Cavarelli slid out of the office, elegant and evil. "Is there a problem?" he asked softly.

"Yeah," Pete said. "I've been stiffed outta three sales."

"But you haven't," Mr. Cavarelli said, fixing his flat predator's eyes on Pete. He smiled. His teeth looked sharp and pointed. "I personally calculated those checks."

Pete shifted uneasily. Maybe he realized he was two hundred and eighty pounds of slow and tasty beef. Maybe he saw the slight bulge under Cavarelli's well-tailored armpit. Helen certainly did. The lizard was lethal. Pete's only weapons were his meaty fists, and they didn't stop bullets.

"Well, it better be fixed next time," Pete said lamely.

"I'll look into it," Mr. Cavarelli said with a flick of contempt.

Pete walked out, shoulders slumped. Zelda and Taniqua followed, too beaten down to protest.

"Wow, that was something," Jack said. "That guy in the suit has real management ability. Did you see the way he handled those malcontents?"

"He had a gun," Helen said.

"You're kidding," Jack said.

Helen wasn't sure he believed her. It was too soon for Jack to get a commission check. He'd learn soon enough about Girdner's curious accounting.

She was carrying her rose in its bottle vase. He blocked her way to the door, awkward as a schoolboy. "Uh, I wanted to see you today, but I can't. I've got an appointment with my lawyer this afternoon. About the divorce."

"I understand," she said.

"And I can't make it tonight, either," he said.

"Jack, you don't have to explain. We're not going steady."

"I want to see you all the time." He looked so sincere, like a little boy all grown up. He was so neat and well-groomed, so different from the boiler-room dopers and losers.

"Helen!" Vito's shout broke into her thoughts. "Thank God you're still here. Can you work the survey side tonight?"

A rose from Jack and a night in survey heaven. Helen was in such a good mood, she decided to call Savannah. She stopped at the Riverside Hotel and used one of the pay phones. Might as well make this call in comfort.

"No word from Miss Debbie," Savannah said. "I called all last night until two o'clock and she didn't answer. That little blond snip is not getting away with this. This is my sister we're talking about. I'll choke the information out of Debbie with my bare hands. I'm going to her apartment. You're off work now, right?"

"Until five," Helen said.

"I haven't had lunch yet, and the boss isn't around this afternoon. I can take a little longer. Let's drive over to Deb-bie's."

"Are you packing a weapon?" Helen said.

"I told you, I don't like guns."

"I'm talking about oven cleaner."

"You got my last can. I'll be outside the Riverside Hotel in five minutes."

Savannah's Tank pulled up in front of the hotel, rattling and rumbling. Savannah put it in PARK, and it farted black smoke. The doorman averted his eyes.

"Nice troll doll." Helen pointed to the orange-haired toy swinging from the rear-view mirror.

"I brought it for luck," Savannah said. "Laredo gave it to me."

There was a sad silence.

"I raised her, you know," Savannah said. "Mama didn't want her. She only had Laredo because Woodbridge Manson wanted a boy child, and she thought she could keep him if she gave him a son. Guess she figured she had a fifty-fifty chance of pleasing him.

"Mama gambled and lost. You can't return a baby like a wrong-size dress. Manson took off when Laredo was two months old. Mama wasn't mean to Laredo or anything. Just not real interested.

"I was ten years old. I thought Laredo was the cutest thing. She was my own baby doll. I liked everything about her. Her baby smell. The way she kicked her little legs and squinched up her eyes when she cried. And her smile. She could light up a room with that smile. She was bald as Dwight Eisenhower until she was almost two. I used to tape a pink bow on her head, so everybody would know she was a girl.

"By the time she turned twelve, they sure knew. She had bazooms out to here, and boys following her like dogs in heat. Laredo had man trouble from then on. I figured it was because she couldn't keep the first man in her life, her daddy, Woodbridge Manson. I was always getting her out of scrapes with boys. She got knocked up at fifteen, but I talked her into getting rid of it. Mama never knew. I went with Laredo to the clinic and held her hand. I thought it was my fault. I didn't raise her right."

"You were ten years old."

"Yeah, well, I was a failure as a mother. I don't have any daughters of my own. Laredo's the closest I'll ever have to a child."

She touched the troll doll. "Maybe she had itchy feet after all. Maybe she's not dead. Maybe she ran off with another man. It wouldn't be the first time."

Helen thought Savannah was trying to convince herself. She knew the truth, and so did Helen. She was glad when they pulled into Debbie's apartment complex. She spotted the waitress's purple Neon in the lot.

"She's home," Helen said.

"I thought so. Little witch wasn't answering my calls."

Savannah grabbed her purse, slammed the car door, and marched up the stairs. Helen ran after her, hoping she'd kept her promise about the oven cleaner.

Savannah rang the doorbell. Nobody answered.

"Ring it again," Helen said.

Savannah did.

Helen did not hear anyone moving around in the apartment.

"Must be taking a nap. This will wake her." Savannah smacked the door with a powerful wallop. It swung open.

"Place smells funny," she said.

They walked in cautiously, Savannah first. "She's a messy housekeeper, too. There are things all over the floor."

Helen spotted a chair lying on its side, stuffing flowing from the slashed seat. A lamp was tipped over, the bulb shattered. "Something's not right here. Don't touch anything."

"You think it's burglars?" Savannah stepped cautiously around a ripped couch pillow. "Or mean kids? They knocked over that knickknack stand and broke everything. Look."

Helen saw a headless china cat, a shattered cupid and a

porcelain hand on the tile floor. The hand looked intact. There were no chips in the pale fingers.

Debbie had uncommonly pale skin, like fine porcelain. Helen froze. Her legs weighed ten tons each. They refused to move.

"What's the matter?" Savannah said. "Did you see this kitchen? Someone dumped sugar all over the counter. She's going to have ants everywhere. Flour and coffee are in the sink. And look at this. They threw raw chicken on the floor. I guess that's the bad-meat smell."

"The hand. Her porcelain hand," Helen said.

"My grandmother had one of those," Savannah said, peering around the doorway.

Helen got her legs to move again, and slowly walked behind the beige couch. The pale hand was connected to a white lace cuff. The cuff was connected to . . . nothing.

"It's just like Grandma's," Savannah said. "Except hers had a china rose on the little finger. And look at that thing on the pedestal. Debbie sure likes body parts, doesn't she?"

It was a heavy-breasted female torso, a plaster copy of something Greek or Roman, Helen thought. For some reason, the vandals hadn't toppled it.

"I bet Debbie's hanging out by the pool. Is she in for a surprise when she gets back," Savannah said.

Helen stepped carefully around some spilled CDs to get into the bedroom. "The covers and pillows are torn off the bed and the mattress is slashed," she reported. "And there's a marble foot by the bed."

"Another body part," Savannah said.

Helen saw that the foot was connected to a long white leg. The leg went up to a flirty cheerleader's uniform and a tangle of blond hair.

"Debbie!" Helen said, her voice sounding small and scared. "Debbie, are you OK?"

Even as she said the words, Helen knew Debbie wasn't. One look at her purple, distorted face told her that. There was a cruel line of bruises around her throat. Her long white-blond hair had been twisted into a silver rope and pulled tight around her neck. Debbie had been strangled with her own hair.

Savannah came up behind Helen and touched her shoulder. "Jesus," she whispered.

Helen jumped at her touch. "You said you wanted to strangle Debbie with your bare hands."

"I didn't kill her. Someone else did." Helen backed away, putting the bed between her and Savannah.

"You strangled her," Helen repeated. She took another step back. Now she could run for the door.

"Hell's bells," Savannah said. "Use your head. If I was the killer, would I drag you to the scene of the crime? I'd let the cops think it was a burglary gone bad and never come back here."

That made sense, but Helen was still wary. "We better call the police," she said.

"Uh, I can't be around the police. Little problem with my former employer," Savannah said.

"I understand." Helen wasn't anxious to contact the police, either. "Let's leave and call them from a pay phone." She wanted out of that place. Now.

"I'm not leaving until I look for Kristi's address," Savannah said.

That declaration convinced Helen: Savannah was either innocent or putting on a good show.

"Don't touch anything. Just stand there. I'll be finished in two shakes." Savannah pulled a pair of yellow rubber gloves out of her purse and began searching. She pawed through the papers scattered on the floor and checked the message slips by the phone. She poked in the wreckage of overturned drawers. She picked through the contents of Debbie's purse, spilled across the bedroom floor.

"Nothing. Either Debbie never had Kristi's address, or it's gone," Savannah said. "We better make ourselves scarce."

Savannah and Helen used their shirttails to wipe the doorbell, doorknob and door. "We didn't touch anything else with our hands. The floor is tile. I don't see where we left any footprints."

"What if the neighbors see us?"

"What neighbors? Everyone's at work."

They stopped at a pay phone on Dixie Highway and called the police nonemergency number. Savannah disguised her voice to sound like an old woman. She said there was a funny smell coming out of apartment 203. No, she wouldn't leave her name, just check it out, please. That's why she paid taxes.

Savannah hung up. The Tank rumbled and bucked down the highway. Helen felt sick and dizzy, but she wasn't sure if it was the lurching car or . . . She saw Debbie again, her blond hair twisted around her white neck. Debbie had used her beauty as a weapon. It didn't save her this time.

Debbie was dead.

And I stepped over her body, wiped my fingerprints off her door, and left her to rot. What's wrong with me? How could I be so cold?

Helen remembered Debbie in the parking lot, flipping her long hair, flirting with the dazzled cook, driving home in her purple jellybean of a car. She was young, silly and sure she could conquer the world—at least the male half.

Like Laredo. And now Debbie was dead. Like Laredo.

A single tear splashed in Helen's lap. She tried to hold the others back. She didn't want to cry, but she couldn't stop.

"What's wrong?" Savannah said.

"Debbie's dead and it's our fault." Helen wiped her eyes with her palms and sniffled back more tears. "She was afraid to tell us anything. She said, 'They'll hurt me. They'll hurt me bad.' If we hadn't forced Debbie to talk, she'd still be alive. We've blundered around and killed another person."

"Excuse me? *We've* killed another person? Where are you getting that crap?"

"I heard a woman being strangled. Now I've seen one."

Savannah turned on her angrily. "You didn't hear a woman being killed. You heard my little sister Laredo die. She had blond hair and the sweetest smile you ever saw. She wanted to be a famous actress and she had a part in a real Shakespeare play. Now she's dead and I can't even find her body to bury her."

The Tank died at a light, and Savannah smashed her foot down on the gas until the car shot forward, belching smoke.

"You want to know why I can't find her? Because Debbie told the police Laredo took off. She took a thousand dollars to say that.

"I'm sorry Debbie's dead, but she made her mistake when she lied about my sister. I didn't kill her and you didn't, either. Debbie's own greed killed her."

Savannah was so upset she ran a light and nearly hit a delivery truck. There was a rousing chorus of honks punctuated by one-fingered salutes, then a long silence.

"Who do you think killed her?" Helen said. "Hank Asporth?"

"He's the most likely candidate," Savannah said. "But why did Debbie say 'They'll hurt me'? Why not 'He'll hurt me'?"

"You think he's working with someone else?"

"I don't know. We need to get in touch with this Kristi. She knows something. But I'm fresh out of ideas."

"I'll call Steve and see if he needs a bartender," Helen said.

"You're going to tend bar topless? Nice lady like you? You'll be too embarrassed."

"I'm beyond embarrassment," Helen said. "I'm a telemarketer."

Chapter 12

It was only two thirty in the afternoon when Savannah dropped Helen off at the Coronado. It seemed much later. Time had slipped sideways in Debbie's apartment. Helen felt oddly boneless. And she was tired, so very tired. She had to get some sleep before she went to work, or she'd never stay awake tonight. Helen set her alarm for four o'clock.

As soon as she crawled under the covers, Helen was wide awake. She saw the dead Debbie, her long hair twisted cruelly around her neck. Helen could not picture her as a blond beauty anymore. Debbie was a bloated face and a bruised neck, a bedroom nightmare.

She rolled over on her back and stared at the ceiling. Maybe she should go see Margery. Her landlady would make a screwdriver that would knock the nightmares out of her head. But she would also tell Helen to quit telemarketing. Look where it got her: working with junkies and bikers and listening to murders.

Helen didn't want to hear that lecture. She turned restlessly in her bed and punched her pillow.

Why didn't she quit?

Helen knew telemarketing was a terrible job. But for some weird reason, she was good at selling septic-tank cleaner. Sometimes, she was ashamed of talking lonely people into buying a product they didn't need. She knew she should get a decent job.

But Helen was stubborn. It was her greatest virtue and her biggest fault. The more her friends urged her to quit, the more she clung to the job out of perverse pride. Besides, the money was better than any dead-end job she'd ever had.

She shut her eyes and saw Debbie again. She hadn't liked the greedy little tease. But no one deserved to die like that. Helen flopped onto her stomach. The sheets were hopelessly twisted. The pillows were squashed into comfortless lumps.

At three thirty, she gave up on sleep and fixed herself a pot of coffee. She drank the whole thing. She'd have to get by on caffeine instead of sleep. At least she was working the survey room. She couldn't take the boiler room's insults tonight.

As soon as the elevator doors opened on Girdner Surveys' luxurious office, Helen felt calmer. Her feet were cushioned by the deep carpets. Her eyes rested on the expensive paneling. She was soothed by the sight of her coworkers: Nellie, the big butterscotch blonde with the creamy voice. Berletta, thin and efficient, with her beautiful Bahamian accent. There was no sign of Penelope, her prissy boss. That was good.

"Tonight's survey is for a disposable-razor company," Nellie said. "Respondents must answer question five and the answer must be yes."

Question five. Helen skimmed the survey. Ah, there it was: "Do you shave your armpits?"

"I actually have to ask women that? That question is the pits," Helen said.

"So to speak," Berletta said.

"Yes, you must ask it," Nellie said. "And remember, we don't want the hairy ones."

"Sweet Gloria Steinem," Helen said. "Women won't answer that question."

Helen sure wouldn't. For her, there was only one correct answer: "Get off my phone, you pervert."

But she forgot she was in Florida. Helen made her first

survey call to Nancy, age thirty-three, in suburban Weston. Nancy lived in a mini-mansion on the edge of the mosquito-ridden Everglades. She sounded awfully chirpy. Maybe she wouldn't slam down the phone when she heard question five. Helen took a deep breath, then asked, "Do you shave your armpits?"

She waited for Nancy to yell, or scream or hang up on her.

"Oh, yes," she said proudly.

Five more women responded with equal enthusiasm, as if they were reporting to the pit police.

The sixth was shocked and angry. "Of course I shave," she said. "Do you think I'm European?"

America: land of the free and home of the shaved.

Helen was working on her seventh questionnaire when her pencil broke again. Surveys had to be filled out in pencil, and the phone-room staff was given cheap orange ones that often cracked under the strain.

"Third time tonight this pencil broke. I hate these things." Helen ground it into the electric sharpener. "I need a break."

"Just like your pencil," Nellie said.

Helen peeked out the phone-room door. No clients. Good. Survey riffraff weren't supposed to be seen by the sacred suits. She tiptoed down the hall to the employee lunchroom for a soda. Maybe she could scrounge a cupcake from a day-shift birthday party. There was always leftover food.

Tonight she found something much tastier on a counter-top: a whole box of shiny black pencils. They were fat and sturdy-looking, a higher grade than the cheap orange ones. They wrote thick and black, not scratchy pale gray like the cheap pencils. They even fit her hand better.

Helen took one pencil. Finally, she could complete a survey in comfort.

She was carrying her prize back to her desk when she ran into Penelope, stiff as a department-store dummy. Her boss's tight mouth was crimped in disapproval. "What are you doing with that?"

"With what?" Helen said.

"That black pencil."

"There's a whole box in the lunchroom," Helen said.

"You obviously didn't know, so I will excuse you this time," Penelope said, clipping each word. "But you are not allowed to use a full-size black pencil. Those are for clients and management only. You may use the black pencil stubs or the orange pencils provided for you."

Penelope held out her small white hand and Helen surrendered the black pencil. How far she'd fallen. In her old job, Helen had once received a four-hundred-dollar Montblanc pen as a gift. Now she was reprimanded for taking a pencil.

"Everything OK?" Nellie asked, when she returned.

"Penelope caught me with a black pencil. She acted like I was stealing the copy machine."

"Oh, hell, honey, that's my fault. I should have told you. Penelope has a bug up her ass about those pencils."

Somehow, those words in Nellie's come-hither voice sounded elegant. Helen laughed out loud and went back to asking strange women strange questions about their underarm hair.

She was on her tenth survey when Nellie said, "Phone call for you, Helen."

"I'm swamped. Can you or Berletta take it?"

"She says she'll only speak to you." Helen heard a slight curdle of disapproval in Nellie's whipped-cream voice. Personal calls were forbidden. Helen quickly finished her survey and picked up the call, her heart beating faster in alarm. Something was wrong. She never got calls at work.

"Helen?" said a distraught voice. "It's Savannah."

"Are you OK?" Helen could tell this was no social call.

"Helen, I know I shouldn't call you at work, but they got my trailer. I got home from my office job about five-thirty and found the door open. Someone jimmied it and trashed my home. They got . . ." She stopped. Helen could hear her swallowing tears.

"Savannah. What happened?"

"They tore up everything in Laredo's room. Slashed the bedcovers. Ripped her Shakespeare book. Smashed a china ballerina she's had since she was eight. Now I don't have anything to remember her by. It's all broken." Savannah wept the hot, harsh sobs of someone unused to crying.

"Savannah, please don't cry. Talk to me. Who did this? Do you think it's the same people who killed Debbie?"

"Definitely. Laredo's room was hit the hardest, but they got my whole place. They slashed the couch cushions and the mattress. They dumped everything out of the drawers and cabinets. Five pounds of coffee were dumped in the sink. There's sugar on the kitchen counter and raw hamburger stinking up the floor."

"Sounds familiar," Helen said.

"It's just like Debbie's apartment. Except they also kicked in my TV. Put their foot right through the screen. Somebody was real mad."

"Savannah, I'm so sorry. Did you call the police?"

"Didn't have to. They hit another mobile home in the same park. The Sunnysea cops were already here when I got home, talking to my neighbor, Randy. He had ten dollars on the dresser and nobody touched it. They didn't even take his camcorder. The police say it was kids tearing things up."

"Do you think it was kid vandals?"

"No. They would have taken the cash. These bustards were looking for something that belonged to Laredo. Her room is slashed to pieces. That other trailer was window dressing to distract the police. Randy's home didn't have near the damage mine did. They broke in his door and over-turned a few things."

"Savannah, I get off work in half an hour. I'll catch a bus and come right over."

"No, don't. That's not why I'm calling. I'm warning you to be careful. They're after us. Both of us. They got me. You're next. Watch your back."

Helen had a jumpy walk home from work. Why would Hank Asporth—or whoever it was—trash Savannah's trailer? What was he looking for? The killer won't bother my place, she told herself. It made sense to search Laredo's home. But Helen didn't have anything of interest.

Besides, Margery was more eagle-eyed than any security service. She knew every alley cat that crossed the yard. No human would slip by unnoticed. Still, Helen was glad when she reached the Coronado. She was even happier to hear Cal the Canadian having a disapproval derby with Fred and Ethel by the pool.

"It would never happen in Canada," Cal said.

"You're right," Fred said. "America is a violent society. Rapes and murders are rampant and nobody gets punished. Why, just the other day . . ."

Three people were within deploring distance. They'd come running if Helen called for help. It would give them more to deplore. She felt safe—until she saw that her front door was slightly ajar. Helen saw the telltale jimmy marks on the door frame. She slowly opened the door. Something white floated out.

A feather.

She saw the smashed lamp first. The boomerang coffee table was overturned. The couch pillows were slashed. Her money was gone. Her secret stash. She'd had almost twenty-three hundred dollars stuffed in those pillows.

She ran to the bedroom. The sheets and spread had been dragged off the mattress. Her feather pillows had been ripped open. The room had snowdrifts of white feathers.

"Thumbs?" Helen said. "Thumbs, where are you? Are you OK?"

The toylike cat with the huge paws crawled out from under the bed and said, "Mrrrw."

"Good boy," Helen said. She picked him up and scratched his soft gray ears until he purred. "At least you're safe."

She was slowly taking in the damage. She ran to the kitchen, remembering Savannah's sugar on the counter and rotting meat on the floor. Thank goodness I don't have to deal with that, she thought. They didn't trash my TV, either.

But in the bedroom, her dresser drawers were open. Her bras were twisted together on the floor. Her panties were spread out on the bare mattress. The creeps had had their hands on her underwear. That violation seemed worse than Savannah's torn books and smashed china.

Underwear. She had seven thousand dollars stashed in the Samsonite suitcase, guarded by a mass of snagged stockings and old lady underwear. What if they got that?

She tore open the utility-closet door. The suitcase was still there. She yanked it open. The money was safe under the pile of elderly intimate garments.

Suddenly, Helen couldn't stay in her home another second. She ran across the lawn and pounded on Margery's door. Her landlady opened it wearing a purple leopard-print shorts set—if there were purple leopards—and kitten-heeled sandals.

"What's that racket? It's ten thirty."

"Someone broke into my apartment," Helen said. "They wrecked it and took about thirty-two hundred dollars in cash."

"Not at my Coronado," Margery said. "We've never had anything like that." The break-in was a personal attack on the integrity of her apartment complex. She crossed the lawn in long, feline strides. A tiger was in those kitten heels.

Margery surveyed the damage to Helen's home. "The miserable buggers broke my lamp. Don't worry. I have another one just like it."

"They had their hands on my underwear," Helen said.

"We'll fix that." Margery stuffed the mauled bras and panties into a shopping bag, then added the sheets and spread. The pillow cases were totaled, but she took them, too.

"Let's go back to my place. I'll throw these in my washer. Damn. The one night I go visit my friend Shirley and this happens. Do you want to sleep on my couch tonight?"

"No, they're not chasing me out of my place. Besides, there are plenty of people around."

"Fine. Let's call the police."

"No!" Helen said. "How would I explain twenty-two hundred dollars stuffed in the couch pillows?"

"You don't have to. They're not the IRS."

"I don't want the police wondering why I have all that cash," Helen said. "They'll never find my money. I can't point to a pile of bills and say, Those are mine. I recognize George Washington's picture.' "

"We can at least ask Cal, Fred and Ethel if they saw anything. Peggy's not home yet."

As they pushed through the poolside palm fronds, Helen heard Fred say, "The government should make those welfare bums work."

"Excuse me," Margery said. "While you were settling the fate of the nation tonight, did you see anyone hanging around Helen's apartment? Someone broke in."

"That's terrible," Ethel said. She was wearing an ASK ME ABOUT MY GRANDBABY T-shirt. Helen would cut out her tongue before she did.

"They get anything?" Fred said.

"Just messed the place up," Helen said. She wasn't going to tell them she'd lost over two grand.

"Kids," Ethel said. Her chins wobbled judicially. "They should be in school, but they're roaming about, not working, everything handed to them. When I was their age—"

"Canada would never—" Cal interrupted.

"Did anyone see anything?" Margery interrupted. "Any strangers on the property or the parking lot? I left about six tonight."

"I didn't get home until a-boot half an hour ago," Cal said. A year ago, Helen would have found that "a-boot" sexy, along with the rest of Cal. Now it was as thrilling as his boiled-broccoli dinners.

"What about you and Fred?" Margery asked Ethel.

"We were otherwise occupied," she said primly.

"What's that mean?" Margery's purple leopard spots quivered impatiently.

"We were getting a little afternoon delight." Fred grinned

and stuck out his gourdlike gut proudly. Helen wondered if another body part stuck out further.

Ethel simpered.

Margery looked disgusted. "Thanks for that information. I better take Helen back to my place and feed her some dinner."

When they were safely in Margery's kitchen, she said, "I was afraid lover boy would start pounding his chest like a gorilla. Let me fix you a drink. I don't know which is worse— Fred and Ethel in the throes of connubial bliss, or your place tossed and robbed."

"How about having my underwear pawed by thieving pervs?"

Margery filled a water glass with about six ounces of gin, then added a shot of orange juice. "Drink that."

She did. Helen felt a pleasant buzz. Three gulps and the Fred and Ethel X-rated movie vanished. The Debbie horror show still played in her head, but it was safely in the background.

Margery handed her a big glass of water next. "Now, drink this. It's a chaser to clear the palate." She pulled a brown box from the freezer.

"DoveBars," Helen said. "Dark chocolate. Yum."

The bar was richly rotund. Helen ate it in greedy bites, cracking the thick chocolate coat.

"Have you had dinner?" Margery said.

"No." Helen deftly caught a chunk of cracked-off chocolate with her tongue.

"I'll get you a sandwich," Margery said.

This struck Helen as funny. After six ounces of gin, lots of things were funny. "You gave me dessert first."

"Of course. Life is short. Turkey OK?"

"For life?" Helen was confused.

"For dinner. I can fix you turkey on whole wheat and salt-and-vinegar chips."

"Hold the chips," Helen said virtuously, then hiccupped. She'd already held four bags that week—and eaten them all.

About halfway through her sandwich, Helen's eyelids began to droop. "Let's get you home. You've had a bad day," Margery said.

"You have no idea." But Helen wasn't drunk enough to tell Margery exactly how bad.

Her landlady disappeared down the hall. While she was gone, Helen pawed through her purse until she found her pay envelope. Finally, something good happened today. She hadn't had time to put it with her stash, thank goodness. She quickly counted her money. Four hundred fifty dollars. Vito had stiffed her an extra fifty. She was too tired to care.

Margery came back with an armload of lavender sheets, a purple blanket and two white pillows. "Ready? Let's fix up your place," she said.

As they passed Phil's apartment, Helen breathed in the sticky perfume of burning weed. "Do you think Phil saw anything?"

"Phil probably saw lots of things, but nothing that can help you," Margery said.

"I don't believe he exists," Helen said.

"Of course he does. I see him when he pays his rent every month, and he's never been late." This was Margery's highest character reference.

"Is he married or single?"

"Don't you have enough problems?" Margery snapped. She examined Helen's jimmied door. "I'll get you a new door and lock tomorrow."

It took almost an hour to put the place in order. They righted the coffee table. Helen swept up the broken lamp and carried the pieces out to the Dumpster. She put her things back in the dresser drawers while Margery vacuumed up the feathers and Thumbs chased them around the room.

Then they made the bed while Thumbs tunneled under the covers.

"He's having a good time," Helen said.

Margery patted the new pillows into place and shooed

Thumbs off the bed. She was not a cat lover. "I'll get you a couple of couch pillows. Sorry I can't replace your stuffing."

Helen examined the reconstructed room. "Something's missing."

"That broken lamp leaves a big hole," Margery said.

"No, it's in here." Helen stared hard at the bed. "It's Chocolate."

"I can get you more chocolate. I have some Godiva."

"Chocolate, my bear. My stuffed bear is gone."

Helen checked under the bed, but she knew he wasn't there. "He had almost a thousand dollars in him. They could have just taken the money, but they didn't.

"They got my teddy bear," Helen said. "Now it's personal."

Chapter 13

They stole her money. They pawed her panties. They took her teddy bear.

A vengeful rage flamed up in Helen. She'd lost almost thirty-two hundred dollars, hidden in her couch pillows and her bear. She thought of all the things she could have done with that money. A few more bucks and she could have bought a decent used car. No more buses and begged rides. A good car was an impossible luxury for someone who worked dead-end jobs. She'd been so close.

It was gone now.

So was her button-eyed bear with the jaunty purple bow. For some reason, that made her angrier than the money. No, she knew why. The bear was one of the few good things salvaged from her old life.

Then she saw Debbie's long hair, the silken weapon she'd used to ensnare men, twisted into a murderous rope. Helen's mind scrabbled away from that and crept back to something safer—her lost money.

Helen thought about what she'd endured to get that thirty-two hundred dollars. She relived every insult, every indignity, every leering pep talk from Vito. She wanted to weep. No, she would not give in to tears. Her anger had burned away soft feelings.

Revenge. She wanted hot, hateful revenge on the man who ruined her peaceful life. She wanted to strip him naked. Take away his money, his honor, his dignity.

She knew who did this: Hank Asporth—or his hired help. She would get him if was the last thing she did.

But it wouldn't be easy. Hank was powerful and protected. He ordered around high-priced lawyers like pin-striped lackeys. There was no way she could get near him. She was a minimum-wage slave. She was invisible. No, worse than invisible. She'd been branded a crazy woman. She'd called the police about a nonexistent murder. She'd wasted the cops' valuable time. She had no credibility.

Helen had to find the mysterious Kristi, the woman who knew about the Six Feet Unders. What was their deadly secret: Murder? Necrophilia? Snuff movies? In South Florida, anything was possible. Kristi worked in that back room with the Six Feet Unders. At least, that's what Debbie had said, but she was now six feet under herself. The only way to find Kristi was to work topless at Steve's next party.

Going undercover was one thing. Going naked was another.

Helen would rather work smart than topless. She knew how to get what she wanted and keep her clothes on. She called Steve, the bullying boss of the bartenders.

"Helen! I've been trying to reach you, but I don't have a number for you." Steve sounded puppy-dog friendly. Did he need topless bartenders that bad?

"You got noticed last time. A guy who saw you wanted your phone number. He's loaded. If you're smart, you'll be nice to him." Helen could hear the wink in his voice.

"It wasn't the old guy with the shamrock—" She almost said shorts, then remembered she wasn't supposed to have seen the second party. "Shamrock cummerbund," she finished.

"You mean ol' Parrish Davenport? Nah, it wasn't him, although I'm sure he'd like you. He never met a girl he didn't like. Joey's nothing like old man Davenport. He's about thirty-five and good-looking. A little rough around the edges, but connected, you know what I mean?"

"He knows all the movers and shakers?" Helen said.

"Uh, something like that. Gimme your phone number for Joey."

"How about if I call him?"

"Here's his cell phone. Call right away, will you? He wants to go to a party Friday night. You promise me you'll call him?" Steve sounded oddly anxious.

"I promise," Helen said.

"Now, about Saturday night at the Mowbrys' house. You wanna work the second party, too? We pay nice money to ladies who are your free spirits—broad-minded, you know what I mean?"

Helen knew exactly what he meant.

"It's a real tasteful atmosphere in your fine private home, not a strip joint or anything. You'll stand behind the bar, no dancing. We pay two hundred for the first party, five hundred for the second. Cash. But I don't want you if you're not willing to work the second party."

"I'll do it."

"You don't mind showing your tits?"

"No problem."

Because it's not going to happen, Helen thought. She would not be taking off her clothes no matter how much Steve paid her. She would find Kristi on the first shift, slip out the service entrance and never work for Steve again. He didn't have her number, and he didn't know where she lived.

Helen dialed Joey's cell phone next.

"Joey here," a man said. Then she heard a screech of brakes and a blaring horn. Joey screamed, "Why the fuck don't you watch where you're going?"

He was back on the phone. "Asshole cut me off. Who are you?"

"I'm Helen Hawthorne. Steve gave me your name. I was tending bar at the Mowbrys' party and——"

"Oh, yeah. I remember you. You're a little older than

some of Steve's girls. But you got something them dumb twenty-year-olds don't."

"Wrinkles?" Helen said.

"Class. Them other girls act like whores when they think a guy's got money. I need someone classy to go to my friend's house. I don't want my date sitting around picking her nose and scratching her ass, or vicey-versey."

"So far, I've never been caught doing either one in public." Helen wondered if this creature left a slime trail.

"Yeah. I knew you'd be OK to take to Hank's."

"Hank?"

"Hank Asporth. You know Hank. All the girls do. Has that big house in Brideport. It's real nice. Nothing like the Mowbrys'. That's a mondo-mansion. Hank just has a big house. Tomorrow night, some of the guys are hanging out at Hank's, drinking some brewskis, talking business. The gals will sit around the pool. Bring your suit. Better yet, don't." Helen could hear the leer.

"That's not classy on a first date," Helen said. Or a last one.

"See? You're a natural when it comes to class. I'll pick you up at your place."

Helen didn't want him anywhere near the Coronado.

"It's a little inconvenient to get to because of construction," she said. "Suppose I wait for you in front of the Riverside Hotel?"

"More class," Joey said. "I'll pick you up at seven o'clock. I . . ." The rest of his sentence was drowned out by angry horns. Joey yelled, "Hey, watch it you dumb—"

Helen hung up before she heard the rest. She had the horrible feeling that going out with Joey would be far more embarrassing than going naked.

She sighed. Friday night with Joey the jerk. Saturday night at the Mowbrys' orgy. Her social life couldn't get any worse. Except the next morning, it did. She had to turn down the one date she really wanted.

Jack Lace was waiting for her outside Girdner Sales at

seven fifty, digging a shoe toe in the dusty asphalt like a little boy. Only good little boys wore such polished shoes and
clean shirts and had their hair combed so neatly.

"I've been waiting for you," he said. "Would you like to
go out Friday night?"

"Wish I could, Jack. I have a previous engagement."

"Is there someone else?" Suddenly the little boy was
gone. This was a man who wanted her.

"Not really."

"It's not a night out with the girls, is it? I can take you to
better places than they can. How about dinner at the Delano
on South Beach?"

The Delano. Possibly the most beautiful of the old Art
Deco hotels. And she would be knocking back brewskis with
Joey the jerk.

"I'd love to, Jack, but I can't. How about next Saturday?"

"That's too long to wait. Let's do lunch Monday. Wear
something nice to work and we'll drive down to South Beach
when we get off at one. We should make it back by five."

"It sounds lovely," Helen said.

It was only after she clocked in and sat down at her desk
that Helen wondered how Jack could afford the Delano. The
valet parking alone cost more than they both made in a day.

She turned to ask him, but her computer had begun making calls in Massachusetts. Helen had to start her spiel.

"How dare you wake me up, you dumb slut?" were the
first words she heard. All thoughts of the Delano, and anything else pleasant, disappeared.

A red Viper with white racing stripes pulled up in front of
the Riverside Hotel at seven o'clock Friday night. It looked
like a Corvette on testosterone. Some cars seemed to an-
nounce, "I have major masculinity problems." This was one
of them. Helen knew it belonged to Joey before he got out of
the car.

Steve had called him good-looking. That didn't begin to
describe the man.

Joey looked like Michelangelo's David, if David wore Armani—and Helen figured he would. His muscles were sculpted. His face was chiseled perfection. The man was marble come to life. Too bad Joey was solid rock between his ears and crude as a prison tattoo.

"Hiya, babe," he said. "Ready to boogie?"

The doorman stared at her date. First, he'd seen her get into Savannah's belching Tank. Now this. Helen blushed as red as the car.

The car had black leather seats and a small, flat TV screen on the dash. Joey watched a boxing match as he weaved in and out of traffic. A muscular black man in baggy gold Everlasts was pounding the bloody spit out of a sweating Latino.

Helen had to shout over the announcer. "So, what do you do to earn this amazing car?"

Joey turned the volume down a notch. "I run the Yellow Pelican resort and marina."

"Very nice," Helen said, as the Latino man spit more blood.

"It used to be. Now I got the Feds crawling up my ass, saying I don't hire enough *melanzanos*. I have plenty of them in jobs they can handle—kitchen work, car parking, janitorial— although the Spics are taking over the cleaning jobs. Spics work cheaper and harder. All you have to say is 'green card' and they almost look like white men."

Joey laughed. A car honked as the Viper cut it off. Joey rolled down the window and flipped off the driver.

Helen wanted to jump out at the first red light. She wanted to tell this racist creep exactly what she thought of him. But she wanted inside Hank Asporth's house even more. So she kept quiet, hating herself and hating him. How could someone so handsome talk so ugly?

Mercifully, they were soon in Brideport. Helen saw the Latino man being pounded into the mat as the Viper roared into the driveway. It was already bumper-to-bumper Range Rovers, Jaguars and Cadillacs. They parked in front of a long, low white house built in the seventies. Joey opened Spanish-style double doors with fake stained-glass insets.

"Go on in," he said. "The guys are in the kitchen."

Helen stopped dead in the hall. Hank's decorator must have been Hugh Hefner. The walls were done in black patent leather, accented with smoked mirrors. There were black leather couches, chrome coffee tables and a flat-screen TV mounted on the wall, tuned to the boxing match. Now a Latino man was beating up a black one.

"Hank's got a lot of money riding on that match," Joey said.

In the patent-leather gloom, Helen saw a mahogany pool table and six colossal LeRoy Neiman paintings. The sports subjects were brightly colored as crayons.

"Look at that," Joey said. "Real art on the walls. Hank's got class, huh?"

"The pink flamingos are a nice touch," Helen said. There must have been twenty of them in the room.

Joey tapped one on the head. "No plastic for Hank. These are genuine hand-painted plaster."

Five men were in the vast kitchen, standing around a stove. An enormous pot of red sauce was simmering on a burner. Helen smelled five brutally strong colognes, overlaid with garlicky tomato. A black-haired man was alternately tasting and stirring the sauce with a wooden spoon.

"You're wrong, Gino," he said. "It's perfect. It's my mother's recipe."

"I don't mean to insult your mother, Hank, but it needs more oregano," said a paunchy man with long, rubbery ears. "Maybe you read her recipe wrong or something."

"I said it's fine," Hank said. He put down the spoon and stepped away from the steamy stove. For the first time, Helen saw his face clearly.

She studied the killer. His thick black hair was coated with something shiny. Did they still make Brylcreem? His skin was pitted by ancient acne scars, like dead volcanic craters. His single black eyebrow crawled across the top of his nose.

He wore what Helen thought of as a mobster knit shirt. It had a collar, a zip front, and black and white panels. His black pants were well cut but shiny. Sharkskin would be the right fabric for this man.

Helen thought his hands were made for strangling. They were blunt, muscular and studded with gold rings like tumors. The wooden spoon, dripping tomato sauce, looked like a bloody weapon.

"This here's Helen," Joey said. The men nodded without interest. Hank didn't even look up from his sauce.

"The girls are out by the pool," Joey said. "We're talking business in here. Why don't you run along and join them?" He slapped her on the rump like a horse.

Helen smiled and thought, I'll get them. I'll get them all. She was furious at the dismissal. They didn't even offer her a drink.

Helen looked out the sliding glass doors. Under a striped awning was a pool with a pink deck. The grass seemed striped, too. It led to a red-striped Cigarette boat. Four bikinied blondes with inflated chests were sprawled on chaise longues, sipping pink drinks. One was filing her nails. All looked terminally bored. Helen decided they wouldn't miss her.

"I'll just go find a ladies room," she said. She kept her purse with her. She wasn't going to set it down around this crowd.

Hank gestured vaguely down the hall, but didn't look up. Joey was respectfully approaching a fat man with bad skin. Helen thought he was going to kiss his ring. She ducked down the hall. This was her chance to search Hank's house. There was just one problem.

What was she looking for? Some trace of the Six Feet Unders? She didn't think Hank would keep a coffin in his house. Not unless it was black leather and chrome.

Laredo. She was looking for some trace of Laredo. She needed a sign that Laredo had actually been in Asporth's house the night of the murder. But how would she find that incriminating evidence?

Helen searched a guest room first. It was fairly tasteful, with a white bedroom suite trimmed in gold and a puffy pink satin spread. The closet was empty, except for several suitcases and some heavy winter clothes. Hank must make trips up north.

The bathroom had new toothbrushes and disposable razors, shampoo and conditioner. There was a fresh white terry robe.

The second guest bedroom was done in flamingos. Even the tall bedside lamps were flamingos wearing slightly crooked lampshades, which made them look tipsy. Helen liked the room. That scared her. She was losing all taste and proportion, living in Florida.

The closet had accumulated odds and ends: an ironing board, two fifteen-pound weights, a briefcase, an old set of encyclopedias. The dresser drawers were stuffed with women's underwear in small sizes. There was no way to tell if it was Laredo's, but Helen doubted it. This was expensive lingerie.

The master bedroom across the hall was a Playboy dream. The round bed was covered with a sable spread. The ceiling and walls were mirrored. So were the lamps.

The bathroom was deep brown, from the Jacuzzi to the commode. The commode sat in a mirrored alcove. Who would want to look at himself on the john?

She opened one side of the double medicine cabinet. It was standard stuff: shaving cream, aspirin, a metal nail file and clippers. The other side wouldn't open. It was locked. Helen saw a small lock on the underside. It looked a lot like the one on her sister Kathy's diary. She reached for the nail file. Yep, it opened just like Kathy's diary.

Inside was Hank Asporth's dirty little secret.

She saw a prescription bottle of Viagra. Another jar of pills was called Last Man. Helen thought she'd seen it on late-night TV being peddled by a former fullback. Creams, pills and gels for "male enlargement" promised "longer pleasure for you—and her. Four inches of penis growth in three weeks or less!"

Helen giggled. Big, beefy Hank suffered from teeny-weenie syndrome.

Then she quit laughing. Footsteps. Someone was coming down the hall. Quickly, she shut the cabinet and slipped into the flamingo guest room. The footsteps were coming closer. Helen opened the closet door and crawled in behind the ironing board.

She cracked the closet door open half an inch. She could see Hank heading for the bathroom. He didn't bother to shut the door. Thanks to the mirrors, she could see his every move.

Please, please, don't use the john, she prayed. He blew his nose noisily, then fished a small key from under the marble soap dish. The locked cabinet swung open when he touched it. Hank looked startled. She wondered if he'd locked it specially because he was having company.

Something definitely made him suspicious. Hank ripped back the shower curtain. He opened the master-bedroom closets and looked under the bed. Helen tried to make herself smaller behind the ironing board, in case he flung open the guest-room closet.

He came angrily out into the hall, heading right for the flamingo guest room, when his cell phone rang.

Helen jumped, and the pile of encyclopedias tilted forward. She caught them before they fell. The briefcase tobogganed down the pile, and she stopped it with her chin. She sighed with relief. She tried to settle back behind the ironing board, but a spike poked her in the back. What was that? She couldn't look now.

"Yeah," Hank said into his cell phone. "No. Yeah." Hank snapped it shut and went back into the bathroom. Helen felt a lot better, except for the spike in her back.

Rattle, rattle. Hank shook a pill out of a prescription bottle. Viagra. Which one of the bored women was the lucky winner of the short trip through Hank's tunnel of love?

Hank locked the cabinet, then walked down the hall. Helen waited a full five minutes before she sat up and got the spike out of her back. She carefully shifted the pile of encyclopedias against the wall. They stayed in place. The briefcase did not slide off the top.

Helen slowly unfolded from behind the ironing board. Finally she could find out what that fiendish spike was.

It was a cheap red high heel. Size six. A scuff on the toe had been covered with red ink.

Laredo, Helen thought. I'll bet anything this is Laredo's shoe. Savannah will know for sure. She picked it up and stuffed it into her purse. She didn't see a second shoe. She checked her watch. She'd been back here for half an hour. She had to get out of this place fast, then get the shoe to Savannah. She straightened her clothes, combed her hair and walked down the hall.

Joey was sitting at the kitchen table with the others. He looked ridiculously handsome next to these men with their big ears, big bellies and baggy skin. But on the inside, he was as ugly as they were. The long-eared man was telling a joke.

"What's the difference between a black man and a large pizza?"

"I dunno," Joey said, playing the stooge.

"A pizza can feed a family of four," Long Ears said.

The men all laughed. Especially Joey. She tried not to show her disgust. He finally noticed her, standing at the kitchen door.

"Hey, honey, why haven't you put on your suit?" There was a touch of impatience in Joey's voice.

"I don't feel like swimming," Helen said.

"What's the matter—embarrassed?" Joey said.

She nodded. She was embarrassed to be with these swine.

"Tits too small, huh? Don't worry. We can fix that."

"What?" Helen said.

"You need a boob job. It will give you confidence. Don't

worry. I'll get you one. I buy all my girls boob jobs. The doc practically gives me a group rate. I see it as investment— something we can both enjoy." He nudged the man next to him and grinned.

Ugh. How could he think she wanted fake boobs?

Because you work for Steve, who hires topless bartenders for charity orgies, she thought.

"Besides, it will help you in your work. Bigger tips with bigger tits."

"Call a cab, please," Helen said. "I'm not feeling well."

"I can drive you, if you want," Joey said. It was a half-hearted offer.

"No, a cab is fine. I need to go home. I think I'm going to throw up."

Chapter 14

"Another young Lauderdale girl is dead," Ethel said. "Murdered. Says so right here in the paper."

American violence was the Saturday evening topic for the tsk-tsk taskforce—Fred, Ethel and Cal. Helen saw them out by the pool as she was leaving for her bartending job at the Mowbry mansion. She planned to pass by the sour trio with a nod and a wave.

"Strangled with her own hair." The paper crackled with Ethel's righteous indignation.

Helen stopped dead.

Debbie. Her murder was in the paper. Of course it would be. She was young, beautiful and worked at a popular restaurant. Helen wanted to run away. She wanted to rip the paper out of Ethel's hands and read every detail.

"How old was she?" Cal asked.

"Twenty-three years old. Isn't that awful?" Ethel's chins wobbled in disapproval.

"It's drugs," Fred said. He'd turned his gourdlike gut into an anti-gay billboard. His T-shirt said, GOD MADE ADAM AND EVE, NOT ADAM AND STEVE. Helen figured Fred was safe from homosexual advances. Hetero ones, too.

"I don't doubt it," Ethel said. "It isn't right, a young girl working at that Gator Bill's. Too many men and too much money. No daughter of mine would work at a place that serves alcohol."

"In Canada—" Cal began.

"Any suspects?" Helen cut short his budding tirade.

"Huh?" Ethel said. Helen was supposed to bash kids or society, not spoil a good discussion with the facts.

"Do the police have any suspects?"

"They don't say anything about them," Ethel admitted.

"They wouldn't," Fred said. "The police only investigate important murders."

"In Canada—" Cal said.

"You'd be freezing your ass off," Helen said. The three stared at her. Helen walked off. Poor Debbie, dead and dissected by these dolts.

"Really, that woman is so rude," Ethel said. "I don't understand how Margery puts up with her."

By the time she was aboard the water taxi, Helen felt better. The evening was a gift and she enjoyed it. She watched the brilliant sunset fade to tender pink and felt the soft, warm breeze. The little taxi churned through the pearly gray water, passing luxurious yachts and splendid homes, until it docked near the Mowbrys' mansion.

A thirty-five-foot Cigarette boat painted with red flames was parked at the Mowbrys' dock. Helen squinted to read the name: *Hellfire*. She was looking at nearly a quarter-million-dollars' worth of boat—about what she'd make in a lifetime of minimum-wage jobs. Penis boats, the sailboaters called them, and made unkind remarks about their owners' masculinity. But Helen figured if you could afford a Cigarette boat, you didn't much care what other people thought.

Tonight's party was supposed to benefit the Broward County Wildlife Coalition. Helen liked that idea—wild life to save the wildlife.

"You're cutting it close," Steve said, when she arrived at the service entrance. "I can't have late bartenders. Got that? Go set up your bar. It's by the pool again."

This wasn't the same man who'd begged her to call Joey. She wondered if he'd heard about their date.

Tonight, the Mowbrys' party area was done in brilliant tropical greens, blues, reds and yellows. Young women in safari outfits walked around with live macaws, spider monkeys and spectacularly ugly lizards. Helen hoped the animals went home after the first party. God knows what would happen to them at the second.

The band did a thumping version of "Baby Elephant Walk" that sounded like it was being played by pachyderms. A different bored newspaper photographer showed up and snapped the same pictures.

It was the same crowd of thin face-lifted women and fat rich men. Helen heard the same conversations as the men lined up at her bar.

"Greatest president we ever had. Bombed those camel jockeys back to the stone age," said a scotch and soda.

"No, he didn't. They were already *in* the stone age," said a bourbon and water. The two broke into braying laughter as they left with their drinks.

Helen poured red wine for a white-haired politician who said, "This is America. If they want to live here, let 'em speak American."

A hatchet-faced doctor agreed, then said, "Some bleeding heart is trying to raise the minimum wage again. Those people don't understand what it takes to stay in business. I'm running an office and barely breaking even." He reached for a fresh gin and tonic. Helen saw that his watch cost more than a minimum-wage worker made in a year.

"You're going to be here for the second party, right, honey?" the doctor said.

"Yes," Helen lied.

He stuffed a twenty in her tip jar.

"You gonna give her a free breast exam?" the politician said.

Helen poured booze until her arms ached and her feet screamed for relief. The next time she checked her watch, it was nine o'clock. She'd seen no sign of Kristi all night. She was getting uneasy.

At ten o'clock, Helen made an excuse to go back to the kitchen for more limes. She wandered through the party, scoping out all the stations. Kristi wasn't working any of the bars or passing around canapés. Now she was worried.

"Where's Kristi?" she asked, when Steve came by at eleven thirty. The first party was ending. Helen wasn't going to panic yet. But she had to find Kristi quick.

Steve counted out ten twenties. "She couldn't make the first shift. She'll be here at the second party. The one you're working."

Helen turned pale.

"You're not going to chicken out on me, are you? If you turn me down, that's it, honey. I don't know your name anymore."

Topless. Helen would have to work the second party topless. There was no escape. Not if she wanted to talk with Kristi.

She couldn't do it.

She had to. Helen thought of Savannah, waiting for her little sister who would never come home. Kristi knew what had happened to Laredo. There was no other way to find her.

She took a deep breath. "Yes," she said.

"Clean up your bar," Steve said. "Then take off your shirt. You gotta show your tits at twelve."

Helen felt like she'd been slapped.

She scrubbed the sticky spilled liquor and soda off her bar while she argued with herself. At midnight, she would be tending bar topless. She'd take off her blouse and bra and parade half-naked in front of strangers. She saw the nuns from her high school staring at her in horrified shame. She heard her mother crying. How could she?

I do what I have to do, Helen thought. I don't know those people. They won't see me. I'll be another anonymous worker. I won't have a face.

I'll be half-naked for a bunch of rich jerks.

I'm forty-two, not some blushing virgin. Besides, there are doctors at this party. They see naked people all day.

But not healthy naked people. They see the sick, the injured and the dying. For them, good health is a turn-on.

Then Helen remembered the way the police had looked at her, as if she was a hysterical woman. That was worse than being naked.

Besides, said a nasty little voice. It's five hundred bucks. After the break-in, she could use the money.

Helen put the lemon peels, lime wedges and maraschino cherries into little glasses on the bar. She checked the ice. She counted the glasses and set out the cocktail napkins.

She unbuttoned her blouse. There were six buttons. She'd never noticed before. Now each one counted.

She was standing at her bar with her shirt open. She looked around. No one was pointing and laughing. The guests were inside the mansion, changing out of their clothes. The other bartenders and servers were already topless, looking like they did it every day.

Helen took a deep breath, removed her blouse and unhooked her bra. She stuck them both in her purse.

Going topless wasn't as bad as she expected. It was a little chilly, since her bar was outside, but that perked things up. The men stared at her chest, which made her uncomfortable at first. Then she felt better. She knew they'd never remember her face. Their eyes would never get up that high.

I'm invisible, she thought. I am a pair of breasts. I have no other identity.

Some guests had stripped to their underwear. Only a few men stayed dressed. Helen was grateful to the guys who kept their clothes on. Clothes did make the man, she thought. Especially when he was over forty.

A skinny woman whose pool house had been featured in a recent Sunday paper strolled by, clad only in pink thong panties and a push-up bra. Helen was pleased to see she had cellulite.

Helen served a beer to a naked politician. He had on a

wedding ring, but he stared at her chest as if he'd never seen a bare one before.

She was getting used to the fat men in their underwear. It wasn't any worse than the beach during tourist season. Most of the sex and drugs seemed to be inside the house, so she was spared those scenes.

It's not bad, she thought.

Then the lizard, Mr. Cavarelli, slithered up to her bar.

"I'm invisible. Management never deigns to notice boiler-room staff," she told herself, as she poured his red wine. And she was. Mr. Cavarelli never looked at her face or noticed her shaking hands. His flat yellow eyes were fixed on her breasts. Helen wondered if he engaged in interspecies sex. Her skin crawled.

What was the boiler-room boss of bosses doing at a society party? He was better dressed and fitter than most of the men. He'd also kept his clothes on. Thank God. She didn't want to look at his lizard hide. Cavarelli took his wine and slid into the jungle of palms near the pool.

Suddenly, she found herself staring at another man's chest. A man wearing a well-cut black sport coat and a black T-shirt that said, CLAPTON IS GOD.

She knew only one person who had a shirt like that. The man she'd wanted to see for more than a year. The man who had eluded her so thoroughly, she'd begun to doubt he existed.

It was Phil the invisible pothead.

He was real after all. And he could see her, too. Way too much of her. Helen grabbed a pair of liter soda bottles to cover her naked chest.

"What are you doing here?" Helen and Phil said simultaneously.

"You're Phil the invisible pothead." Helen had waited so long to see him, and now she couldn't look at him. Instead, she talked to his chest, the way the men talked to hers.

"I'm your neighbor, yes," he said. His voice was soft and

low. Another time, it would have been sexy. Now, it was like being doused with cold water. "What are you doing here?"

"Tending bar," Helen said. She could feel a full-body blush creeping down past her shoulders. She adjusted her soda bottles to make sure they covered as much chest as possible.

"Helen, you—"

"How do you know my name?"

"Margery told me. I pulled you out of the fire, remember? Does she know you're here tonight?"

"She's not my mother," Helen said.

"She loves you like a daughter," Phil said. "This stunt would worry her sick. You've got to get out of here. It's dangerous."

"Don't be such a guy. I have a job to do." It was hard to look serious with two soda bottles stuck on your chest.

A fifty-something man in blue boxers interrupted. "Hey, what do I have to do to get a drink?"

"Sorry," Phil said. "You'll have to use the other bar. My friend is going home. She has a chest cold." He took off his sport coat and threw it over Helen. It felt soft and warm.

"Oh, no, you don't," Helen said. "You're not pulling that big brave male stuff on me." She wanted to hand back his coat, but she couldn't let go of the bottles. She shrugged it off instead.

Phil caught it and said through gritted teeth, "Helen, look at me."

She'd waited a whole year for this moment. She'd sneaked peeks out her mini-blinds. She'd risen at dawn and stayed up late, hoping to catch a glimpse of him. Now he was standing before her and she couldn't look at him.

Slowly, she raised her eyes to his. They were electric blue with long dark lashes. Sparks were flying everywhere.

This man was worth waiting for. He was in his forties, with a thin, sensitive face. His nose was a little too long and made a slight jog to the left. She wondered how it had been broken. He had deep laugh lines. His skin was tanned and his thick white hair was pulled into a ponytail. The effect was devastating. He looked like an actor or a rock star.

"I'm not being sexist," Phil said. "I'd advise a man to do the same thing: Get out of here. Now will you listen to me?"

"I need Kristi's address," she said in an equally low voice. "She's the blonde who works in the back room. I'm not leaving until I get it. Period."

"I know who Kristi is. I'll get her address from Steve. I'll tell him I'm taking you home. It happens all the time. He'll give you brownie points for pleasing a customer. But you've got to leave. Now. Please." He put the coat back around her shoulders. This time, she left it on.

"Alright, but I have to put the bar away in the storage room."

"Fine. I'll track down Steve and square your absence with him. I'll meet you back here in ten minutes."

Helen broke down her bar and wheeled it to the storage room. She wouldn't be missed. The second party was in full swing and the guests were occupied with more exotic activities than boozing.

The Mowbry mansion was a labyrinth of halls and cul-de-sacs. On the way back, she must have turned left when she should have gone right. Two more wrong turns, and she knew this was not the way to the pool. At the end of the hall were two massive mahogany doors, twelve feet high. The doorknobs and hinges were solid gold. Dragons and demons danced on the door panels.

Was this the fabled back room?

Helen wouldn't need Kristi. She could see for herself what went on in there.

The heavy double doors were shut, but not locked. Helen slid them open an inch and peered inside.

The room was dense black. Tall candles flamed on silver stands. The air was thick with incense and license. Bodies writhed in the corners. A naked couple opened a teakwood box that held white powder, a mirror and a tiny silver spoon. The flickering shadows were fantastic and evil.

Helen couldn't take her eyes off these scenes. Then suddenly, she heard the music, a swell of powerful sadness. A requiem. Brahms, she thought. Next, she saw the heavy black velvet curtains across the back wall. They seemed to absorb the candlelight.

An ebony coffin stood in front of the black curtains. It was flanked by seven-foot candles and serpentine vases with dead white flowers.

In the coffin was a blonde wearing a white lace dress and holding a bouquet of lilies.

It was Kristi.

Chapter 15

Kristi was in a black coffin, with white lace and lilies. No one cried. No one cared. No one even looked at her. But Helen could not stop staring.

Kristi blond hair was fanned out on a silk pillow. Her massive chest was modestly covered with white lace. Her skin was as pale as her lily bouquet.

Now a man rose out of the flickering shadows and approached the coffin. His dark hair stood in peaks like horns. He had thick black hair all over his back, like a pelt. His studded leather codpiece seemed more perverse than nakedness.

The leather man ran one finger down the curve of Kristi's bare white throat. Helen shuddered. The finger traveled downward over the white lace. Then both his hands grabbed Kristi's breasts. The man moaned and pressed himself against the black coffin.

Helen watched in horror. It was obscene. The woman was lying in her coffin. How could he touch her like that?

Then Kristi sat up, tossed the bouquet aside and pulled the man into her black coffin.

Helen gave a little shriek, but no one heard her. The coffin rocked slightly as the leather man climbed inside, his horned hair making devilish shadows.

Helen did not want to see any more. She slid the great

paneled doors shut. Their dancing demons and dragons grinned at her as she turned and ran back to meet Phil. This time, she had no trouble negotiating the mansion's maze of halls. Helen arrived at the pool, panting and white with shock.

"What's wrong?" Phil said. "What did they do to you?"

"I saw Kristi in a coffin. What was she doing?"

"Exactly what you think," Phil said.

"The Six Feet Unders. That's what they are. Debbie told me about them right before she died."

"We don't have time to sit here and chat," Phil said. "Let's go."

"Do you have Kristi's address? I'm not leaving without it."

"Here." Phil handed Helen a white card. "Steve told us to have a good time. He gave me your money, too. Five hundred bucks. Now let's go."

"Turn your back," Helen said.

"What? Why?"

"I have to put on my blouse. It will just take a second." It was ridiculous to insist on modesty after she'd spent the night half-naked, but Helen couldn't put on her clothes in front of Phil. He turned his back and mercifully didn't say a word. The man was a gentleman.

"Thanks for your jacket," she said, when she was decent again.

"Why don't you keep it until we get home? It's chilly after midnight." That sentence soothed her humiliation. She wasn't a topless slut. She was shivering in the night air and a man offered her his jacket.

As they walked to his car in silence, Helen studied Phil by the streetlight, drawn to those deep blue eyes and that tanned face framed by the startling white hair. She wanted to trace her finger along his slightly crooked nose. He looked like an eighteenth-century swashbuckler. She could imagine him with a sword, in satin knee breeches. She could imagine him without those breeches, too.

How could a man this good-looking live right next to her and she never knew it?

Because he didn't want you to know, she thought. So don't go daydreaming. You've had enough man trouble without falling for a druggie.

But Phil's eyes were clear and so was his skin. He was fit and muscular. His gut did not have the telltale liver bulge of longtime drug users. He didn't use drugs.

"You're undercover, aren't you?" Helen said.

Phil said nothing.

"DEA?"

Silence.

"FBI? ATF? Local?"

The silence grew, blacker and heavier. Phil said softly, "This is not a game. People are getting killed."

"I know," Helen said. "That's why I was at the party. I heard a woman die. She was strangled and I couldn't stop it. Her name was Laredo Manson. She worked the back room with Kristi."

"How did you hear her die?"

"I'm a telemarketer and—"

"A what? Where?"

"For Girdner Sales."

"Oh, my God. They're owned by the Mob."

"I figured. Either that or the boss, Vito, was hanging around with the cast of *The Sopranos*."

"Will you quit joking?"

"Will you quit flying off the handle? I'm a grown woman. I've taken care of myself for a long time."

Phil took a deep breath. "OK," he said. "I'm sorry. Let me take you home and you can tell me what happened."

Phil drove a beat-up black Jeep, dusty and stripped to the essentials. Helen liked the zippered windows. This was a working vehicle, not some yuppie fantasy. When they were out of the maze of Brideport streets, Phil said, "How did this Laredo woman die?"

"I was working on a vodka survey. I called a man who

lived in Brideport. He started to answer my questions, then put down the phone. Next, I heard him arguing with a woman."

"What about?" Phil said.

"I don't know," Helen said. "At first the woman sounded defiant. She said he'd better give her what she wanted. I couldn't hear what the man said but he seemed angry. She was pressuring him. She called him a liar and yelled other things I didn't understand. Then she became afraid and screamed, 'No, Hank!'

"Her scream was cut off and she made this terrible gurgling noise. It was a sound I've never heard anywhere else. He strangled her. Then he hung up the phone."

Helen felt the hot tears rise up. She would not cry in front of Phil. It was weak and useless. She swallowed her tears. They tasted like bitter medicine, but they did not make her feel better.

"I called 911 and the police went to the house. They didn't find any sign of a struggle. There was no body, no blood, no strange cars in the driveway. The police searched his house, cars and boat. Nothing.

"The guy claimed I'd heard a movie, and the cops believed him. They acted like I was a nutcase. But that was no movie. I heard that horrible sound and I heard her call his name."

"His name was Hank? Hank who?"

"Hank Asporth."

She studied his face. Phil gave no indication that he knew Asporth.

"Hank Asporth sicced his lawyer on me to shut me up. But I searched the computers at work. A woman named Laredo Manson was supposedly living with Asporth. I called her number and got her sister, Savannah. She said Laredo was missing. The police weren't looking too hard for her. A woman who worked with Laredo at Gator Bill's restaurant said she was restless and took off.

"The waitress's name was Debbie. She was a nasty little

tease with long white-blond hair. I mean, it went all the way down to her waist. Must have taken all day to dry. Debbie got a lot of tip money making middle-aged men crazy with that hair and her body."

I'm babbling, Helen thought. I don't know this man. I did some pretty dicey stuff with Debbie. It could get me arrested.

She studied Phil's handsome, offbeat face. Could a man with a crooked nose walk the straight and narrow?

"What's the matter?" Phil said. "Why did you suddenly stop?"

"I'm trying to decide if I can trust you," Helen said. "What if I told you I did something bad? Would you turn me in to the cops?"

"Did you commit a murder?"

"No!" Helen was shocked.

"Do you deal drugs?"

Helen was outraged. "Are you nuts? Would I take abuse as a telemarketer if I could make good money dealing?"

Phil grinned. That was slightly crooked, too. "Then the answer's no. Besides, Margery would skin me alive if I turned you in."

He was right. Margery trusted him. She could, too.

"Savannah and I went to Debbie's apartment. She told us Hank Asporth paid her a thousand dollars to lie about Laredo."

"She told you, huh? This Debbie sounds hard as nails. She was paid to lie, but she volunteered information out of the blue?"

"Her long hair didn't work on us. And we were persuasive," Helen said.

"I bet," Phil said.

"Do you want to hear this or not? Debbie said Savannah's sister worked the charity orgies in the back room. Debbie claimed she didn't know what went on in there, except that it was some group called the Six Feet Unders. She said Kristi would know the details because she worked there, too. Debbie was going to get Kristi's address for us, so we could ask her some questions. Except somebody killed her first. We found her dead when we went back to her apartment. Debbie was strangled with her own hair."

"Did you tell the police what you know?"

"We called them from a pay phone so they'd find her body, but we didn't say anything else. Savannah'd had a little problem with the law."

"I'm not surprised, being as she's so persuasive. What about you? Did you call the police?"

"Uh, it wasn't a good idea for me, either."

"You've got a little problem with the law?" Phil looked amused.

"I've got a big problem with an ex-husband." Also with the court, but Helen didn't want to get into that. She kept talking, hoping to slide over that sticky subject.

"Anyway, I managed to get into Hank Asporth's house and search it. He has a fur bedspread, mirrors on the ceiling and penis extenders."

Phil burst out laughing so hard he had trouble downshifting. The gears ground and the Jeep lurched forward. "So you were working undercover on your own?" he said.

"This isn't funny. I found a red shoe tossed in the back of a closet that I think belonged to Laredo. That's proof she was in Hank's house. I snuck it out."

"You removed it from the scene?" Phil was serious now. "It's useless as evidence."

"What evidence? Do you think the police will search the Asporth house again on my say-so?"

"May I ask how you got into Hank's house?" Helen noticed Phil had called him Hank. Did he know Hank Asporth or not?

"I went as the date of a guy named Joey. Drives a red Viper."

Phil stared at her. "You dated Joey the Model?" A car behind them honked. They'd been sitting at a green light.

"Is that his name? I couldn't stand the guy. I pretended I was sick and he sent me home in a cab. He was awful."

"You could say that. Joey the Model has murdered six people that we know about, two of them women he dated. He beat them to death."

"Oh," Helen said. "I knew there was something wrong with him. That's why I was working that awful topless party. It was the only way I could get Kristi's address."

"You are really something," Phil said. "But what it is, I don't know."

When Phil pulled into the Coronado parking lot, Helen jumped out and handed him his coat. "Thank you very much," she said, leaving him standing there. She ran all the way to her apartment.

What's the matter with me? she asked herself. Why didn't I stay and talk with Phil? I've told him everything—well, a lot anyway—about me. I have plenty of questions for him. But I ran like a rabbit. At least I could have let Phil walk me to my door.

But Helen knew the reason: She was afraid he might kiss her good night. She was afraid he might not.

It felt strange passing Phil's door without the familiar pot smog. It felt stranger still to have a face for the man in the Clapton T-shirt. Phil was no longer invisible. He wasn't even a pothead. But he was still a mystery.

Who was he? Who did he work for? Why did he create that druggie persona? What was he doing at that charity orgy?

Once inside her apartment, Helen began shivering uncontrollably. She fixed a cup of decaf coffee and sat in the turquoise Barcalounger with her cat on her lap, absently scratching Thumbs' ears until he rolled belly-up in ecstasy.

The cat and the comfortable chair could usually lull her to sleep on the most restless nights. But not tonight. Helen kept flashing on Kristi with her white lace and lilies, and the heart-stopping moment when she sat up in her coffin.

Then she thought of sassy little Laredo, with her yellow hair and red shoes. There would be no surprise resurrection for Savannah's sister.

Helen sat up until the night sky turned into gray dawn, drinking decaf and asking questions she couldn't answer.

Where was Laredo's body? Did the Mowbrys' parties have something to do with her death? Did Savannah's sister see something that got her killed? Had she been blackmailing someone? Or had Laredo stumbled onto something stranger with the Six Feet Unders?

The coffin scene made Helen believe this was way beyond anything her Midwest imagination could conjure up. The Mowbrys' guest list read like a South Florida who's who—with one slithering exception. Why was Mr. Cavarelli, the boiler-room reptile, mixing with the movers and shakers at a charity orgy?

There was one more guest who didn't belong in that crowd. A slim, muscular man with white hair, blue eyes and a lean, tanned face.

Chapter 16

"You look stunning," Jack Lace whispered in her ear. "All set for lunch at the Delano?"

Helen nodded. She was wearing her best black Ralph Lauren suit. Both she and the outfit looked slightly shopworn in the bright morning light. The suit was too shiny. She was too dull.

After that long slow night, morning came rushing straight at Helen. As soon as she clocked in at the boiler room, the staff was crammed into Vito's smelly little office for another pep talk.

Jack boldly sat on the edge of Vito's dusty desk. The room was so crowded, Helen was practically in Jack's lap. The prospect was not as pleasing as she thought it would be. Jack's cologne was overpowering in the hot room. His hair was suspiciously black. His manner seemed smarmy.

Vito started marching up and down behind his desk, a plump pink piglet on parade.

"Listen up, people. I don't have to tell you these are tough times for telemarketers. The Feds are making it harder for us to call people. Millions of people have signed up for the National Do Not Call Registry so far. Freaking millions. Our database is shrinking. With so many people on the do-not-call list, who's left for us to call? The stupid, the old, the lonely, and the technologically challenged.

"How are we going to sell to someone too dumb to put their name on a national no-call list? These are the dregs.

"Wrong. They are the cream—and the government skimmed it off for us. These people are our natural customers. We want them. We got them."

"You may want them, man, but they don't want us." Rico was a skinny, pimply kid who'd started three days ago. "People hate us. All day long, they say, 'Why do you telemarketers bother me?' "

"And what do you tell them?" Vito asked.

Rico shrugged. "I say I'm a telemarketer. I can't help it."

The room laughed.

"Here's what you say: 'Sir, please don't call me a telemarketer. I'm a technical advisor for a company that sells a product for septic-tank systems.' "

"Technical advisor," Rico repeated. "I like that." Even his spots looked brighter.

"You are also a surgeon," Vito said. "Bet your mama always wanted a surgeon in the family. Know what kind of surgeon you are, Rico? A wallet surgeon."

More laughter. Vito was warming up, his porcine body pacing faster. He waved his meaty arms, exhorting them like a TV evangelist.

"Get those prospects to say yes. If they say yes three times, the sale is yours. Get those sales, and I'll get you out of here."

The telemarketers looked startled.

"You heard me right," Vito said. "This is boot camp. The worst of the worst. If you survive this, I'll put you in the promised land."

Vito paused dramatically. "I'll let you call Canada. Canadians are polite and courteous. They don't have many telemarketers up there. No one has harassed them like in America. In Canada, they listen to you. In Canada, they talk to you. They're lonesome. It's winter. They're frozen in with nothing to do. They want to talk. Canadians are like little virgin girls, tender and sweet."

Vito, the fat pervert, was practically drooling. Was he planning to sell to the Canadians—or sauté them?

"Now get out there and sell. And if you keep selling, you'll have little Canadian virgins all day long."

That's disgusting, Helen thought, as she filed out.

"That's terrific," Jack said. "That man has a real way with words."

"You've got to be kidding."

"Well, maybe it was a little politically incorrect, but he knew how to talk to his audience. They're inspired."

"I'm not inspired by little virgin girls," Helen said. "Vito sounds like a child molester."

"That's the problem with you women. No sense of humor."

"What did you say?" Helen said.

But Jack was already oozing into his phone. Probably anxious to get those Canadian virgins, she thought sourly.

Helen didn't get any virgin on her first call. She had an irate veteran in Maryland. "Why are you calling me?" the woman demanded. "My name is on that national no-call registry. I'm reporting you."

"When did you sign up?" Helen said.

"Six weeks ago."

"Ma'am, it takes up to three months for your request to go into effect."

"Three months? Three months of you waking me up on my day off? I'm not waiting another minute. I keep a shotgun right here by my bed—"

Helen hung up before the woman shot her ear off.

All morning the calls were like that. She talked to the addled and the angry. The lunch at the Delano shimmered before her like a mirage in the boiler-room desert. Helen was miffed at Jack for his asinine remark, but the Delano would be a mini-vacation. Instead of dirty carpet and scruffy walls, she'd be in exquisite surroundings, waited on by an attentive staff. Sigh. She could have that life again, if she would only . . .

No. She had her pride. She was not giving one penny to that lying, no-good—

"Jack Lace!"

The voice was so loud it cut through the boiler-room racket. "Is there a Jack Lace here?"

Jack hung up his phone, jumped up, and waved his hand. "I'm right here."

"Come forward, Jack Lace," the voice said. Helen saw a man in a brown uniform standing by the door. There was almost a skip in Jack's step as he ran up there. Strange.

"Is he being arrested?" Helen asked Taniqua. But she knew he wasn't. Jack looked too happy.

Taniqua had the mirthless laugh of a much older woman. Even in the dreary boiler room she was beautiful. Why was she so bitter?

"Arrested? No. He should be. I told you, he a bailiff boy."

"I don't know what that is," Helen said.

Taniqua opened a pack of Famous Amos chocolate-chip cookies. "Want one?"

Helen shook her head. She'd already decimated a drawer full of salt-and-vinegar chips.

"Aren't you lucky?" Taniqua said. "Ask Marina. She knows." Marina made a face but kept talking on the phone. "That's why her baby boy Ramon be crawling on this nasty floor. Cause his worthless daddy a bailiff boy."

Taniqua somehow managed to get down on all fours in her tight black chiffon dress. She gave the little boy a cookie.

"Cookie!" Ramon said happily and smashed it into his truck. Helen wanted to smash something, too. How much longer was Taniqua going to stall?

She ate another cookie, then said, "A bailiff boy cheats his family. When a bad man gets a divorce, he don't care no more about his wife and family. He don't want to give them no money, no matter how much he be making. He want it all for hisself. So he find hisself a lawyer who be as low as he is. Then he quits his job and works at a place like this. He don't want no real money cause his wife and kids might get it. He flip burgers, wash dishes or sell septic-tank cleaner. He probably slip Vito money to give him this bad job."

Helen thought Taniqua was right, although she couldn't say anything. Vito helped himself to a hunk of Helen's bucks because she needed cash under the table.

"Then the bad man dress up real poor-like and tell the court he can't afford to pay hardly no child support cause he lost his good job and he be working as a telemarketer. The court send out a bailiff to his new job to check on him. The bailiff see him working here, and then the bad man is gone. You never see that bailiff boy here again."

"But what happens to his good job?"

"He go right back to it. Plenty of bad men out there, helping other bad men. Bad women, too, hurting their sisters. His poor wife have to go back to court to get more money out of that lying cheat, and it cost her more lawyer bills. She got kids to feed and put through school. She can't afford to chase the bad man around the court. Most of these men get away with it.

"I warned you. You caught yourself a bailiff boy."

Taniqua's even white teeth cut a cookie viciously in two.

Pieces of Jack's conversation came floating back to Helen. Jack took her to the dazzling Pier Top Lounge over-looking Lauderdale and said, "Helen, I promise you, the telemarketing is only temporary. I'll be back on top of the world soon and you'll be with me."

Jack was curiously unworried about paying for their De-lano lunch.

Jack talked oddly about his children. "It's like they aren't even my kids anymore." Jack hadn't used their names. They were no longer people to him.

Helen looked toward the dirty boiler-room door. The man in the brown uniform was gone. Jack was bouncing back down the aisle to his seat with a big grin on his face. Taniqua gave him a look that should have turned Jack's black hair snow white. She pointedly turned her back on him and picked up her phone.

"What's her problem?" Jack said.

"Is it true?" Helen said. "Are you working this job to cheat your family out of child support?"

"My wife turned the boys against me," Jack said. "Why should I bust my butt for them?"

Helen felt sick. How could she have thought this worm was attractive?

Jack gave her a grin that showed too many teeth. "Hey, the law favors the mother. It isn't fair. She doesn't have to account to me how she spends my money. She could spend it on studs for all I know."

"You scumbag," Helen said. "You're going to deprive your own children so you can lunch at the Delano."

"Relax, babe. Those boys are spoiled rotten. It's good if they don't get everything they whine for. They may have to get a summer job or something. It will make men out of them."

Helen's rage flared up like a red geyser. She slapped Jack across the face so hard her hand stung. "Nothing," she said, "will make a man out of you."

When her rage cleared, she saw Jack rubbing his cheek. Taniqua was laughing and clapping her hands. Vito came out of his office and said, "Hey, Helen, what's the matter? You on the rag or something?"

"I'm sick," she said. "I'm leaving now. I won't be in tonight."

It was three minutes to one. She clocked out early and stomped up Las Olas, cursing Jack and her own gullibility. The rat. The black-hearted, black-haired creep. Cheating his own children. How low could a man go?

She noticed something wet on her cheeks. Tears? It couldn't be. She was not going to cry over Jack. He wasn't worth it. She stopped in front of a shop window to check for runny mascara. It was a shoe store, featuring a clever display of red high heels.

Red heels. She still had the red heel she found in Hank Asporth's house. It was in her purse. She stopped at a pay phone to call Savannah and told her about her date with Joey the Model.

"I found this shoe tossed in a closet. It's a cherry-red spike heel. Size six with a scalloped edge and a scuff on the toe colored in with red ink."

"That's it," Savannah said. "My sister used that ink trick ever since she saw the Julia Roberts' movie *Pretty Woman*. Drove me crazy. Laredo would borrow my good shoes and scuff them up. She was too lazy to polish them. I used to yell at her all the time. Guess I won't have that problem any more."

There was a sad silence.

"Laredo loved those red shoes," Savannah said. "She would never have left that shoe behind at Hank's house. It won't convince the police, but I know she was there. It's time to get in touch with that Kristi person. What are you doing this afternoon?"

"Looks like I'm tormenting Kristi."

"I can't get away until about three. I'll pick you up at your place."

The call to Savannah cured Helen of any lingering grief about Jack Lace. Savannah had real problems. Helen did not. She was lucky. She hadn't dated Jack. She hadn't slept with him. He wouldn't be back to the boiler room. What was the big deal?

I was a fool once again, she thought. Why am I such a bad judge of men? Is that all that's out there?

There's Phil. Your next-door neighbor who looks like a rock star, a small voice whispered. She tried to ignore it.

It was one thirty when she reached the Coronado. Cal, Fred and Ethel were having another slamfest by the pool. Helen caught the words, "We would have never been allowed . . ."

Helen waved at them, then knocked quickly on Margery's door before they could trap her in a conversation. It was a fine day, a sunshiny seventy-two degrees. Her landlady was sitting in her kitchen with the blinds pulled, avoiding the dreary threesome by the pool.

"You want a bologna sandwich with ketchup? It's all I've got in the house," Margery said.

Helen thought of her lost lunch at the Delano, the exquisite plates, the fine wine. "Sure. But no whole-wheat bread. Bologna has to be served on white pillow bread."

"Coming up, Julia Child," Margery said. "You want salt-and-vinegar chips with that?"

"Why not?" Helen said. Why worry about love handles when she had no lover?

The bologna on pillow bread with Heinz ketchup was wonderful. It's your childhood on a plate, Helen thought. Maybe the Delano should add it to the menu. Nah, they'd ruin it by making the chips out of sweet potatoes or something.

"I met Phil last night," Helen said, taking another bite of her sandwich. "You knew he was no pothead, didn't you?"

"Of course. Do you think I'd rent to a drug user?"

"Why not? You've rented to everything else," Helen said.

"You're just bitter about Fred and Ethel," Margery said.

"You bet I am. It's a perfect day, but I can't sit by the pool with the temperance society out there. Admit it. You hate them, too."

Margery sighed. "I should have known normal wouldn't cut it in South Florida. I went to my lawyer and tried to get their lease broken, but they haven't done anything wrong."

"And they aren't likely to," Helen said. Her sandwich was disappearing fast.

"We're stuck with them until March," Margery said. "I won't renew their lease. I promise."

"Have you thought of an exorcism for 2C? The place is possessed."

They stared morosely into space. Then it dawned on Helen she'd been adroitly steered off the topic of Phil. "He's undercover, isn't he? Who's he with?"

"Can't say."

"Can't? Or won't?"

"I keep my promises to you. I keep my promises to him," Margery said.

Fair enough, Helen thought, as she munched her bologna.

"Is he married?"

"No."

"Single? Divorced? Straight?"

"Divorced. Definitely straight. And much too dangerous for you."

Helen left her potato chips untouched on her plate.

Chapter 17

"Promise me that you will not carry any oven cleaner," Helen said. "I'm not doing hard time for Easy-Off."

"No oven cleaner," Savannah said.

"No guns, either," Helen said.

"I hate guns," Savannah said.

"Do you swear?"

"I swear on my sister's grave, if she had one, that I do not have oven cleaner or a gun on me." Savannah put her work-worn hand on her heart.

Helen studied her thin, freckled face. Savannah seemed serious. "Okay, I'll go with you to see Kristi."

She got into the belching, lurching Tank. The car seemed to have deteriorated since the trip to Debbie's. It shimmied so bad at stoplights that Helen felt seasick.

"The Tank needs a bath," Savannah said.

"A bath?" Helen said. "This car needs to be junked."

"Careful. You'll hurt its feelings. You must have noticed that a car runs better when you wash it. I parked the poor Tank under a tree, and the birds got it. It'll run better after I clean it up."

A red warning light popped on in the dashboard. Helen thought she'd better change the subject. "It's two o'clock in the afternoon. How do you know Kristi's home?"

"I called half an hour ago and pretended to sell her a newspaper subscription. She told me to do something nasty. Is that what you go through all day?"

"Yep."

"I don't know how you stand it."

"No matter what they say, they can't shoot me," Helen said. "It's your part-time job that scares me, working nights at a stop-and-rob on State Road 7."

The Tank did a smoky cha-cha as they passed through the glass-brick pillars of the Palmingo Apartments. Cuddling in a coffin must pay well, Helen thought. Kristi's building was a sleek white stucco and glass affair overlooking a palm-lined canal. White-clad couples played tennis. Bikinied men and women lounged by the pool. No one swam in its outrageously blue water. True Floridians never went in a pool.

Luckily, the building did not have a doorman. He would have never allowed the Tank to leak oil and transmission fluid in the parking lot.

Helen and Savannah checked the directory in the lobby. "She's on the third floor. I'll get us inside," Savannah said. "She may recognize you and refuse to open up."

Savannah stood in front of the door and knocked politely. She looked deceptively harmless.

The door opened a few inches. Helen saw one suspicious blue eye.

"Hi," Savannah said brightly. "I'm collecting for the—"

"We don't want any," Kristi said, starting to slam the door.

"Oh, yes, you do." Savannah hit the door so hard it smacked Kristi in the face. She pushed her way inside. Helen followed.

"You hurt me," Kristi said, rubbing her face like a little kid. "I could get a black eye." There was already a red mark. Kristi didn't seem afraid. Maybe in her line of work, she was used to rough treatment.

"Your kinky customers would probably like that." Savannah, freckled and stringy, towered over the lush little blonde.

Kristi's hair tumbled down her shoulders. Her breasts threatened to spill out of her hot pink halter top.

"Who are you?" Kristi demanded, looking as fierce as her five-feet-four frame allowed. "Get out before I call the cops."

"Go ahead and call them," Helen said. "I'm sure they'd love to know you make your living doing the horizontal bop in a coffin. So would the IRS."

Kristi went pale as death.

The white living room increased her corpselike color. It was done in Beach Bauhaus. The white overstuffed couches and love seats had swooping curved arms. The carpet, curtains and lamps were white. So were the silk flowers and plaster seashells on the coffee table.

The plaster seashells were the essence of the Beach Bauhaus style. The beaches were littered with real seashells, but Floridians adored fakes, and paid good money for them.

In the midst of this arctic wilderness, Kristi seemed small and scared.

"I was at the party last night," Helen said. "I saw you in the back room."

Kristi grabbed a white chair arm for support. Savannah took two steps forward. Kristi took one back.

"We want to know about my sister, Laredo," Savannah said. "We heard she worked with you."

"I don't know anything about Laredo except she's gone," Kristi said. A lock of blond hair flopped in her eyes. She pushed it away defiantly.

"She's gone, all right," Savannah said. "She's dead. And you're going to tell me everything."

"I didn't kill her," Kristi said.

Savannah made a buzzing sound. "Wrong! The correct answer is, 'I thought she left on a trip.' You just told me you know way too much."

Savannah reached into her bottomless black purse and brought out a plastic bottle filled with a clear liquid. She stuck it in Kristi's face. The dead-white woman whimpered.

"Savannah, you promised," Helen said.

"I promised no guns or oven cleaner.

"This is ammonia and bleach," she said to Kristi. "It forms a highly toxic chlorine gas. If I squirt it, you die."

Kristi put her hands up to protect her face.

"We all die," Helen said. "You brought your own chemical war."

"Nope," Savannah said, tossing her a white mask. "Put this on. I am trained in the use of household cleaning products."

Helen fitted the mask over her face. She wasn't sure how much protection it was, but she wasn't taking any chances. Kristi looked frantically for some escape from the living room, but Helen and Savannah blocked the only exit.

"Sit down." Savannah gestured toward the couch with the bottle. The white mask took the humanity from her face and the country softness from her voice.

Kristi started to tremble.

"I said, 'Sit down.' "

Kristi sat on the puffy white couch. The love seat was covered with clothes. Helen wondered if Kristi had been sorting things for Goodwill. These outfits looked too sedate for a sexy young woman. Heck, they were too conservative for Helen. Their high necks, long sleeves and long skirts were more suitable for a grandmother on her fiftieth wedding anniversary.

Helen picked up a gray wool dress. It was slit down the back and had a brownish stain near the waist. Odd. Who would want that? Next, she examined a pale blue dress. It, too, was cut down the back.

Kristi moved uneasily and started to say something, then clamped her mouth shut.

"What's going on here?" Savannah said. "Why are those clothes slit down the back?"

"I don't know." Kristi's eyes darted like fish in a pond.

Helen picked up a scissors with a scrap of pale blue fabric stuck in the blades. "I think you know." She sounded like an android in that mask.

Savannah had the spray bottle in Kristi's face again. "I think you're gonna tell me."

Kristi hesitated. A thin sheen of sweat broke out on her forehead.

"They're corpse clothes," Kristi blurted.

"What?" Helen and Savannah said together.

"They were worn by dead people. They're slit up the back, because that's how you dress a corpse."

Helen dropped the blue dress and wiped her hand on her pants. Now she was glad for the mask. "Where did you get them? Are you robbing graves?"

"I bought them from a funeral home. The families changed their mind before the bodies went on view."

"What's that mean?" Helen said.

"They decided the blue dress didn't look good on Aunt Tillie, so they brought the yellow suit for her to wear instead. The family doesn't take back the blue dress. They can't. It's been on a dead body. Someone who worked at the funeral home sold it to me."

Helen was so creeped out, she could hardly look at the gruesome pile of clothes. Savannah was motionless. Her finger was still on the trigger.

"What do you do with it?" Helen said.

"Corpse clothes go for major money," Kristi said. Helen studied her pale face. The mouth was pinched. The eyes were hard and shiny as coffin handles. "Some guys like a woman to wear corpse clothes when they do her."

That was kinky even for Florida.

"I can't believe funeral homes make all these mistakes." Helen pointed to the pile of slit dresses.

Kristi shrugged, as if she didn't care what Helen believed.

"You're not telling us the whole truth." Savannah pointed the spray bottle at Kristi's hard blue eyes.

"Not my eyes. No, please," Kristi pleaded. She was ghost white. "I'll tell you. I only bought one real dress worn by a dead person. I made the others myself."

"You counterfeit corpse clothes?" Helen said.

"I have to. The demand is greater than the supply. Besides, buying corpse clothes is risky. A funeral director could lose his license if he's caught. So I go to the resale shops and buy good secondhand clothes. I never pay more than thirty-five dollars. I slit the dresses up the back. That's what I was doing when you knocked on the door."

"What are those stains?" Helen said, pointing to the brown spot on the back of the dress.

"They're supposed to be formaldehyde. Sometimes it, you know, leaks from the bodies. The freaks pay extra for that. I stain some clothes with unscented hair spray and food coloring and say it's formaldehyde. People don't know what formaldehyde looks like.

"My biggest sellers are the white lace dresses. I get a thousand dollars for those, twelve hundred if they're stained." She sounded proud of herself.

"What's the big deal with white lace—a bridal thing?"

"No, it was the dress on the corpse in the opening of *Six Feet Under.*"

Helen flashed on Kristi with her white-lace dress and lily bouquet, inviting the leather man into her coffin. Of course. It all made sense.

"That's why you had white lace and lilies last night," Helen said. "The Six Feet Unders. What exactly do they do?"

"Not much." Kristi rolled her eyes. "It's some kinky old guys and a couple of weird women. They like to screw in a coffin. They're old and boring and think it's a big deal. Maybe it is for them. They'll be in their own coffins soon enough."

"One question," Helen said. "You don't have to answer if you don't want to. Is it comfortable doing it in a coffin?"

"It's not bad, once you get over the idea. It's roomier than the back seat of a Toyota but not as big as a twin bed. It's got a mattress. The springs don't squeak, either."

Savannah interrupted in a flat, dead voice. "My sister was doing this? Wearing grave clothes and . . ." She couldn't bring herself to say the rest.

Helen suddenly felt ashamed for asking about sex in a coffin.

Kristi smiled, showing small pointed teeth. It was a predator's smile. She would enjoy hurting Savannah.

"For awhile she was real popular. Those fat old guys go for the spunky blondes. She had big tits, too. The geezers like to grope those."

Savannah's hand trembled on the trigger, and Kristi realized she'd gone too far.

"But she stopped," she said, quickly. "She really did."

"When?" Savannah said.

"Just before she disappeared. She said she found something that was going to change her life. Something big. Laredo said she wouldn't be just a pair of tits. She'd be somebody important. She'd get married and live in a mansion."

"What did she find?"

"Uh . . ."

"Tell me what you saw or you'll never see another thing." Savannah's finger twitched on the trigger. Helen held her breath. If she lunged for the bottle, Savannah would shoot Kristi for sure.

"It was a computer disk." Kristi's voice was a high-pitched shriek of panic. "It was red. Plain red. She showed it to me. I saw it. She said that little disk was her winning lottery ticket."

"What was on it?"

"I—" Kristi started to cry.

"Answer me, or you'll really have something to cry about."

"It was stuff from Hank's computer. She said he'd been laundering money. He was into some other fraud, too. She said I'd be surprised at who was involved. Big names. That's all she said."

"What did she do with the disk?"

"She put it in her purse. Later, she told me she hid it."

"Where?"

"If I knew that, it wouldn't be hidden, would it?"

Savannah moved the spray bottle closer to Kristi's eyes. "I didn't want to know," Kristi said. "Laredo was gone and Debbie was dead. I was afraid I'd be next." She was crying hard now. Her white face was now an ugly red. Her nose was running. "You can point that thing at me all day, but I don't know any more."

"You got any family?" Savannah said.

"A sister in Missoula."

"I suggest you take a nice long visit home. The last woman we talked to wound up wearing real corpse clothes."

Chapter 18

"Some of the greatest actors of all time had a period of hired sex in their past," Savannah said. "Marilyn Monroe, for instance."

Helen said nothing. She was still shaking from the encounter with Kristi. Or maybe it was from riding in the Tank. The car was shimmying like Elvis' hips. The troll doll was dancing from the rearview mirror. Her stomach was in a spin cycle.

"My sister wasn't a hooker." Savannah sounded like she was trying to convince herself. She clutched the bucking steering wheel with both hands. If she held onto it, she might hold onto her sanity.

"Savannah, I work rotten jobs just like you," Helen said. "Dead-end jobs hurt your body. They grind down your spirit. Anyone who talks about the dignity of labor has never worked them. After a day on the phone in the boiler room, I can hardly move my neck, it hurts so bad. I come home at night and fall into bed—alone. I don't have the time or the energy to date.

"I'm tough. You are, too. But someone as young and pretty as your sister might do anything to escape."

A single tear slid down Savannah's dry, freckled face, as if she had no more left. Helen could hardly bear to watch its slow progress. "Laredo put on those weird clothes and climbed into a coffin with flabby old men. My little sister. How could she?"

"She must have been a great actress," Helen said.

Savannah seemed to find Helen's comment comforting. They rode in silence for a mile or so, if any time in the jiggling, jittering Tank could be called quiet. An SUV driver gunned her engine and drove around them, narrowly missing the Tank's bumper as she flipped them off.

"Can I ask you a favor?" Helen said. "Can we pull over and ditch that spray bottle? It makes me nervous. If we have an accident, bleach and ammonia are a highly volatile substance."

"It's just plain ammonia," Savannah said. "There's no bleach. I wasn't going to take a chance like that. I told you I'm trained in the use of household products. I brought the masks for effect. They scared Kristi good."

"Scared me, too," Helen said.

"Sorry about that. I wouldn't really use such a dangerous substance. But I knew Kristi wouldn't tell me the truth. I had to frighten it out of her. She's a hooker, however much you dress it up in white lace and lilies. Hookers are good at lying. It's what they do for a living."

More silence. Laredo, the pinup-pretty blonde with the sassy red high heels, was in the car with them. Helen could almost see her laughing—and lying to her sister. Even the rattling Tank couldn't shake their sadness.

"Well," Savannah said, because she couldn't say anything else. "Wanna get something to eat?"

Helen realized breakfast had been her last meal, and it was four o'clock. "Sure. My treat."

"No, mine. I ruined your appetite. Least I can do is help you get it back."

They pulled into the Heywood Family Diner, a mom-and-pop place on U.S. 1. Exactly what we need right now, Helen thought. Hot buttered grease. Waitresses who call us "honey" and bring us comfort food.

Savannah got out, unscrewed the top on the spray bottle, and dumped the contents on the parking lot. Then she tossed the empty bottle in the back seat. It landed on a pile of yellowing newspapers and old takeout bags. She threw the two masks in the restaurant Dumpster.

Inside, the Heywood diner looked exactly the way Helen hoped it would. There was a long row of blue plastic booths. Comfortable-looking waitresses carried pots of hot coffee. The daily specials were chalked on a blackboard. The air smelled of fried eggs, fresh biscuits and hot coffee. Home. They found a booth in a corner shielded by a glass-brick planter filled with dusty fake ferns.

"Coffee?" the waitress said. She carried two hot pots at once, a feat Helen could never master.

"You bet," Helen said.

The waitress poured and said, "We got a tuna-melt special with cole slaw and fries for four ninety-five. A bread-pudding dessert comes with that."

"Sold," Helen said. "My grandmother made terrific bread pudding. I love the stuff."

"Make that two," Savannah said. "We're easy."

Their food was on the table ten minutes later. "This is just what I needed," Savannah said.

The world did seem brighter with hot food. Savannah quit gnawing on herself and worked on her tuna melt. Helen ate everything down to the last salty fry. The waitress brought another round of hot coffee and bowls of fragrant bread pudding.

"They used lots of cinnamon," Savannah said. "This is the good stuff."

"What do you call that yellow sauce on your bread pudding?" Helen asked.

"Hard sauce," Savannah said.

"That's what my Southern granny called it. Nobody else knows what I'm talking about."

When they pushed back their bowls and had more coffee in front of them, Savannah was ready to talk about Laredo.

"What do you think my sister really had on that disk? Kristi said it was money laundering and some fraud with big names. I can't imagine what she means."

"How much did Laredo know about computers?" Helen said.

"A lot more than I do. Computers are second nature to someone her age, and she was darn good. She could have had a career in them. But she said computer jobs were boring and didn't pay enough. Plus, she thought the guys were geeks."

"Did your sister mention anything about breaking into Hank's computer?"

"No," Savannah said. "But she didn't always tell me everything."

That was the understatement of the year, Helen thought.

"Laredo did tell you something: Hank treated her like dirt at his house and she got mad. She also got even. She told you she used his computer for video poker. I bet she was playing a more dangerous game. She broke into his financial records. She could have been blackmailing him."

"But what did she find—and why would the names surprise us?" Savannah said.

"Hank goes to parties at the Mowbrys', and they're connected to some powerful people in South Florida. Maybe he's mixed up with the Six Feet Unders. He could be in some weird business like snuff films. People who like sex in coffins may also get off on watching people die."

Savannah shivered, and Helen didn't think it was the air conditioning. "God, I hope you're wrong. Could you go back to Hank Asporth's house and check out his computer?"

"No way I'll ever get in his house again," Helen said. "Not after my date there. Besides, Hank isn't stupid. Once Laredo threatened him, he'd have gotten the incriminating records out of there.

"We have to find Laredo's disk. It's important. Hank hasn't found it yet, or he wouldn't have trashed your place, my place, and Debbie's apartment. Where did your sister hide things?"

"In her shoes," Savannah said. "She used to keep rolled-up money in the toes of her high heels. But all her shoes and clothes are gone."

"She couldn't hide a computer disk in a high heel. It would be too easy to see."

Savannah sipped her coffee and thought for a minute. "When we were little, she used to hide stuff in her mattress. She'd cut a hole in the side and slide it in. When she was thirteen, she stashed her diary in there. I found it and read all about her adventures in Jeremy Ames' red pickup. I gave that boy what-for and he never came around again. After our trailer got trashed, that's the first place I looked. Nothing."

"Any other favorite places?" Helen said.

"Her car. Under the floor mat and in the trunk under the spare. But her car is gone, too. There's nowhere else I——"

Helen looked up and nearly dropped her coffee. Fred and Ethel had walked in.

"Oh, God," she whispered and ducked down in the booth.

"What the matter?" Savannah said.

"It's the awful couple in 2C. I don't want them to see me. They'll invite themselves to sit with us and never leave. They're so boring they make my socks roll down."

Savannah peeked over the dusty ferns. "She the gray-haired lady wearing the WORLD'S BEST GRANDMA T-shirt? And he's the guy with a gut? His shirt says, SORRY YOUR GOD IS DEAD—MINE'S ALIVE AND WELL."

Helen groaned. "It's Fred and Ethel, all right."

"You're safe," Savannah said. "They can't see you behind the planter."

But Helen could hear them. Their voices were so loud, she felt like they were sitting in her booth. She wanted to flee, but she couldn't leave while they were there.

They both ordered tuna-melt specials in booming voices. "We don't like bread pudding," Ethel said. "Can we have rice pudding, instead?"

"Sorry, ma'am," the waitress said. "No substitutions,"

"Can you take fifty cents off the price?" Ethel said.

"Nope. Can't do that, either."

"Some people are so cheap," Helen whispered. "Can you believe that?"

"They do throw pennies around like manhole covers." Savannah took another peek over the booth top. "But they've got their food already and they're really chowing down. It won't be long before they're gone. I'll get us more coffee. Just relax. It will be over soon."

"That's what my dentist says."

There was a fearful scream.

"Good lord," Savannah said. She looked over the fern barricade. "It's Ethel. Blood is gushing from her mouth."

Helen poked her head up through the ferns. "Do you think her tuna bit her?"

Ethel was moaning and holding her jaw. Blood dripped through her fingers and onto her T-shirt.

The waitress came running over. "What's the matter, ma'am? Are you hurt?"

"This piece of metal was in my tuna melt," Ethel said. "I bit right into it. I'm cut bad."

"I'm taking my wife to the emergency room," Fred said. "What's your manager's name?"

"Mr. Wilson," the waitress said. "He's in back. I'll get him."

Fred helped Ethel up and put his arm around her. She was dabbing at her face with a napkin, smearing the blood around.

The manager came running over. He saw bloody Ethel and turned the color of yesterday's oatmeal.

"My wife hurt herself on a piece of metal in your food," Fred said. "Look how she's bleeding. I'm not a suing kind of man. But she needs to be stitched up and I got a four-hundred-dollar deductible for my emergency room insurance."

"I'm sorry, sir," the manager said, wringing his hands like an old dishrag. "If you'll bring your receipt from the ER, we'll be happy to pay the deductible."

"In cash?" Fred said.

"Absolutely," the manager said. "Here's my card. Just call and we'll settle up. I hope your wife will be OK. We're so sorry. Next time, your dinner is on us."

Ethel was still holding the bloody napkin to her mouth and dripping dramatically. Helen saw she developed a limp as Fred helped her out to the car. Strange. That metal had been nowhere near her foot.

"There's something funny going on," Helen said. "Let's see if they really go to the emergency room."

Savannah threw down some bills and they ran to the Tank. Fred and Ethel didn't notice the lurching, smoke-belching car. They went nowhere near a hospital. Instead, they drove straight to the Coronado. When Ethel got out of the car, there was no blood on her face. She was smiling. A blue windbreaker hid her bloodstained shirt.

"I knew it," Helen said. "She faked that injury."

They drove past, so Fred and Ethel wouldn't see they were being followed. A half an hour later, Savannah dropped Helen at the Coronado. The sunset had painted the sky a glorious rose-pink. Wild parrots settled into the rustling palms. The soft evening breeze was scented with chlorine and Coppertone.

This was Helen's favorite time of day. A few months ago, she would have been sitting by the pool, toasting the sunset with white wine. Margery and Peggy would have been relaxing on chaise longues, Pete patrolling Peggy's shoulder while she discussed her latest lottery scheme. Margery would snort and smoke and ignore Pete's squawks. They would all be laughing.

Now Peggy and Pete sulked inside. Margery was barricaded in her home.

Their poolside evenings had been hijacked by Cal, Fred and Ethel. The couple claimed to be teetotalers. Helen thought they were drunk with disapproval.

Florida was warm and accepting, more interested in committing sin than condemning it. Fred and Ethel's moral superiority had soured too many evenings. Ha. They were nothing but small-time scam artists.

Helen banged on Margery's door until the jalousie glass rattled. Helen knew her landlady was home. Her car was in the lot.

"Margery, it's me," Helen said.

The door finally opened. Swirls of cigarette smoke poured out. Helen choked.

"Quiet. I'm avoiding the pool party," Margery said. "They've already complained twice. Fred said the chlorine was too strong in the pool. Ethel saw a palmetto bug."

"Only one?" Helen said.

Even in the darkened kitchen, Helen could see Margery was a mess. Her purple shorts were wrinkled. Her red lipstick had crawled up into the cracks in her lips and her nail polish was chipped. She was drinking a screwdriver that didn't even have a full shot of orange juice.

"You need your vitamin C," Helen said, heading for the fridge. She poured a hefty jolt of juice into Margery's half-empty glass of booze. Then she opened the blinds.

"Let in some light. We need to celebrate. We're getting the fun couple out of here. I caught Fred and Ethel in a big fat fraud."

Helen gave Margery the details. She could see her landlady perk up with every sentence. By the time Helen finished, Margery looked ten years younger. The wrinkles were even gone from her shorts.

"Are you working tonight?" Margery said. "No? Good. It's the Mertzes' bingo night. They leave about six thirty. We'll wait until they're gone and check out their place. I have a passkey."

At six twenty-six, Fred and Ethel left. Cal trailed along with them. Margery and Helen heard two cars start on the parking lot. They waited another half hour to make sure the trio didn't come back. Then they crossed the yard and went up the steps to 2C.

Fred and Ethel's apartment was a furnished unit, done in

wicker and seashells. "She keeps the place clean, I'll say that for her," Margery said.

The living room was tidy, except for the wicker couch. It was covered with stacks of newspapers. The coffee table had a pile of torn-out restaurant ads, mostly for family restaurants.

"The next victims," Helen said.

The kitchen table had been turned into a desk. A laptop and laser printer were set up on it. "Bet that's where they do their fake emergency room receipts," Helen said.

Next to the printer was a pill box.

"Wonder what drugs they're taking?" Margery opened the pill box. "My, my. Fred and Ethel figured out how to turn base metal into gold. These aren't pills. They're metal slivers. Ethel probably carried some in her purse and slipped them in her food. And what's this?"

She opened a small brown paper bag and pulled out a package.

"Fake-blood capsules," Helen said. "The kind kids use on Halloween. See, the package says, 'Bite me for that vampire look.'"

"'Bite me,'" Margery said. "That's how Ethel had blood running out of her mouth. She used fake Halloween blood."

"'Not harmful to humans or animals,'" Helen read from the package. She slipped one blood capsule into her pocket, and put a pinch of metal slivers in an envelope.

"Those cheap bastards. That's really cruel, scamming little restaurants for cash," Margery said.

"And free dinners," Helen said. "This routine could be pretty lucrative. Hit two restaurants a week, and they'd make eight hundred dollars in cash, tax free. They pick mom-and-pop places that are afraid of lawsuits. These little restaurants are happy to pay four hundred cash and avoid big legal bills."

"If we can catch those crooks in the act, they're outta here," Margery said. "And I know how to do it. Fred brags how often he takes Ethel out to dinner. 'I don't want my

Ethel slaving over a hot stove,' he says. 'I'm retired, so she is, too.'

"I'll find out when they're eating next at one of these little places. We'll go there and catch them."

Helen felt a huge weight lift from her spirit. She was going to get back her tropical nights by the pool.

Margery was nearly dancing with glee. "I can't wait to throw out Fred and Ethel. By the way, why did you think there was something wrong in the first place?"

"I don't trust a woman who doesn't like bread pudding," Helen said.

Chapter 19

Mother Nature made a mistake. Helen should have had Margery for a mother.

Helen admired her landlady's courage, her candor and the way she held her liquor. She liked Margery's purple shorts and sexy shoes. She was touched when Margery defended and protected her.

But Helen already had a mother, and though she tried to deny it, Helen loved her. She thought her mother's problems started with her name: Dolores. That name would make any woman sorrowful.

Dolores was small and fearful. She lacked the courage to sin, but lived in terror that she would lose her soul. Helen thought it might slip away, like an escaped mouse.

Dolores never made it into the twentieth century, much less the twenty-first. She disapproved of Helen's corporate career. "A woman's highest calling is a wife and mother," she said.

Dolores told Helen she had a duty to take back her unfaithful husband, Rob. "If you hadn't spent so much time at work, he might not have strayed. Men are different."

"Only because we let them get away with it," Helen said.

Her mother burst into tears, making the conversation even more dolorous.

Dolores believed what the old priests told her: Birth control was a sin. Wives should endure their husbands' faults, from alcoholism to adultery. Catholics who divorced and remarried would burn in hell. Helen was on the path to perdition.

Each month, when she hung up on her tearful, fearful mother, Helen told herself this was the last call. But thirty days later, she called her mother again.

Helen had a ritual to help her through it.

She took her old Samsonite suitcase out of the closet, crammed with rump-sprung cotton panties and circle-stitched Cross Your Heart bras that were gray as grandmothers. Thumbs jumped up on the bed and began playing with a dangling bra strap. Helen tossed her cat off the bed. She was in no mood for frivolity.

Helen had bought that snake-tangle of old lady lingerie at a yard sale, hoping it would scare away any thief. Underneath it, she hid her remaining money, a little over seven thousand dollars. She also buried a cell phone bought under a fake name in Kansas City. Helen had sent her sister Kathy a thousand dollars to pay the phone bills. She only used the cell phone once a month to call her mother and her sister.

Each month, Helen hoped her mother would miraculously become a strong, independent woman who believed in her daughter. But in case that didn't happen, Helen also brought out a piece of pink cellophane from a gift basket.

Helen always called her mother on the same day at the same time: seven P.M. She dreaded this one call more than a whole day in the boiler room.

This time, Helen got a recording, one she heard a dozen times a day. "The number you are calling does not accept unidentified calls. If you are a solicitor, please hang up now."

My own mother has blocked me out, Helen thought.

"Helen, is that you?" her mother said. Dolores sounded frailer than the last time.

Helen could see her: a withered woman wearing a luxuriant brown wig. Helen wanted to rush home and fold her small, faded mother in her arms. But she knew that was hopeless, too. Dolores would turn Helen over to the court and send her back to her cheating ex-husband.

"Helen, I have good news," her mother said.

If the news was good, why did she sound so tentative?

"I'm seeing Mr. Lawrence Smithson."

Lawrence? Helen flashed on a bandy-legged old man in baggy shorts and a flat yellow cap, mowing his lawn at six A.M.

"You're dating Lawn Boy Larry?" Helen said. "The guy who trims his lawn with nail scissors? I can't believe you're going out with that geezer."

"Don't call Lawrence that," Dolores said.

"That's what Dad called him," Helen said. "My father was a real man." A real unfaithful man, but no one ever questioned his virility. "Lawn Boy just wants to get his hands on your dandelions."

What's wrong with me? Helen thought. Why do I care who my mother dates, if he makes her happy? It's none of my business. My father's been dead for ten years.

"I have no one to talk to," her mother said. "Your sister Kathy has Tom and the children. You're living God knows where. You won't even tell your own mother."

"It's better that way." Rob would charm the information out of Dolores. She still saw him.

"Lawrence has been so helpful," Dolores said. "He fixed my toolshed. He mows my lawn every Wednesday. He cleans my gutters."

"Does he grease your griddle and haul your ashes?"

"Don't be disgusting."

"I'm sorry, Mom. I'm happy that you have a romance."

"It's not like that," her mother said. "I'm too old for romance."

"You're only seventy, Mom."

"I won't live much longer," her mother said. "I want you to come home."

All aboard for the guilt trip, Helen thought. "Mom, I can't go back to Rob, not after what he did."

"You didn't try," her mother said.

"I did," Helen said. "But every time I looked at Rob, I saw her."

It was worse than that. Every time Helen looked at Rob, she saw him naked with their neighbor, Sandy.

Helen had come home early from work and found them on the deck. At first, Helen couldn't make sense of the tangle of Rob's hairy legs and Sandy's waxed ones. Then she understood all too clearly. That's when Helen picked up the crowbar and—

"You should have offered it up."

Helen had a vision of Rob and Sandy humping away, while she knelt by the teak chaise longue and prayed.

"Offered what up?" she said.

"Your suffering. The saints did it. I did it for forty years with your father."

"Did you offer it up when Dad died at the Starlite Motel with the head of the St. Philomena Altar Society?"

There. She'd said the words that had been buried for a decade. She expected Dolores to burst into tears. But her mother said with simple dignity, "Yes, I did. It was my duty as his wife and your mother."

"Well, I'm no saint," Helen said. "And I've got the police report to prove it."

Helen had brought the crowbar down on the chaise with a loud *crack*! Rob jumped up and ran for his Land Cruiser, locking the doors and abandoning his lover.

Sandy, naked as a newborn but not nearly as innocent, scuttled toward her cell phone and called 911.

Helen started swinging. The Land Cruiser's windshield cracked into glass diamonds. The side mirrors disintegrated. She trashed the taillights and smashed the doors, while Rob cowered on the floor and begged for his life.

"You tried to kill your own husband," her mother said.

"I wasn't going to kill the SOB. I wanted to wreck his SUV. That was his true love. And I bought it for him."

She'd told the cops the same thing when they pried the

crowbar from her hands and pulled a buck-naked Rob from the wreckage. She could see the cops fighting back snickers.

Rob and Sandy didn't press attempted-assault charges. Sandy was afraid her husband would find out what she'd been doing when Helen started swinging that crowbar. He did anyway.

"I know you were upset, dear," Dolores said. "But now you've had time to cool off. Rob just made a mistake."

"Not a mistake, Mom. A bunch of mistakes. He hopped into bed with women I knew at the tennis club, the health club and our church. He's an incurable adulterer."

"You must hate the sin, but not the sinner," her mother said. "You promised to love, honor and obey Rob forever."

"And what did he promise?" Helen said. "After he lost his job, I supported him for five years while he did nothing."

"He looked for work, dear. He talked to me about it."

"He talked to everyone. He just didn't do anything."

But Rob had worked hard during the divorce, spreading his lies. His lawyer portrayed Rob as a loving househusband married to an angry, erratic woman. When he showed the photos of the smashed SUV, the judge winced.

Rob got his old girlfriends to testify to the work he did around the house. No one mentioned that Helen paid a contractor to finish his botched handyman jobs.

Helen wanted her lawyer to ask these women if they'd had a sexual relationship with her husband. But her attorney was too much of a gentleman.

Helen prepared herself to lose the house she'd paid for. But she didn't expect the judge's final pronouncement. She could still see him: hairless, smug and wizened, like E.T. in a black robe.

"This woman is a successful director of pensions and benefits, making six figures a year," his honor said. "She earns that money because of her husband's stabilizing influence, because of his love and support. He made her career possible at the expense of his own livelihood. Therefore, we award this man half of his wife's future income."

A red rocket of rage shot through Helen. She must have stood up, because she could feel her lawyer trying to pull her back down into her seat.

Helen grabbed a familiar-looking black book with gold lettering. She put her hand on it and said, "I swear on this Bible that my husband, Rob, will not get another nickel of my salary."

Later, the black book turned out to be a copy of the Missouri Revised Statutes, but Helen still considered the oath binding. She also believed the judge had been dropped on his head at birth.

Helen slipped out of St. Louis, packing her clothes and her teddy bear, Chocolate, into her car. She left everything else behind. She didn't tell anyone goodbye, except her sister, Kathy. Kathy was a traditional wife and mother, but she understood Helen's anger.

"I wouldn't have bashed in his SUV, Sis," Kathy had told her. "That poor Land Cruiser didn't do anything. I'd have taken that crowbar to Rob's thick skull."

Kathy was the only person on earth who knew how to find Helen. She had zigzagged across the country for months, trying to evade any pursuers. She didn't know how far the court would go to track down a deadbeat wife, but she knew that Rob would go to the end of the earth to avoid work. He wanted her money.

Sometime during her flight, Helen traded her silver Lexus for a hunk of junk. It finally died in Fort Lauderdale, and that's where she stayed. Now she worked for cash only, to keep out of the computers. Her dead-end jobs brought her a kind of freedom: no memos, no meetings, no pantyhose. She would never go back to corporate America. If Rob did find her, he'd get half of nearly nothing. Her old life and her old ambitions had vanished in easygoing South Florida.

"Helen, are you listening to me?" her mother said. "I can help you. I can make your problem go away."

"I won't go back to Rob, mother."

"You won't have to, Helen dear, if you're really determined. Lawrence and I have been talking it over. He has some friends in the archdiocese and I have some money. We want to start the proceedings for an annulment. It would be like your marriage never took place."

"But it did," Helen said. "For seventeen years."

"Well, you'd still have a civil divorce. But if you got an annulment, in the eyes of the Church your marriage never happened."

"But it did," Helen said. "I have the pictures to prove it. Mom, an annulment won't erase my marriage. It renders it sacramentally invalid. It's nothing but a divorce for rich people, and in my opinion, it's for hypocrites."

"Helen, I'm trying to save your immortal soul." Her mother started crying. She was terrified her divorced daughter would go to hell.

"Mom, I was married. You can't say I wasn't. I slept with the guy all those years. You can't save my soul with a lie."

"You're stubborn," her mother said angrily. "You don't want to be helped."

Helen had to end this hopeless conversation. She brought out the pink cellophane from the gift basket and crackled it near the phone.

"Hello, Mom? We're breaking up. I have to go now. I love you."

Helen pressed the END button. The last thing she heard was Dolores' heartbroken weeping.

Helen found she was clutching the phone and her cat. As she stroked Thumbs's soft, thick fur, she wondered:

What if my mother had believed in me more and the Church less? What if she'd said, "Rob is a rat. Pack your bags and come home to your mother, where you belong"?

Then I would not have had that screaming scene in court.

I would never have run from St. Louis.

I would not be living in South Florida.

I would not have this dead-end job.

I would not have heard a woman die.

Chapter 20

Someone had sucked all the air out of the room.

Helen couldn't breathe. She couldn't stop thinking about her mother, pulling strings to make Helen's marriage disappear. Dolores had denied her husband's infidelity for forty years. Now she was denying her daughter's failed marriage. Helen felt as if her mother was trying to wipe her out.

She ran outside. It was only eight o'clock. The winter evening was velvety warm, scented with night-blooming flowers and Phil's pot smoke. Phil. Now there was a man worth thinking about. Except Helen had a perfect record of picking losers.

"You going to stand there like a lawn ornament?"

Helen jumped. Margery had materialized in a cloud of cigarette smoke. Her landlady was in deep purple down to her ankle-strap platforms. Those shoes took guts. Helen would kill herself walking in them.

"Sarah called," Margery said. "You want to use my phone to call her back?"

Once they were inside, Margery said, "Sarah did call, but I wanted to tell you about Fred and Ethel. They're going to the Happy Cow tomorrow. I'll pick you up outside your office."

"Let's hope they bite," Helen said.

"Is that a pun? And will you stop pacing?"

Helen realized she'd been marching back and forth across Margery's kitchen.

"You're wearing me out watching you. Sit down. You look like hell. Have some chocolate." Margery handed Helen a Godiva truffle, like a doctor dispensing a pill.

"Should I take two and call you in the morning?"

"Wake me up and you're a dead woman. Now make your call."

Margery tactfully left the room. Helen settled into the puffy purple recliner. Her landlady's vintage lavender Princess phone was on a metal TV tray. It had been awhile since Helen had used an actual dial. It felt heavy and awkward.

Sarah answered on the third ring. "Helen, have you seen the paper today?"

"Not yet."

"See if Margery has one."

Margery either had powers of divination or she was listening on the extension. She plopped a paper in Helen's lap.

"What was the name of that guy you were calling when, uh, everything started?" Sarah asked.

"Hank Asporth."

"There's a story about some big society party in the feature section. I think his picture is in there."

Helen found the party story. "Holy cow. It's the Mowbry mansion," she said.

In the newspaper photos, the place looked like a museum. The furniture was so gold-trimmed and gaudy she knew it was either really cheap or really expensive.

"Helen," Sarah said, "did you say Mowbry? I thought his name was Asporth."

"The Mowbry mansion is where this party took place. These photos make it look even spookier than when I was there."

The guests were pretty frightening, too. The women's surgically stretched, chemically peeled skin made them look like burn victims. The men were old and dissipated.

Helen was fascinated to see Parrish Davenport, the jowly old man in the shamrock shorts, identified as a lawyer with a major Lauderdale firm. He was holding a drink. The pouches in his puffy face proved he'd held a lot of them.

"I'm impressed," Sarah said. "How do you know what the Mowbry mansion looks like?"

Helen was still staring at the pictures. Good Lord. The lecher who tried to squeeze her breasts was a prominent plastic surgeon. Maybe he wanted to know if they were real.

The woman in the La Perla panties was a real estate agent who sold multimillion-dollar properties. In the photo, her real estate was covered with a chic black dress.

And there was Hank Asporth, with his oiled hair and eyebrow like a furry black caterpillar. He was in another mobster knit, this one gray with black trim. He had one arm around an overdieted society type, a stick figure with blond hair and balloon breasts. Her dress was weirdly exaggerated, the way only couture can be. It was the party's hostess, Mindy Mowbry.

Hank Asporth had his other arm around a man, identified as Mindy's husband. Helen could identify him, too. He was the guy with the tan and the too-white teeth. He'd burst in on her in the bathroom and asked, "Wanna get it on?"

"Dr. Melton Mowbry (left), a partner in the Prestige Perfect Plastic Surgery Group. Mr. Asporth (center), a Brideport financier, is an investor in Dr. Mowbry's enterprises," the newspaper cutline said.

Hank Asporth definitely knew Melton and Mindy Mowbry. Probably in the biblical sense.

"Helen, are you there?" Sarah said. "You seem distracted. Have you really been to a party at the Mowbrys'? You didn't tell me you moved in such exalted circles."

"I've been to a couple of parties there," Helen said. "But not as a guest. As a bartender."

"There's a bartender in the photo on the right. Well, part of one. I see the arms and chest. Is that you?"

"I doubt it," Helen said, absently, still studying the photo of Hank Asporth draped around the Mowbrys like a fur stole. "I don't think the paper runs pictures of topless bartenders."

There was a loud clunk. Margery must have dropped the phone.

"I'll be over in fifteen minutes," Sarah said.

Uh-oh. Helen wished she'd thought before she spoke. Margery was standing over the purple recliner. "Would you care to explain why you were tending bar topless?"

"I'm forty-two. I don't have to explain."

"I don't care if you go streaking buck-naked down Las Olas," Margery said. "But I know you too well, Helen Hawthorne. There's only one reason why you'd work a job like that. You're trying to solve that girl's murder, aren't you? You've set something loose. That's why your place was torn apart. The Coronado never had a break-in before. You've brought those people onto my property. You better tell me what they're looking for."

"Can I wait until Sarah gets here, so I don't have to tell the whole thing twice?"

"No. Start talking."

Helen obeyed. Those purple platforms made Margery look ten feet tall.

She told her landlady everything from Debbie's death to Kristi in the coffin. When Sarah showed up, she started over again. Margery listened with her arms folded over her chest and her mouth in a tight line.

"And I thought society parties were boring," Sarah said.

"They are boring," Helen said. "Those people aren't any more interesting naked than they are clothed."

"They're deadly boring," Margery said. "We've got two young women strangled and two ransacked homes. Those killers have been at the Coronado. What are you going to do about it?"

"They're trying to find that red disk," Helen said. "That's

why they trashed my place. I don't know everything that's on it, but they want it bad. I have to find it first."

"And how are you going to do that, Sherlock? I assume you're not going to the police?"

"That's a lost cause. The cops think I'm a nutcase," Helen said. "I have to find it myself. I'm going to take another look in the Girdner computers. I'll use the names in this newspaper story and see what I can find out about these people. There are all sorts of useful tidbits in the Girdner database. There have to be some connections between these people at the party."

"It's a start." Margery's mouth was no longer a straight line. She'd unfolded her arms. She was coming around.

"Here's my plan," Sarah said. "I'm taking Helen to Jimmie's in Dania Beach. She can use a little chocolate therapy." Sarah looked like a bonbon herself in a pink caftan frosted with a white turquoise necklace.

"I've already had Godiva." Helen pointed to the gold wrapper on the TV tray.

"Chocolate isn't like booze. You can mix," Sarah said. "And Jimmie's chocolates are pure South Florida."

When they were in Sarah's Range Rover, Helen said, "I've been eating a lot of junk lately. I'm not sure—"

"Oh, please, Helen, don't fall into the great American pastime of obsessing about food. I may be fat, but I'm not boring."

"You're not fat," Helen said. "You're just you." Sarah, like Pavarotti, looked best as a person of size.

Jimmie's was in a little pink house with a candy-striped awning. Above the door, an evergreen wreath framed three white plastic swans. Pink flowers bloomed everywhere.

"This place looks like it was made out of gingerbread," Helen said.

"Are you going to be the witch?" Sarah said. "Jimmie's has champagne. I think you need some."

"Is that chocolate-covered, too?"

"Just breathe in the air. You'll feel better."

Helen had never seen so much chocolate, ribbons and flowers. It was as if her favorite maiden aunt was a chocoholic. There were mounds of rum, piña colada and key lime truffles. There were shelves of dark chocolate turtles, hand-dipped Oreo cookies, and chocolate-covered pretzels. Rows of chocolate-covered fruit: kiwi, pears, oranges. The chocolate-dipped strawberries were big as peaches.

"They're dipped first in white and then in dark chocolate," the salesperson said.

"Try the chocolate-covered orange peel," Sarah said. "It's tart—a word that seems to describe you lately."

Helen made a face, then took a bite. The orange peel was not sweet. It was rich, with a nifty little zing that was almost alcoholic. "Oh, my. If I had Jimmie, I wouldn't need other men. This is better than . . ."

"Sex?" Sarah said.

Helen thought of Phil, the visible non-pothead.

"Almost anything else," she said.

"OK, who is he this time?" Sarah said. "Let's go over to the café side and discuss this."

Sarah ordered champagne and more chocolate, which gave Helen time to collect her thoughts. A waitress brought two glasses and a cold bottle of champagne.

"Nobody," Helen said. "My romance was over before it began. I took your advice and went out with a guy from the boiler room."

"Not the boiler room." Sarah slammed back a surprising gulp of champagne. "I wanted you to meet a decent man."

"Well, I didn't. I need a chocolate-covered strawberry before I can go any further."

Helen told Sarah about Jack the bailiff boy between bites. The story didn't seem so bad. Champagne was the right accompaniment for a romance gone wrong.

"I am sorry," Sarah said. "But you handled the whole thing well. Your exit line was perfect. Besides, you don't sound too broken up. I know there's someone else."

"I'm not dating him. I just saw him."

"Who?" Sarah's champagne glass hung in midair. "Don't let me sit here sounding like an owl."

"I've finally seen Phil the invisible pothead."

"After all this time? I want details."

"He looks like a rock star. Dark-blue eyes, slightly crooked nose, long hair, lean face, nice muscles, good tan."

"All this and a druggie, too," Sarah said.

"But he's not. It's an act. He's undercover. Margery knew all along he wasn't a pothead. That's why she rented to him. She won't tell me which agency he's with. She says he's single, straight and dangerous."

"Sounds like your kind of man."

"Not according to Margery. You disapprove, too, don't you?"

"You'd be bored with a nice, safe man," Sarah said. "If he's good enough for Margery, he's good enough for you."

"That's practically an endorsement," Helen said.

They clinked champagne glasses.

"Always agree with the customers."

Vito was giving another pep talk in his dingy office. He was the televangelist of telemarketing, exhorting his ragtag flock to salvation. If they didn't sell more, they were damned to eternal unemployment.

"If someone says, 'I don't buy over the phone,' what do you say?"

The boiler-room crew looked up hopefully.

"You say, 'I agree, ma'am. You don't buy. First, you use our product for thirty days. Then you buy it.' See, you're agreeing with them."

Helen was fascinated by Vito's round head and spherical muscles. He was a bundle of ovoid energy.

"If they say, 'I can't afford it.' You say, 'I agree. You can't afford it. But you can't *not* afford it. If your septic tank backs up, it will cost you seven thousand dollars to dig up your yard. Seven thousand dollars.'

"First, sell them fear. Then, sell them peace of mind. Be

like the guy who has three cups and puts the bean under one. Keep moving that argument."

Vito raised his muscular arms toward heaven—or at least the cobwebs on the ceiling. "Now, go out there and sell. And remember, never, ever give out our toll-free number."

When Vito finished talking, Helen wanted to buy the product, and she didn't even have a septic tank. She made six sales that morning, beating her all-time record.

Vito sent her to survey heaven. She could do her research on the Mowbrys' party that night.

It was easy work on the survey side. Helen had to sign up people with in-ground swimming pools. In Florida, everyone who was anyone had a concreted, chlorined hole in their yard. Helen was back in the A-list, the richest of the rich. It was her natural hunting ground. But she couldn't start checking the newspaper yet. She had to sign up survey customers first.

She read the personal information on the first pool subject on the computer screen:

"Angela Hawson. Birth date 2/16/76. Single. No children. Occupation: Tax lawyer. Income: $100,000-plus. Number of computers in home: Three. Number of swimming pools: Two, one indoor. Pets: Two cats. Cars: Drives a 2002 Lexus. Suffers from depression. Takes Prozac. Has a weight problem."

Helen was amazed what people told survey takers. She'd tear out her tongue before she'd tell a stranger she was taking mood-altering prescription drugs. But phone-survey takers heard more secrets than priests in the confessional. People told her they were in rehab, bipolar, being treated for venereal disease. Helen thought they were too trusting.

"Hi, Angela. This is Helen with Girdner Surveys. We're conducting a swimming pool survey that pays—"

"I told you to take my name out of your database," Angela said. "I don't want your annoying calls."

"Yes, ma'am, I'll make a note of it."

But I won't take your name out, Helen thought. I couldn't,

even if I wanted. Angela didn't understand that once she gave her name to a survey taker, it was in the database forever. Now it would simply have a notation: "Do not call."

Even death would not remove Angela. When she turned up her toes, her entry would say, "Dead. Do not call."

A database was faithful unto death.

After she'd made enough survey calls to meet the minimum quota, Helen started checking the names in the newspaper story.

Ten of the twelve names were in the Girdner database. The real estate agent in the La Perla panties was divorced, made two hundred thousand a year, and had a hysterectomy.

Parrish Davenport was mortgaged to his shamrock shorts. Helen wasn't surprised. Girdner's records showed he'd been married four times. His current wife was twenty-eight. Helen suspected she was real tired of shamrocks.

Dr. Melton Mowbry wasn't in the database, but Mindy was. She used tampons and kept tropical fish. She drank beer, wine and liquor. She was allergic to shellfish, which disqualified her for many restaurant surveys. She had three cars and a Cigarette boat. Helen wondered if she really drove the boat or if Melton had put it in her name for some tax dodge.

The lecherous plastic surgeon, Damian Putnam, was the most interesting entry. Helen was surprised to see that he was sixty-three. She'd thought he was about forty. He must be into recreational nips and tucks. He was a partner in the Prestige Perfect Plastic Surgery Group. Where had she seen that name before? In the newspaper. That was Dr. Melton Mowbry's company. Interesting.

Dr. Putnam lived on the mansion side of Brideport, a finial or two from the Mowbry house. The database thoughtfully provided his address, all four phone numbers and his wife's name.

Was she at the party, too? Helen checked the newspaper. That was her, in a shiny evening suit of silk shantung. Helen had seen that facelift before, in the back room. Dr. Putnam's wife had been with another man. While her husband was grabbing tits like a dairy farmer, she and a naked man were playing with a custom coke kit. Nice couple.

She was forty-one—the perfect age for her husband's art. She owned a Pekinese. She'd also kept her own last name, which was unusual for a doctor's wife: Patricia Wellneck. That name was familiar. There was a chain of South Florida funeral homes called The Wellneck Group. And wouldn't you know it? The database said Patricia was its CEO.

Helen wondered if she gave the Mowbrys a good price on an ebony coffin.

Chapter 21

The Happy Cow belonged to the suicidal animal school of advertising. The restaurant's neon sign featured a beaming bovine in a chef's hat, eager to plunge a knife and fork into its own breast.

"If you think about it, this is a weird place," Helen said.

Margery made a left-turn through the traffic on U.S. 1, and pulled into the Happy Cow parking lot. "What's weird about an all-you-can-eat buffet in South Florida?"

"That cow. It's dying to become your dinner. How many happy cows, cheerful chickens, perky pigs and smiling shrimp have you seen, all thrilled to death because they're going to wind up on your plate?"

"So what do you want on the sign? A cow cowering in the corner while the butcher attacks it? That will sell a lot of steaks."

"No, I just wonder if people stop to think about it, that's all."

"The only thing these old farts think about is getting home for a nap before they go out for the early-bird special."

Helen didn't mention that some of the people coming out of the restaurant were younger than Margery. Some, but not many. The predominant customer hair color was snow white. At one-thirty in the afternoon, most of the walkers and canes were heading out the front door. The lunch hour was winding down.

"Do you think we've missed Fred and Ethel?" Helen said.

"Nope. Fred said they were going to a sale at Sears, then getting a late lunch here. I figured we should wait in the parking lot until they go inside. I don't think anyone will notice my car."

Margery parked her big white Cadillac between a big white Lincoln and a big white Buick. The parking lot looked like a pod of white whales. Helen could never figure out why, once you turned seventy in Florida, you bought a large white car. It must be some biological urge.

Helen and Margery watched the clientele totter out. "There are more chicken necks here than at a soup factory," Margery said. "This place must depress the hell out of you."

"Not me," Helen said. "Usually I feel old. I'm a hot babe in this crowd."

Margery snorted. "You young people. Always talking about being old. You don't know what age is. You *are* a hot babe. By the time you figure that out, you won't be one anymore."

Helen looked in the side mirror. She could practically see her chin and chest sliding south. She could also see Fred and Ethel pulling up in a big white Chevy.

"They're here." She ducked down in the seat, a decision she regretted. She got a cold blast of air conditioning in the face. By the time Fred and Ethel climbed out of their car, she'd have frozen to death.

Helen poked her head above the window to keep her eyebrows from frosting up. She saw Fred first. An AMERICA— LOVE IT OR LEAVE IT T-shirt was stretched across his melon belly.

"That's a Nixon-era slogan. Where did he get that?" she said.

"I think they're bringing it back," Margery said.

Ethel toted a fat black purse the size of a carry-on suitcase. She wore a GOD BLESS AMERICA T-shirt with a sequinned flag on her chest.

"Patriotism is the last refuge of these scoundrels," Helen said. "I guess we should wait five minutes for them to get seated before we go inside."

"Good. It will give me time for a last cigarette, now that you can't smoke in a Florida restaurant." Margery rolled down her window and lit up. "I've been thinking how this should go down. I know the layout. I've been here with my bridge club."

"I didn't know you played bridge."

"I don't. We play poker, but restaurants don't like that. So we tell them we're playing bridge. We bring bridge pads and set them out. Nobody ever checks. We sit in the bar and play cards and drink enough manhattans to keep the help happy. Fred and Ethel are militant nondrinkers. They won't go near the bar. We can sit in there and watch them where they can't see us. You got the stuff?"

"Right here." Helen patted her pocket. "Let's go."

Helen loved the bar at the Happy Cow. Its generous, curving black leather booths, dim lights and red-flocked wallpaper reminded her of the great old steak houses in St. Louis. The bar smelled pleasantly of mold, Lysol and stale cigarette smoke. That smell lingered long after the smoking ban.

The two women sat on heavily padded black barstools and ordered white wine. The bartender, a woman about Margery's age with an impressive figure and a blond beehive, was fast and efficient.

Margery had picked a good spot. They could see the whole place in the mirrors behind the bar. The restaurant was long and narrow, with a soup, salad and dessert bar running down the middle. A soft-serve ice cream station and soft-drink section were against the wall. The walls were decorated with Florida beach scenes and NO DOGGY BAGS signs. The waitresses took the orders for grilled steaks and chicken. Then the diners raided the salad bar.

The Happy Cow did not have fashionable food. Its clientele wanted a steak tender enough to chomp with dentures and food that filled them up: potato salad, macaroni salad, rice salad, green bean salad, black bean salad, corn salad, carrot salad with raisins. The bread was hot, white and puffy. Lettuce was covered with croutons and creamy dressing. Baked potatoes were piled with butter and sour cream. This crowd did not worry about cholesterol. They had already outlived the weak sisters with heart trouble.

"Fred and Ethel are experienced all-you-can-eat restaurant goers," Margery said. "They skip the starchy salads and bread and go for the expensive fruit and vegetables. Fred's got at least five bucks' worth of produce on his plate."

Fred's plate was loaded with salad, sliced mushrooms, fresh strawberries, cantaloupe and pineapple chunks.

"What's Ethel doing with those mounds of potato salad and bread?" Helen said.

"Getting tonight's dinner. Watch."

Back at their table, Ethel slid into the booth first. Fred's paunch provided privacy, but Helen could see over it on her tall barstool. Ethel opened her purse and eased most of the potato salad and bread inside.

"That's disgusting. She's putting food in her purse." Helen imagined it landing on hairbrushes and old Kleenex and nearly gagged.

"Relax," Margery said. "Her purse is lined with Ziploc bags. Look around the restaurant. Everyone is doing it."

Sure enough, when the waitresses turned their backs, satchel-sized purses snapped open and swallowed salads, vegetables and bread. Sugar and sweetener packs disappeared off the tables. Butter pats and creamers, ketchup and mustard packets all went into the leather maws.

When Ethel's steak arrived, she cut it in two and dropped half in her purse. Her baked potato went the same way.

In fifteen minutes, Fred and Ethel put away enough food to feed a frat house. Fred ate his. Ethel stuffed most of hers in her purse. She did have a bowl of clam chowder, along with her half-steak and half-potato. She hit the dessert bar three times. The first time, a big gooey chocolate brownie went into her purse. The second time, she ate the Key lime pie. On the third swing through, she got the bread pudding and slathered it with sauce.

"She's going for it," Helen said.

Margery asked for the bar check. They watched as Ethel chewed her bread pudding. She gave a muffled shriek, then grabbed her cheek dramatically. Bright red blood gushed from her mouth.

A woman with a macaroni salad screamed, "Help! Somebody call an ambulance."

"No ambulance!" Fred roared.

"You bet he doesn't want one," Margery said. "That would ruin everything." She put a twenty on the bar, but kept watching the drama. A worried waitress ran over to Fred and Ethel's booth. The manager, a thin woman in a blue blazer, sprinted behind her.

"Time for us to go to work," Margery said.

They started for the booth. The waitress was mopping up the blood with napkins. The manager was wringing her hands.

"I'm not a suing kind of person, but I'll have to take my poor wife to the emergency room," Fred said. "And we have a four-hundred-dollar deductible on our insurance."

"Why, Fred and Ethel, what a surprise," Margery said. "Is something wrong?"

Fred looked up, startled. Ethel choked, but quickly recovered. The manager looked ready to leap in and do the Heimlich maneuver.

"Ethel bit down on that metal in her bread pudding." Fred pointed to a piece of metal about half an inch long, lying in a pool of blood. "She's hurt bad. Look how my poor wife is bleeding."

"Wow," Helen said. "Ethel must have magnets in her teeth. That's the second time this week she's found metal in her food. I was in the diner about two miles down the road when she got metal in her meal. You wanted four hundred dollars for your emergency room deductible there, too. Cash only. I don't see any stitches from that accident, though. And Ethel bled all over. She was eating bread pudding that time, too. What a coincidence. I bet that piece of metal Ethel found in her food looks a lot like this."

Helen produced the sliver of metal she'd lifted from their kitchen and put it on the table next to Ethel's bloody exhibit. They were identical.

Fred's jaws were working, but no sound came out. The waitress stared at Helen and Margery. The manager stopped wringing her hands. She had an idea where this was going.

"My, my," Margery said. "Ethel is a regular horror show. Lotta blood running out of her mouth. Of course it looks worse when you smear it all over your face like that. What blood type are you, Ethel?"

Helen took a blood capsule from her pocket, held it up for everyone to see, then squeezed it. Fake blood squirted richly across the sequinned flag on Ethel's chest.

"F-positive," Helen said. "I'm positive you're a fraud."

The waitress gasped. The manager smiled.

"What do you think you're doing?" Fred said. "I'll sue you for slander. I'll call the police. I'll—"

As he talked, he and Ethel eased themselves out of the booth and down the aisle. Margery blocked their way.

"I won't have you two crooks on my property. You have twenty-four hours to pack up and get out, or I'll call the police and tell them about your hobby. Don't even think of asking for your deposit back."

Fred and Ethel scuttled out.

"My name is Gladys," the manager said. "Can I buy you lunch and a drink?" With the tension gone from her face, she looked years younger.

"No, thanks. We have to be about our business," Margery said. Helen thought she sounded like a gunslinger leaving town after rounding up the cattle rustlers.

"I can't thank you enough," Gladys said. "Let me give

you two free dinner certificates to the Happy Cow. Come back any time. We'd be honored to have you."

"Thank you, ma'am," Helen said. "We'll just be moseying along." Margery glared at her.

On the way out to the car, Helen said, "Well, we got rid of Fred and Ethel."

"I promise I'll never rent to anyone normal again," Margery said.

Chapter 22

"Hold it. Stop right there. I've got a gun."

That was Margery. Something was wrong at the Coronado.

Helen sat up in bed, sending the cat flying into the dark. What time was it? She stared blearily at her bedside clock. It was one twenty-seven in the morning.

"I won't hesitate to shoot," Margery said.

The killer. Margery had caught the killer. He'd come to murder Helen and Margery surprised him in her yard. Now her seventy-six-year-old landlady was trying to hold him off with a gun. She saw Margery, frail but fearless, an ancient revolver in her liver-spotted hands.

Margery didn't have a chance. He'd strangled a strong young waitress with her own hair. He would walk up and rip the gun from an old woman.

A weapon. Helen needed a weapon. She grabbed a butcher knife from the kitchen counter, threw on a robe and ran outside. Low-lying fog swirled and drifted across the grass, turning the night into a slasher-movie set. She felt foolish creeping down the sidewalk, kitchen cutlery in hand, but she didn't know what else to do. She had to save Margery.

She heard the rattle of a jalousie door and jumped.

Phil slid out of his apartment wearing black jeans, sandals

and no shirt. All her senses were on red alert. She noticed his broad shoulders, narrow waist, and intimidating weapon. What was that thing? Some new federal experiment? It looked like a ray gun from a fifties science fiction movie.

"I didn't realize you had nuclear capability," Helen whispered.

"What are you going to do with that butcher knife—make cutting remarks?" he said.

"I said drop it." Margery's voice cracked with anger.

Helen and Phil looked at each other, then sprinted across the wet grass toward their landlady's apartment. Margery was standing on her doorstep, wearing red curlers and a purple chenille bathrobe. A loose curler flopped over her left ear. The .38 Special looked enormous in her bony hands.

It was pointed at Fred and Ethel Mertz. Fred was carrying a TV set, balanced on his enormous gut. Ethel was wheeling a bulging black suitcase toward the parking lot. They looked angry but unafraid.

"What's going on here?" Helen asked.

"They're walking off with my TV and God knows what else." Margery waved her weapon at the suitcase. "Two C is a furnished unit. Or used to be, before these two stripped it."

"Open the suitcase," Phil said.

"I don't have to," Ethel said. "You don't have a search warrant."

"Don't need one," Phil said. "I've got this." He raised his ray gun. Helen hoped he would vaporize Ethel in her WORLD'S BEST GRANDMA T-shirt. Fred, too, while Phil was at it.

Ethel looked at Fred. He nodded. She unzipped the suitcase. It was brimming with purple terry cloth.

"My new towels," Margery said. "I just bought them for that unit this season. That's my bath mat, too. And my clock radio. Damn tourists. Can't have anything nice or they take it."

Helen thought of the couple's sanctimonious speeches on America's declining morals. They'd ruined so many evenings by the pool. "In my day," she said, "respectable retired people did not steal towels and TV sets."

"We're not stealing." Fred pointed his finger dramatically at Margery. "She is. She won't give us back our deposit and last month's rent. We're out eighteen hundred dollars."

"I'm out more than that," Margery said. "It's only November. You signed a lease for the season. You owe me through March."

"We would have paid you through March if you'd let us stay." Fred was shouting, beet red with anger.

"I won't have thieves on my property," Margery said. "You stole from those poor little restaurants and now you're stealing from me. I ought to pop you on principle. I could say my finger slipped on the trigger. Poor shaky old lady. Do you think a Florida jury would convict me?"

Margery grinned crazily.

For the first time, Fred and Ethel looked frightened. Helen was scared, too. Margery was quite an actress. Helen could imagine her crafty landlady crying before a jury of her trembly peers. "I didn't mean to kill that couple, even if they were robbing me blind. Something went wrong and . . ."

"Should I check their car?" Helen said, hoping to distract her landlady. "Just in case they've helped themselves to more of your things."

"You bet. We'll all go. Come on." Margery pointed the gun toward the parking lot. Fred and Ethel quietly abandoned the TV and the suitcase on the sidewalk and Helen breathed a little easier.

"Margery, don't you think you should aim that gun at the ground? What if you trip and it accidentally goes off?" Phil said.

"Then it won't be my fault," Margery said. "Listen, sonny, don't patronize me. I'm old but I'm not stupid. Come on, you two. March."

The Mertzes reluctantly walked toward their car, while Margery held the gun on them. Phil followed, looking faintly amused, his ray gun at his side. If he tripped, he'd vaporize the sidewalk. Helen was last in line, clutching her kitchen knife and debating whether the back or the front view of Phil was better. The front, she decided. She liked those raised eyebrows.

"Why, you thieving buzzards," Margery said.

Fred and Ethel's big white Chevy looked like the Clampetts' truck from *The Beverly Hillbillies*.

Roped into the trunk was a wicker rocking chair from the living room. Through the rear window, Helen could see three plastic wastebaskets, two pillows, and a purple blanket.

Margery ran to the car and peered inside. "They even took my shell mirror."

This time, her weapon did wobble. How hard did Margery have to squeeze the trigger to plug the couple? Fred held his wife protectively, but Helen noticed he was standing behind her sturdy figure. If the shooting started, she'd make a handy shield. Phil moved in closer, as if deciding whether to grab the gun from the outraged Margery. If he was really a cop, shouldn't he take it from her? What was going on here?

"Do you want me to call the police?" Helen hoped that would make Margery put down the gun.

"I can settle this without the cops," Margery said. "What if they keep my stuff for evidence? I've got my own way of dealing with thieves."

"We aren't thieves. We didn't take a penny more than we were entitled. This all came to eighteen hundred dollars," Fred said righteously.

"Wholesale or retail?" Margery snarled. She held the .38 on them while Helen and Phil started carrying the swag back to 2C. Helen gently unloaded the mirror with its frame of delicate seashells. Fred and Ethel had packed it in pilfered bath towels.

When Phil picked up the heavy rocker, Helen noticed how his shoulder and back muscles rippled. His abs were absolutely flat. The wrong men got naked at the Mowbrys' party.

Helen hung the mirror back in 2C, then dragged an army green footlocker out of the Mertzes' car trunk. Over Fred and Ethel's protests, she opened it.

On top was a purple oven mitt. "Is this yours?" she asked Margery.

"Yep. And that's my new Martha Stewart kitchenware." She pointed to a set of beige mixing bowls under the mitt.

"Martha has been convicted. Is it stealing to take her stuff?" Helen said.

"She was framed," Margery said.

Helen didn't argue with a woman holding a gun. She piled Margery's belongings on the grass.

Crammed in the footlocker was every tourist T-shirt sold in Florida, especially the disgusting ones. "Did you or Fred wear this?" Helen held up a T-shirt that said: DON'T FOLLOW ME. I JUST FARTED A BIG ONE.

The Mertzes maintained a dignified silence. Phil was stone-faced, but Helen thought his lips twitched.

Helen pulled out a pair of jockey shorts with HOME OF THE WHOPPER across the front.

"You should have gotten the T-shirt instead, Fred," Margery said.

Even Phil couldn't keep a straight face that time.

Under all the clothes, Helen found a black Bible. "What about this?"

"It's not mine. I'm not running a hotel," Margery said. "Besides, they need it more than I do. Maybe they'll read the part about 'Thou shalt not steal.'"

"We weren't stealing," Fred said. "I told you—"

That's when Helen saw the brown furry ear in the footlocker. She tugged on it and a stuffed animal popped out.

"My teddy bear," she said. "You took my bear, Chocolate. You broke into my apartment and stole my money. That was you sneaking around my window when I got money out of my bear. You saw me and ransacked my place for cash."

"I—" Fred said.

"We—" Ethel said.

"Shut up," Margery said. "You broke my lamp when you trashed her apartment. You owe me for that, too."

"You had your hands on my underwear, you perverts."

Helen was glad she was no longer holding the knife. She wanted to plunge it in Fred's fat gut.

She picked up her bear and patted it. Chocolate was oddly lumpy.

She reached into the slit in the bear's back. Instead of money, she felt . . . a plastic bag. Helen pulled it out. It was stuffed with long plastic objects. Salt-and-pepper shakers?

"Those are my love toys," Ethel said, indignantly.

A bag of vibrators. Helen dropped it. She had a sudden searing vision of Fred in his HOME OF THE WHOPPER underwear and Ethel in a flag-draped negligee.

"Where's Helen's money?" Margery said. "Don't make me use this." The gun was right in Fred's face, and this time Helen didn't care if she fired it. "What did you do with it?"

"It's gone," Fred said. "We went on the gambling boats."

"You blew my money gambling?" Helen thought of the brutal hours she'd worked to earn that cash. Now it was all lost. Only suckers played the gambling boats. The Mertzes might as well have dumped her hard-earned money in the ocean.

"Open your wallets," Margery said. "Get them out. Right now."

"What? You can't do this." But Fred and Ethel fished out their wallets and handed them to Margery. She looked through Ethel's fat wallet first, pulling out a driver's license. Then she searched Fred's wallet.

"There's two sets of ID in here," Margery said. "Are you Fred and Ethel Mertz—or John and Mary Smith?"

"Our real name is Smith," Ethel said. "But it's so common. It was embarrassing when we checked into a motel. We had trouble cashing checks. We got tired of the jokes and changed our names."

"You're *I Love Lucy* fans?" Helen said.

"We never watched that silly show," Ethel said haughtily. "I named myself for Ethel Merman. He's a Fred MacMurray fan."

"So why aren't you Mr. and Mrs. Fred MacMurray?"

"That would make us into a joke," Ethel said. Helen gave up.

"Quit gabbing," Margery said. She seemed to have borrowed her dialogue from late-night movies. "Phil, will you search their car for cash?"

Phil pulled everything out of the Mertzes' Chevy, even the backseat. He checked the glove box, the wheel wells and the spare-tire compartment. He felt under the seats and dash. He even took off the door panels. Helen went through every box and suitcase in the car. They didn't find another nickel. Helen's thirty-two hundred dollars was gone for good.

Margery found five hundred dollars in the Mertzes' wallets. She extracted a twenty.

"That will pay for my broken lamp," she said. "Here, Helen, the rest is yours. I'm sorry I couldn't get it all back."

"I never expected to see this much," Helen said.

"Hey, how are we going to buy gas?" Fred said.

"In my day," Margery said, "people worked for their money. You might try it."

Phil announced that the car search was over. "What can they take with them?" he asked.

"They can keep the suitcases with their clothes," Margery said. "But I'm confiscating all those tourist T-shirts. People think Florida is tacky enough without Fred and Ethel wearing those shirts back home."

Margery also kept a citrus juicer and a blender, both in the original boxes. "Those are ours," Fred insisted.

"Show me the receipts," Margery said.

"I didn't keep them," he said.

"Then I keep these," Margery said. "I'll use them to make me some interesting drinks. Screwdrivers with fresh orange juice. Margaritas and strawberry daiquiris. Lighten up, Fred. Fresh fruit is good for you. Alcohol is a preservative."

Fred and Ethel bristled like wet cats.

Finally, they were allowed to get in their car. "Don't ever come back," Margery said. "Do you understand?"

Fred and Ethel had all the expression of crash-test dummies. They nodded but said nothing. Fred started up the ghostly white car. The foggy night quickly swallowed it. Helen, Margery and Phil watched the crooked couple disappear.

"Whew, glad that's over," Margery said. "This thing is heavy." She tossed the gun onto the concrete. It spun crazily, like a lethal party game. Helen and Phil leaped backward as the barrel pointed in their direction.

"Careful," Phil said.

"It's OK," Margery said. "It's not loaded. Never was. I don't even keep bullets in the house."

"Margery, that doesn't make any difference. You have to treat every gun like it's loaded." Phil was a shade paler.

"I hate guns," Margery said.

"Maybe you should start packing oven cleaner," Helen said.

Chapter 23

Margery stood like a triumphant queen in her purple robe, with a crown of red sponge curlers. Her enchanted kingdom was restored. She had banished the trolls, Fred and Ethel. Her plundered treasures were back in apartment 2C.

The Coronado was in deep-night quiet. The other residents slept as if under a spell. White fingers of fog wrapped themselves around the palm trees and snagged on the bougainvillea spikes. The pool lights glowed, magical in the mist.

Phil gave a small, neat yawn, like a cat. Helen was afraid he would disappear into the fog, along with his wizard weapon. Phil had been invisible for more than a year. It could happen again. She blocked his way. "You owe me an explanation."

"I don't owe you anything. And I can't tell you anything," he said.

Helen could feel the heat from his bare chest. The odd, hazy moonlight turned his hair to spun silver

"Margery will vouch for me."

Her landlady pulled her purple robe tighter to ward off the chill, then picked a loose curler from her hair. "Listen, Phil, if you told me, you can tell her. She's in the middle of it, anyway. It's better if she isn't blundering about, causing more trouble."

"Thank you for that vote of confidence," Helen said, stiffly.

"Come back to my kitchen. We can get warm and talk," Margery said. "I'll make some coffee, unless you'd rather have a drink."

They settled for decaf and warm brownies at Margery's kitchen table.

"These brownies are terrific," Phil said. "Are they home-made?"

He ate neatly. Helen's ex-husband, Rob, had dropped crumbs all over the table and the floor, like a messy child in a high chair.

"Nuked them with my own two hands," Margery said. "Now, why don't you quit wasting your breath praising my box brownies?"

"I'm not sure where to start," Phil said.

He was stalling. "Let's pick up where we were the other night," Helen said, helpfully.

"Good idea. Take off your top." Phil grinned.

Helen flushed red with anger and disappointment. The man was a slob after all. "That was below the . . ."

"Belt?" Phil raised one eyebrow.

"That was beneath you." Helen wished she didn't find that eyebrow so sexy. She was suddenly aware she wasn't wearing anything under her short robe. "You were a gentleman at the Mowbrys' party. Now you sound like a pig."

"Helen, since you were half-naked when you met the man, it's difficult to take the high moral road," Margery said.

"I was undercover," Helen said.

Margery snorted like she'd run the Triple Crown. Phil started talking, possibly to cover his embarrassment—and Helen's. "I'm sorry. I shouldn't have said that."

He apologized neatly, too, Helen thought. He could have said he was tired and it was late. But Phil gave no excuses. She liked that. Besides, he was cute when he was contrite.

"I'm undercover," Phil said. "I can't tell you the name of the government agency I'm working for, but I'm not a police officer or a federal agent. I'm an outsourced contractor."

"What's that?" Helen said.

"I'm a private eye. The government hired my firm to do undercover work."

"I thought the federal government couldn't hire detective agencies," Helen said. "I remember reading that somewhere."

"They can't," Phil said. "That's why Pinkerton dropped the word 'detective' from its name years ago, so the Department of Defense could hire their agents as independent contractors. My company did the same thing. I investigate defense-contractor fraud."

"For the DoD?" Margery asked.

"I didn't say that," Phil said.

He didn't deny it, either, Helen thought.

"You're an investigator?" The last thing Helen wanted was an investigator poking around, especially with her past. Phil misinterpreted her interest.

"Yes, but it isn't as romantic as it sounds," he said.

Helen wished he didn't *look* so romantic, with his silver-white ponytail, bare chest and blue eyes. All the man needed was one of those full-sleeved pirate shirts. Actually, he could skip the shirt and stay the way he was.

"All that means is I generally work as a janitor in a small town in the middle of nowhere."

"Aren't you kind of noticeable with that hair?" Margery said.

"When I'm on a job, I cut it short and dye it no-color brown. Nobody notices me."

Helen doubted that.

"My last investigation was in Rowland, Missouri. A company there makes copper components. The government suspected the copper was being siphoned off and sold elsewhere. They were right. I found out how the thieves did it after I worked there for six months as a janitor. They put the stolen copper in a Dumpster. Their accomplices picked it up late at night."

"So what happened?" Helen said. "Did the crooks go to jail?"

Phil shrugged. "No. My investigation was buried in paper."

"Were you disappointed?"

"They stopped ripping off the company," he said. "That was my job and I did it. You get used to nothing much happening in government work.

"My next investigation took me to New Jersey. Some generator parts were getting sidetracked. I traced the shipments down to the Miami–Fort Lauderdale area. I thought it was going to be another version of the copper ring, but it was more than that. When the shipments were found, there was evidence that drugs had been in the packing cases.

"That led to undercover work down here for more than a year. The case has turned out to be complicated. I can't give you the details, but the Mowbrys are involved. That's why I was at the party. That's why I wanted you to leave it."

"They're loaded," Helen said. "Why would they be involved in an illegal operation? Melton Mowbry is a doctor and his family is richer than God."

"Wrong," Phil said. "The Mowbrys used to have money. It's long gone, but most people don't know that. Here's something else they don't know: Mindy Mowbry's maiden name is Cavarelli."

"She's related to the lizard?" Helen said.

"Would you care to explain that?"

"There's this scary-looking guy at the boiler room. I nicknamed him the lizard. He's from the New York headquarters. When he visits our office, even Vito is scared of him."

"Vito should be. That's Carlo Xavier Cavarelli, Mindy's first cousin," Phil said. "The family is connected. Mindy got her Florida mansion the same way her granddaddy got his on Long Island—by breaking the law."

"Does it involve those charity orgies?"

"The parties bring in big bucks. Some of the money goes to the charity. The rest goes to the Mowbrys for upkeep on that mansion."

"Are they blackmailing people?" Helen studied Phil's slightly crooked nose. She liked the way it veered to the left. She wondered why little flaws made a man more interesting.

"No," Phil said. "They're providing a recreational opportunity for broad-minded bigwigs. Remember when those schoolteachers got caught at a Broward County swingers' club? There was a big scandal, even though the teachers were consenting adults doing something that was not illegal in Florida. Same thing here. Broward County's movers and shakers can't be caught at an orgy. They need a safe place to play. They pay well for that peace of mind."

"Enough to buy the Mowbrys a mansion?"

"Not that much. The Mowbrys also have an interest in that boiler room where you sell septic-tank cleaner."

"They're laundering money, aren't they?" Helen said.

Phil raised both eyebrows.

Margery smiled. "That's my girl. She notices things, Phil."

Phil said nothing.

"I bet you if Mowbry is a doctor, he's involved in Medicare fraud," Margery said. "It's a big temptation for those doctors. He'd have to find a way to launder that money."

Phil still said nothing, but his eyes bulged a bit. Helen figured Margery was on target.

"I know how they do it," Helen said. "There was a near riot last payday. About five or six staffers, including this big biker, complained they'd been cheated out of their commissions. They'd been shorted two or three sales."

"Don't they have records?" Phil said.

"Yes, but not good ones. The telemarketers keep track of their own sales. But there are no sales logs or official company forms. Everybody writes down their sales on scrap paper. There is no supervisor's signature or date to verify the sales."

"Interesting," Phil said.

"From the way everyone was complaining, I gather they were ripped off pretty regularly. But this time, the staff rebelled. They finally had enough. I thought they were going to beat up Vito. But then Mr. Cavarelli appeared. They all backed down when they saw the lizard. Even the big biker was afraid of him. I think Cavarelli had a gun."

"So what did the staff do?"

"Nothing," Helen said. "What can they do? The biker is an ex-con. Who else is going to hire him? The others are desperate for different reasons. Most people who work in boiler rooms are trapped. That's why it's a perfect place for money laundering. The bosses can put any numbers they want in the computer for our sales. They're also stealing the staff's commissions. All the telemarketers have are their scrap-paper lists. Those would be useless in court. At least I know now why Cavarelli was slithering around the Mowbry party."

It made Helen sick, when she remembered the party. The Mowbrys' obscene luxuries were stolen ten dollars at a time from single mothers and high school dropouts. She thought of Marina's little boy, Ramon, playing on that filthy carpet. And Nick the junkie, borrowing quarters for orange soda to feed his sugar blues. She saw the other faces in the boiler room, young and old, listening to Vito's pep talks, desperate to hang on to their last-chance jobs.

And then she saw something else: those papers on Vito's desk.

"They're scamming another way," Helen said.

"The last time I was in Vito's office, I saw some papers on his desk. Vito's kind of a slob. He leaves things around. The papers said there were ninety people working in the boiler room and listed their names and addresses. But I know there are only sixty telemarketers. That's how many phones we have. Vito created thirty phantom employees. I bet he gave them phony sales. That's another way to launder money."

"That's the kind of information I need," Phil said. "Looks like I'll be working in the boiler room."

"You can't," Helen said. "You've been to the Mowbrys' parties. Cavarelli will recognize you."

"Not when I cut off my hair and dye it brown."

The thought of amputating that ponytail was painful to Helen.

"There's no need," she said. "I know what those papers look like. They're probably still on Vito's desk. We're always being dragged into his office for pep talks. I can find them."

"No," Phil said. "It's too dangerous."

"Don't pull that big strong male routine on me again, Phil. I'm a telemarketer, and a good one. Besides, I'm already in place there."

"You shouldn't be," Phil said. "What if the boiler room gets raided?"

"Exactly what I've been telling her," Margery said.

Whose side was Margery on? First she praised Helen for noticing things on the job. Now she said it was too dangerous.

Helen shrugged. "I haven't done anything wrong."

"Do you think Cavarelli cares what happens to you or anyone else? You said he was armed. He could start shooting. He could take hostages."

Helen shivered at the thought of Cavarelli's flat yellow eyes. She could feel his reptilian hands, dry and pebbly, as he clutched her for a human shield.

"You haven't told Phil why you were bartending topless," Margery said. "There's two dead girls mixed up in this, Phil. Helen forgot to mention that." She handed Phil a brownie the size of a potholder.

He didn't touch it. He sat there, waiting for Helen to talk. His stillness was uncanny.

"I told you about Laredo," Helen began. "I heard her die while I was making a call for Girdner Surveys."

"Tell me again," Phil said. "I want to hear it all from the beginning."

She told him the whole story. Each time, it seemed a little less shocking to her. Phil listened with that full-body concentration, occasionally interrupting to ask a question. He believes me, Helen thought. If the police had shown this kind of interest, Debbie might still be alive.

Helen noticed something else. She thought there was a layer of loneliness under Phil's professional manner, like a vein of something soft running through granite.

"And you think Laredo was killed for that computer disk," Phil said, when she finished her story.

"Yes. I think she used it to blackmail Henry Asporth. She pushed too hard and he killed her. But that's where Asporth made his mistake: He thought Laredo had the disk with her when she came to his house. Laredo was smarter than that. She hid it. Her last words were 'It's the coffee.' Her sister Savannah and I can't figure out what that means. The disk is supposed to prove that Hank was laundering money and mixed up in a fraud with some big names. Laredo called it her lottery ticket."

"You've searched her home?"

"Yes. So has the killer."

Suddenly, a thought slammed into Helen. "The break-in here. It was Fred and Ethel."

"I thought we'd already established that," Margery said, dryly.

"But that means I didn't bring the killers to the Coronado. They don't know about me. I'm safe. We're safe."

A weight the size of a stone sofa was lifted from her. She'd been sick with guilt since the break-in, thinking she'd exposed Margery and the Coronado to danger. But Fred and Ethel had trashed her apartment and taken her money. That fact put a different light on her investigation, too. She wasn't on Hank Asporth's radar. She was still invisible.

Margery yawned, but it was not dainty and catlike. She looked like a hibernating bear.

"It's four o'clock in the morning," she said. "I'm throwing you both out so I can get some sleep."

"I have to be at work in four hours," Helen said.

As she walked across the foggy courtyard with Phil, Helen was not tired. She didn't want this night to end. Phil lingered, too. The hazy moon silvered his biceps and shimmered in his hair. Helen thought of that poem she had to memorize in high school, about the moon being a ghostly galleon tossed upon cloudy seas. *"A highwayman comes riding, up to the old inn-door."*

Phil looked like the highwayman.

"Can I have one last question?" she said in a whisper. They were standing so close, they were almost touching.

"You can have anything you want," Phil said, and raised that eyebrow again.

Helen wanted him to kiss her. She wanted him to wrap her in his big strong arms and rip her clothes off. She wanted to drag him into her bedroom and lock the door. Helen wanted sweaty, twisted sheets. She wanted beard-burn all over her body and cheap champagne for breakfast.

Her lips parted slightly. She tilted her head upward, so he could kiss her more easily. She was ready for mad, impulsive sex. She said the first thing that came into her head.

"What is that ray gun thing?"

Phil looked surprised. But not as surprised as Helen. Why the hell had she said that? Some alien had taken possession of her body.

Phil became all business.

"It's a target pistol with a red-dot sight," he said.

"That's all? It looks like it could vaporize buildings."

"It made Fred and Ethel disappear," he said. "That was enough."

Helen woke up the next morning on sweaty, twisted sheets. She'd tossed and turned all night after she went to bed alone.

Chapter 24

"So how did you two make out last night?" Margery said. "You were drooling over Phil like a pup with a porterhouse. That's why I left you alone."

Helen didn't want to talk at seven thirty in the morning. She didn't want to talk about Phil any time ever. She stepped around Margery and plowed toward the sidewalk, head down.

"I can't stop now," she said. "I'm going to be late for work."

But Margery was not to be ignored—not in purple clamdiggers and red tennis shoes. She stomped right along-side Helen, keeping up with her long, loping strides. Smoking Marlboros didn't slow her down.

"I'll walk with you," her landlady said. "I'm going in the same direction."

"Then you're going nowhere," Helen said. "That's where we went last night. You know why? Because I opened my big mouth. We were all alone in this romantic setting, sur-rounded by fog and flowers. He moved in closer. I was sure he was going to kiss me. And do you know what I said?" She glared at Margery until the glaze on her good cheer cracked.

"Do I want to know?" Margery said.

"I asked him what kind of gun he had."

"That science fiction thing? What did he answer?" Margery was genuinely curious.

"It's a target pistol with a red-dot sight. But that's not the point. He went all business on me, Margery. He spent half an hour talking about that stupid gun. Excuse me, weapon. It was as romantic as a night at the Bass Pro Shop. I ruined the mood. I've been so long without a man, I panicked and turned into a porcupine. I'm so freaking stupid."

"I think you were smart," Margery said. "Women used to know how to play hard to get. He was probably expecting you to fall into his arms. Instead, you threw him off balance. A man like Phil is used to getting any woman he wants. It will do him good."

Helen's cheeks were bright red, and not from the brisk walk. "Do you really think so?"

"I just said so." They were in front of the sidewalk restaurant at the elegant Riverside Hotel. Margery eyed the tanned busboy in the white jacket and tight pants.

"I hear the buns are great here." She grinned wickedly.

"Margery!" Helen said.

Margery put on her best innocent old lady face. "I'm having a leisurely breakfast as a privilege of my age. You, young woman, should go to work. Build up that Social Security fund."

Helen didn't remind her landlady that she was paid in cash under the table. The only thing she contributed to was Vito's slush fund.

As she walked the rest of the way to the boiler room, Helen decided she was a failure in the womanly wiles department. She'd have to impress Phil with her detecting skills. Maybe she could steal those papers off Vito's desk. She knew how to do it without getting caught.

As Helen clocked in, she felt her spirits sink lower. The boiler room was dingy with ancient dirt. The night shift had left half a bag of Cheetos on her computer. Helen popped a handful in her mouth. They were stale. Her phone was coated with bright orange-yellow Cheetos' residue, like an exotic pollen. She cleaned it off and threw away the bag.

Ramon, Marina's little boy, overturned her trash can. He found the stale Cheetos and started eating them.

"No, no," his mother said, taking away the bag. Ramon sat on the floor and screamed.

Helen heard more screaming on the phone. Her first call was to a Rhode Island man who snarled like a rabid dog. "You got a lot of balls calling me at eight thirty in the morning, lady."

"I've got guts, not balls," she said, but the guy hung up on her. *Comeback interruptus,* Helen thought, a major cause of frustration in telemarketers.

When the customers weren't yelling, Vito was. He patrolled the aisles, shouting, "Loud and proud, people. Let's hear you. Let's get those sales."

All Helen got was the green weenie in her ear. The nicest thing anyone did was hang up on her. For three hours she listened to the same old insults, and those were hard to hear with little Ramon howling for his lost Cheetos. Finally, Helen sneaked some out of the bag in the trash and fed them to the boy. Stale Cheetos wouldn't hurt the kid, she told herself. She'd eaten them herself. Besides, he shut up.

At eleven thirty, Helen finally heard something she wanted:

"All right, people," Vito said, "everyone in my office for a pep talk."

Helen grabbed a pen and some paper. She jumped over little Ramon like a hurdle, then sprinted into Vito's office. She was the second person in the room and snagged a seat on the corner of his desk. The other telemarketers pushed in, until Vito's office was crowded as a Beijing bus. Good. The others would screen her.

Helen pulled out the paper she'd brought with her and began making notes. "Buy cat food. Throw out old takeout in fridge. Or feed to cat." It was a list of things she had to do on her afternoon break, but she looked diligent from a distance.

Vito, pink and porcine, stalked up and down the room.

"You're not selling, people. And if you're not selling, you're not telling the right things about our product. What do we know about Tank Titan? Here's a refresher course:

"Tank Titan eats sludge like Pac-Man."

Vito demonstrated with greedy chomps until the telemarketers were giggling. Helen glanced down at the boss's desk. It was a landfill. With a fingernail, she lifted the top sheet of the paper pile nearest her. It was a stack of articles on the do-not-call law, printed off the Internet. Nothing she could steal there.

"Tank Titan is so good it's like being on the city sewer," Vito said. He quit chomping. Helen went back to scribbling.

"And it's all-natural. Your baby could eat it for breakfast, and it wouldn't hurt him."

Vito grabbed Ramon from his mother's arms and grinned at the boy like a deranged kiddie-show host. Helen noticed guiltily that Ramon's mouth was yellow with stale Cheetos. Ramon burst into sobs, squirming to get away from Vito. The kid's instincts were good.

Vito said, "Of course, you'd be changing a lot of diapers for a couple of days, but Tank Titan is harmless." He handed Ramon back to his mother like a rejected package. While Marina carried her sobbing child from the room, Helen examined the next paper pile: a stack of time sheets and racing forms. Nothing again.

"Helen!" Vito said.

She jumped.

"Name two things that we *never* say to customers."

"You can send the product back," Helen said. "And, we will send you a free sample."

"Very good," Vito said. "See? The lady pays attention."

Fat lot he knows, Helen thought, as she went back to her list of things to do. She looked at Vito's well-packed form and wrote, "Buy ham."

Vito tormented three more telemarketers, who hadn't a clue about what they should not say—or should, for that mat-

ter. Helen poked through more paper stacks. She found over-
due invoices, ads for hair transplants, blank employment ap-
plications. Nothing.

"Remember, you're not a telemarketer," Vito said.
"You're an insurance agent for their septic tank. And how
does a good agent sell? With fear. Make them afraid *not* to
buy our product. Tell them, 'If your septic tank backs up, and
a backhoe rips up your lawn, that's five thousand dollars
down the drain.' Fear sells, folks. Fear is the great motiva-
tor."

It is for me, Helen thought, as she inched toward the last
heap of paper. It was blank copy paper. Damn. The desk
search was a bust. Then she saw a stapled corner sticking out
of the pile. Blank paper didn't have staples. She gave the corner a tiny tug.

Vito shouted, *"What's the most important thing to remember?"*

Every telemarketer knew that answer: *"Never, ever give
out our 800 number!"*

Vito clapped his hands. The telemarketers applauded
themselves. Helen gave the stapled corner a good yank and
pulled it out. She caught the paper tower before it toppled.
She had the list of phony employees. It was covered with
dust and coffee rings, but she had it. She stuck her to-do list
on top of the stolen paper.

The pep talk was over. Helen joined the crowd surging for
the open door.

"Helen!" Vito called.

Helen froze.

"Can you come here?" Vito didn't look porcine anymore.
He looked like a mass of robust muscle. Even his eyebrows
were muscular.

"I saw what you were doing." Vito cracked his knuckles.
Next, he'd crack every bone in her body.

Helen was too frightened to talk. He knew. He saw her
steal that paper. What would he do next? Beat her up? Shoot
her? Burn her with cigar butts? She could stand anything, as

long as he didn't lock her in with Mr. Cavarelli. Please don't call in the lizard, she wanted to beg, but her mouth wouldn't work.

"Taking notes is a good idea," Vito said. "Sets a good example for the other telemarketers. Makes 'em take me more serious-like." His smile showed sixty-four teeth.

Helen nodded. She still didn't have her voice back. She fled the room, the purloined papers in her hand.

Helen went home at lunch break and fed Thumbs the leftover Cantonese chicken with water chestnuts. Her cat ate around the water chestnuts just like she did. Helen made herself a peanut butter and strawberry jam sandwich, but couldn't finish it. Her encounter with Vito had ruined her appetite. The terror diet, she thought, an effective new weight-loss program.

She tried to take a nap, but she was too charged with adrenaline. She knocked on Phil's door to give him the stolen list, but he wasn't home. She slid the list under his door with the phantom employees starred.

Three hours before she had to be at work. Helen paced restlessly, wondering what to do. Then she had an inspiration.

The wife of Damian Putnam, the horny plastic surgeon at the Mowbrys' party, was the CEO for a funeral-home chain. Helen had seen her picture in the society story.

What was that woman's name?

Patricia Wellneck, that was it. The funeral home chain was called The Wellneck Group. Helen had heard their ads on the radio, with a professionally lugubrious announcer intoning: "The Wellneck Group. We're here when you need us."

Helen needed Patricia now.

She checked the phone book. The Wellneck headquarters were in Lauderdale, a half-hour bus ride away. Helen put on a black pantsuit. The bus pulled up to the stop as she arrived, a good omen. Even better, the bus stopped right in front of the pink stucco funeral home.

Florida funeral parlors looked about like the ones in Helen's hometown of St. Louis, with one major difference: they were preternaturally sunny. No matter how thick the curtains, a Florida funeral home was flooded with sunshine. In the softer St. Louis light, you could say, "He looks so natural" with a straight face. But the relentless Florida sun was the enemy of the mortician's art. It cruelly revealed the corpse's makeup, the sprayed hair, the too-stiff stiff. Helen thought that was why there were more closed-casket funerals down here.

The casket in Slumber Room A was mercifully shut. It was pinkish bronze with a red carnation cover, like a flower blanket on a Kentucky Derby winner. Helen thought the red carnations clashed with the casket color, but it was fairly tasteful for Florida.

She tiptoed past Slumber Rooms B and C, both empty, and found the office. A young woman in a somber navy suit said, "May I help you?"

Her soft, solemn voice made Helen want to clutch a tissue.

"I'd like to see Patricia Wellneck about some pre-need arrangements."

"Do you have an appointment?"

"No. But if I don't make them now, I'll never have the courage again," Helen said.

Ms. Solemn Suit knew better than to let a live one get away. "I'll see if she's available."

Patricia Wellneck was back in two minutes. She photographed better than she looked in person. She was so thin, she looked like one of her coffin candidates. Her yellow-blond hair was upswept, and in the harsh light of day, facelift scars were visible behind her ears. She also had an eye-job slant. Her husband had been whittling on her, Helen thought.

"Now, how may I help you?" Patricia gave a death's-head smile.

"I'm looking into some pre-need arrangements," Helen said. "For myself. I want to buy a coffin."

"And your name is?"

What's my name? Helen thought. Patricia's skeletal smile made her panic. I can't use my real name. Who do I want to be in this place?

"Rob," Helen blurted her ex-husband's name.

"Yes, Ms. Robb. You are wise to make your choice now. We have a full line of caskets. Many younger people, like yourself, prefer our theme line."

"Theme caskets," Helen said. She flashed back to those awful corporate theme parties from her former life, where unhappy servers had to wear lederhosen for unfestive Oktoberfests and cowboy hats for dreary chuck wagon cookouts.

Patricia pulled out a catalogue. "These," she said, "are dignified but distinctive."

She showed Helen a casket covered with Monet's water lilies. It looked like a giant jewelry box. "This is from our Eternal Masters series. It makes a comforting statement for your family. This is a quiet reflection of a full life."

Helen looked at the water lilies and thought of groundwater seeping around her body. Florida flooded a lot.

"Uh, no thanks," she said.

"If you are religious, we have many beautiful expressions of faith. Like this one."

Helen saw a sky-blue casket covered with flying seagulls. She looked for the telltale white splotches left by seagulls, but apparently that didn't happen in heaven. Two curlicued words announced, "Going Home."

Helen thought of herself stuck in her mother's home for all eternity and shuddered.

"There's also this one with Raphael's angels on the casket." The two cherubs, who looked like winged juvenile delinquents to Helen, stared out from the coffin lid. Helen had also seen them on umbrellas, cocktail napkins and candles. She felt like a gift-shop special.

"Pretty," she said. "But I don't think I'm the angelic type."

Patricia was not discouraged. "If you have a profession," she said, "we have many choices to honor it. This model is for firefighters."

The bright red casket was covered with fire trucks, which Helen liked a lot. But she thought the flames were asking for trouble.

"Veterans prefer this model," Patricia said, showing Helen a coffin with the Stars and Stripes, an abandoned rifle, and an empty helmet. What a way to go: at war, with a permanent reminder of defeat.

"Very patriotic," Helen said. "But the only place I ever served was a Greek diner. I was a waitress. I had to fight off the owner, so maybe I qualify as a combat veteran."

Patricia didn't laugh.

"Did you attend college?"

"University of Missouri at Columbia."

"Then perhaps you'd like a college scene or your school colors on your casket."

Mizzou had never cared two hoots about Helen until she started making a hundred thou a year. Then the alumni association dunned her for contributions until she finally wrote "deceased" on their begging envelopes. Now the university could follow her to the grave. She would never be free.

"Do I need ivy on my tombstone?" Helen said.

"I see you have a sense of humor," Patricia said. "This model might be the one for you. It packs you for the trip home, so to speak."

The casket was a giant brown package stamped with "Express Delivery" and "Return to Sender." Great. She could be an eternal joke.

"Elvis fans would like it, too," Helen said. "But I'm more of a Clapton fan." Or a fan of a Clapton fan. Helen knew where she'd wind up if she had a black coffin emblazoned with "Clapton Is God"—some place even hotter than Florida.

"These are certainly unusual," Helen said. "But perhaps I'm more of a traditionalist than I thought."

"We have many traditional styles. Some have the newest features, like memento drawers. That's if you want to send something special with your loved one: a photo, medals, letters. We've had wedding photos, jewelry, children's drawings and many other meaningful keepsakes."

She showed Helen a bronze casket with a flat pullout section at the bottom, like a pencil drawer on a desk. Helen had slipped a six-pack of Falstaff beer into her grandfather's coffin, along with a bottle opener and a bag of Rold Gold pretzels. The drawer didn't look big enough for her kind of memento.

"I have an odd request," Helen said.

"We will do our best to accommodate your wishes." Patricia smiled her skeleton grin.

"Could I have the coffin delivered to my home? Before I'm dead."

Patricia didn't bat an eyelash. Maybe she couldn't with her tight eye job.

"Well, yes, you could," she said. "The casket company does not like to deliver to private residences. You'd have to order it from us and have it delivered here at the funeral home. Then you'd pick it up from here with your own truck. Are you interested in one of these models?"

"I was thinking of something in wood," Helen said.

"Pecan, pine, cherry or walnut?"

"Ebony," Helen said.

"Fine woods such as ebony are very expensive," Patricia said.

"I bet they are," Helen said. "But I saw one at a party and really liked it."

Patricia turned white as a satin lining. Her surgery scars glowed red with rage. She rose like a zombie from a new grave.

"I don't believe I can help you after all," she said. "My assistant will show you out."

"I believe you can, Ms. Wellneck. Tell me about the Six Feet Unders. Drop-dead sexy, aren't they? Especially in coffin clothes. Did they buy them here?"

"I have no idea what you're talking about." Patricia stepped around her desk and clamped her hand on Helen's arm. It was cold as ice, but steel-strong. Patricia could have been a South Beach bouncer. She'd spent years dealing with the overwrought at wakes and funerals. She knew how to subdue someone while making it look as if she was helping the person out of the room.

Helen struggled to get free, and Patricia changed her grip. Pain shot up Helen's arm. Patricia dragged Helen out of her office.

"Buying a casket can be an emotional experience," Patricia said. "Perhaps you would like to rest a moment in our family comfort room. I'll bring you a cup of tea."

She steered Helen toward a gloomy green-curtained area with a dark door. Helen knew if she went through that door, she'd come out feet first. She took her size-eleven shoe and stomped down hard on Patricia's foot.

"Bitch," Patricia said and relaxed her grip for a split second.

Helen pulled free and ran. Out the door and down the hall. Past the empty slumber rooms. Past the bronze casket, where dying carnations covered a dead man. Through the double front doors and into the hot Florida sun.

Chapter 25

Helen shivered in the blazing sun.

It was ninety degrees. The sidewalk sparkled and shimmered in the heat. But she felt bone-cold after being strong-armed by the coffin pusher, Patricia Wellneck.

I imagined that scene, Helen told herself. I was never in any danger. Patricia Wellneck is a respected funeral director. She thought I was upset because I'd been looking at coffins. She offered me a comfortable chair and a cup of tea.

But the bruises on Helen's arm were already turning purple.

After she ran out the front door, Helen hid behind an SUV in the parking lot for fifteen minutes, waiting to see if Patricia Wellneck would come after her. No one left the funeral home. But three people arrived in somber black. Patricia had funeral business, Helen decided. And she figured I got the message.

Helen didn't feel safe catching a bus in front of the funeral home. She ran half a mile before she waited at a bus stop. That left her panting and out of breath, but it didn't warm her. Now Helen was pacing anxiously, peering down the sun-hazed street, praying her bus would come soon.

The street was deserted. No one was following her. The

land was flat as a kitchen counter. There wasn't a bush to hide behind. She should feel safe. But she didn't.

Get a grip. Quit behaving like a wimp. Patricia doesn't even know your name.

But Helen knew where that ebony coffin came from. She wondered if Patricia and her horny husband were connected with the boiler room. Were the Mowbrys laundering cold cash from her funeral homes—or sawbucks from her sawbones spouse? Did they know about the murdered Debbie? Were they in on her murder?

No, she decided. Patricia would never leave a body unburied.

Helen should feel triumphant. She'd found an important connection. Instead she was uneasy. Casket shopping would give anyone the shivers, she decided. Fashionable caskets were even creepier, as if death were a *Vanity Fair* feature. Eternally cool.

At last, she heard the screeching rumble of bus brakes. Helen climbed on, sat down and sighed with relief, glad to be on her way. It was only three o'clock. Two more hours before she went to work at the boiler room. She wondered how much more trouble she could get into.

Might as well call Savannah. Helen had a lot to tell her.

The bus let off Helen in front of a convenience store. She went in to buy a large coffee, determined to throw off the graveyard chill.

"You don't want to drink the stuff in that pot. It's turned to sludge," the woman behind the counter said. She was a scrawny fifty and moved like her feet hurt.

"It's OK." Helen poured herself a big cup of something drained from a crankcase. "I'm not going to drink it." She carried it to the cash register, wincing when she saw a bucket of "love roses" next to the beef jerky.

"I'm not charging you for that stuff," the footsore woman said. "I was going throw it out. Just don't tell anyone you got it here."

Helen thanked her and stood outside the store, holding the

hot foam cup. She wondered how the woman stayed so nice in these depressing surroundings. The parking lot was littered with trash, spilled drinks and fluids she didn't want to examine.

When her fingers were warmed enough so she could punch the buttons, Helen walked over to the pay phone. It was encrusted with chewing gum blobs like fake jewels. She dialed Savannah's number.

"We need to meet."

"I can't. Too busy," Savannah said. She'd even speeded up her drawl. "See you at the Floridian after we both get off work tonight."

She hung up before Helen could answer.

Savannah didn't show up at the Floridian until nearly eleven p.m., which gave Helen plenty of time to contemplate the cheap champagne breakfast for two on the menu, and wonder if she'd ever have anyone to share it with. She sucked up coffee till she was jittery as her old junkie seatmate, Nick.

Finally, Savannah arrived, trailing apologies and excuses. She wore the same seat-sprung jeans and scuffed cowboy boots. She looked thinner. Her face was more lined, as if it had been freeze-dried. Her eyes were tired. Her sister's death was taking its toll.

This time Savannah did not pick at her food. She ate like it was her last meal before a seven-year famine. She ordered an astonishing four fried eggs, a ham steak and a loaf of buttered toast. Helen felt positively virtuous with her single egg and English muffin, so she added a chocolate-cake chaser.

When their food arrived, Helen told Savannah everything.

Well, almost everything. She did not mention Phil. But she said she'd heard some things at the party: The Mowbrys could be involved in drugs and money laundering and so, possibly, could their good buddy, Hank Asporth.

"So you think that's what my sister had on that disk? She was going to nail the Mowbrys and that murdering buzzard Asporth for drugs and money laundering?" Savannah stabbed the ham steak through the heart. Her egg yolks bled onto the plate.

"That's my best guess," Helen said. "It would be infor- mation worth killing for. If Laredo had the facts and figures on interstate drugs and money laundering, Hank Asporth could do federal time. No more parties in Brideport. No more barbecues for mobsters, or bimbos in bikinis sitting around his pool. No wonder she called it her lottery ticket. Hank As- porth killed her for it. He must have thought she had the disk with her the night he strangled her."

Helen instantly regretted her brutal words. But Savannah was busy tearing apart her toast and smearing it with blood- red jelly.

"Laredo got her revenge. She hid the disk well. That's why Asporth ripped your trailer apart. He was looking for it."

"Listen, did your sister have a favorite coffee shop she hung around?"

"Laredo? No, she liked bars with rich men, not coffee shops with poor college students."

"I keep going back to her last words, 'It's the coffee.' I thought she might have hidden the disk at a Starbucks or something."

"Laredo wouldn't pay that kind of money for coffee," Sa- vannah said. "But I guess that's why whoever trashed my place dumped my can of Folger's in the sink. They were looking for that disk. They didn't know Laredo drank instant. There's no coffee connection I can think of."

"Any other ideas where your sister could have stashed it?"

"Her car, maybe," Savannah said. "She used to hide things under the spare tire. But we can't find that, either. God knows how a car that color yellow could disappear, but it has. What if she hid the disk at the Mowbrys'?"

"Then we'll never find it," Helen said. "That place has a zillion bedrooms and acres of reception rooms. It could be anywhere there."

"But my sister wasn't," Savannah said. "Laredo wasn't a

guest. Most of the house would be off-limits to her. She tended bar. She pretty much stayed in one spot all night."

"Except when she worked the back room," Helen said.

"But she stayed in one place there, too."

Yeah, a coffin, Helen thought. But she couldn't say it. That would be too cruel.

Savannah took her silence for assent. "If she hid the disk at the Mowbrys' place, wouldn't it be in one of those rooms?" she said.

Unless someone took her upstairs to a bedroom, Helen thought. But Savannah didn't need to hear more dirt about her sister. Instead, she said, "Those are good places to start."

"Maybe she hid it in her portable bar at work."

"The bars have lots of cubbyholes," Helen said. "But if she hid it there, the disk would have been found weeks ago. The bus staff takes the bars apart to clean them. They have to. Drinks are sticky. They attract ants and roaches. Bugs would be all over those bars if they weren't cleaned thoroughly. I don't think a portable bar would be a good hiding place."

Helen was distracted watching Savannah eat her ham. First, she sliced all the round edges off the steak, reducing it to a square. She ate those slices first. Then she cut her steak into stamp-sized pieces with surgical precision. It was as if she could reverse the chaos in her life by squaring that steak.

"What about that back room?" Savannah said, between neat bites.

"There wasn't much in there but flowers, candles and that black coffin."

Helen could see its polished darkness, absorbing the flickering candlelight. She saw Kristi with her white lace and lilies. The devil-horned man in the leather harness was climbing inside . . .

"Wait!" Helen said.

Savannah jumped, sending her fork skittering over the side of the table. She fished around for it on the floor, then asked the waitress for a new one. It was several agonizing minutes before Savannah went back to her squares of ham steak, and Helen could continue.

"You said Laredo liked to hide things in mattresses. The coffin's got a mattress. It has a lining, too, with lots of tucks and folds. There would be plenty of places to hide a disk."

Something zinged in Helen's brain. Maybe it was because she'd spent the day looking at caskets, but Laredo's last words finally made sense. "That's it." Helen slammed her hand down on the table. Savannah's fork went flying again, but this time she didn't notice.

"I heard her wrong," Helen said. "Laredo wasn't saying, 'It's the coffee.' She was trying to say, 'Coffin.'"

Helen stopped just in time. She was going to say that Laredo's words were cut off by a scream. She would have been really hurting to scream like that. Poor Laredo, struggling to choke out the words that could have saved her life.

Helen and Savannah were both silent. The remains of the ham steak, squarely subdued, sat untouched. The cheerful noise of the restaurant flowed around them. Life went on. But not for Laredo. She'd told Hank, but it was too late.

Savannah did not ask for another fork. Their silence grew larger and heavier, until it seemed to sit between them. At last they understood what had happened. Laredo had desperately wanted to live. She'd tried to say the words that would stop her killer, but she'd been fatally misunderstood.

"Can I get you anything else?" the waitress said. She was brisk and chipper. The heavy silence disappeared.

"No, I think we have all we need," Savannah said.

When the waitress left with a pile of their plates, she said, "How are we going to check that coffin?"

"Looks like I have to go to another orgy," Helen said.

Chapter 26

The second time at an orgy was boring.

Helen had seen better bodies in the dressing room at Loehmann's. Too many of the naked people here tonight had wrinkles, flab and hairy patches on their hide.

Taking off their clothes didn't make them more interesting or improve their conversation. Just like being half-naked didn't make Helen a better bartender.

When this is over, I'll probably join a convent, Helen thought. My ex-husband will never find me there, and I won't have to worry about my next meal. Except didn't nuns have jobs now? Maybe so, but she didn't think there were many nun-telemarketers. Or topless bartenders, for that matter.

She did feel a sizzle of excitement. But it wasn't sex—it was stealing. God knows what would happen if she was caught prowling the Mowbry mansion. But she was going to find Laredo's disk in that coffin.

As Helen sprinted across the park-sized lawn, she stumbled over a copulating couple. They grunted, but paid her no attention. She passed a daisy chain that included two lawyers and an insurance executive. She hoped they got mosquito bites in places they couldn't scratch. Helen didn't know anything about orgies, but she suspected this one would not be very shocking in New York or L.A.—or even Miami. Broward County would put on a suburban satyricon.

She saw the Cigarette boat, tied up at the Mowbrys' dock. Its flames looked like a childish cartoon.

No one was near the mansion's service door. Helen walked in as if she had every right. So far, the party goers had acted as if she were invisible. Her disguise was working.

Helen had refused to go naked this time. She couldn't take off her shirt again, no matter how she rationalized it. Instead, she'd come up with a good way to keep her clothes on. At least, she'd thought so back at the Coronado.

Now that she was sliding along a dark corridor in the depths of the Mowbry mansion, Helen wasn't so sure. It was midnight. Somewhere, a clock bonged twelve gloomy notes. Black shadows stretched down the corridor. She could hear party laughter, but the sound was distorted. It sounded demonic. She was afraid the boredom underneath it would suck her bones dry.

Helen counted at least six doors on the long corridor. About half opened onto lighted rooms. The rest were dark. She didn't know which looked more ominous.

It had been easy to find out when the next charity orgy was. She'd called Steve for a bartending job. "I could use you tomorrow night," he'd said. "Wanna work? I hear you were a hit with a certain guest."

"He was pretty cute," Helen said. Cute? Where did that come from? What was this, high school? "But I'm booked tomorrow night."

"Suit yourself," Steve said, his voice like a slap. "Don't call again unless you want to work."

That was Steve, always ready with a threat or a putdown. She was glad she'd never work his parties again, even if they paid obscenely well.

It was also easy to find the clothes for her disguise. Helen had a pair of beige khaki pants in her closet and sensible shoes from another dead-end job. She borrowed a khaki work shirt from Margery. It had BILLY sewn on the pocket. She knew better than to ask her landlady who Billy was.

All she needed to complete her scam was a toolbox. She used the gray metal box she kept under the kitchen sink. No one would know it held only a hammer with a duct-taped handle, a screwdriver and rusty pliers. She added enough cash for a water-taxi ticket, so she wouldn't have to carry her wallet. While she was rooting around in her purse, Helen found the can of oven cleaner she'd confiscated from Savannah and threw that in. She might need it for protection.

In her pocket was the envelope with the rest of Fred and Ethel's metal slivers. They were going on a final fraudulent mission.

"What in hell's name do you think you're doing?"

Helen nearly dropped the toolbox. She recognized that bullying bark. It was Steve. She froze against the wall, hoping the shadows would hide her, knowing they wouldn't.

I'm caught, she thought. He'll see the toolbox and think I'm a jewel thief or something. I'll spend the night getting cavity-searched at the city jail.

"I told you before," Steve said, "Wedges and peels. Wedges and peels. We don't use lemon slices at a service bar. The limes are wedges. The lemons are peels. Always. Only. Why can't you get that through your thick head?"

Steve was screaming at some hapless bartender.

The door to the next room was partly open. Helen caught a glimpse of a bare-chested blonde and a red-faced Steve. The bullied blonde cringed against a supply rack as Steve whipped her with his words. Helen felt sorry for the woman, but she had to get past that open door.

Don't stop yelling now, she thought, as she sidled past the doorway. But Steve didn't see her. He was too busy badgering the bartender.

Helen almost made it when her toolbox banged against the doorframe with a loud clunk.

"Who's there?" Steve said.

Helen ducked into the next open door, one of the dark ones, and bumped against someone. "Sorry," she whispered.

No answer. She could feel hard, pointed breasts jutting into her back. This woman was packing serious silicone. Why didn't she say anything? Was this another kinky game?

Steve went back to verbally beating the bartender. He'd forgotten about the noise.

Helen's eyes slowly adjusted to the dark. She was in a closet. She could see brooms, mops and buckets. Her back was pressed against a strange woman's chest. A woman who wasn't talking. Helen was afraid to turn around, in case she knocked over something noisy. She carefully moved her hand back a few inches. She felt a leg. In black leather. It seemed lifeless and rigid.

The hair went up on the back of Helen's neck. Was she in a closet with a dead body? Helen stepped back and hit something metal with her foot. It felt like . . . a stand.

Helen almost giggled. She was up against a department-store dummy. There's another big dummy in here, she thought. Dead body, indeed. I should know better. A real leg doesn't feel like that.

Helen wondered what the Mowbrys were doing with a dummy, and decided she didn't want to know. By the time she could breathe normally, Steve and the freshly battered bartender were gone. Helen started down the hall again, keeping her toolbox away from the wall. The corridor stretched endlessly. How long was it? She'd taken shorter walks down Las Olas Boulevard. Her neck and shoulder muscles ached from tension. The toolbox weighed a thousand pounds.

Three more doors to go. She scooted past another one, then saw that the next opening wasn't a door. It was a window. What did her mother always say? God didn't close a door without opening a window. Helen had had a roommate like that. It was annoying.

This window was at least seven feet high and gave Helen a good view of the pool area. She leaned out the open window and looked down on the party. From this height, the writhing couples in and around the pool were white and wormlike. She recognized a few. Mr. Shamrock Shorts was pawing another waitress.

Helen was relieved she didn't see Patricia Wellneck, theme funeral planner. She wondered if Patricia had ever buried any of her surgeon husband's mistakes. She was even happier to see no sign of the boiler-room reptile, Mr. Cavarelli.

But she did spot Phil, with his shining silver-white hair and black jacket. He was talking to the real estate dealer in the La Perla panties. Tonight, she was wearing a hot-pink thong. Ms. Realtor kept rubbing Phil's arm like she was releasing a genie from a bottle. Phil had his hands wrapped around a beer, but he was smiling at the little—

Helen heard a noise. She saw a semi-naked couple walking down the far end of the hall. The woman's high heels clicked on the floor. The man padded alongside her barefoot. They seemed to see only each other, but Helen wasn't taking any chances. She streaked down the corridor and shot around the corner.

At last. There were the mahogany doors with the dancing dragons and demons. She'd reached the back room. The gold knobs gleamed in the shadows.

Helen opened the double doors. The blackness drew her in.

She saw the ebony casket, surrounded by flickering flames and white flowers. It held a pale woman in a white lace dress, with hair like a dandelion. Helen didn't recognize her. Good. Kristi must have left town. At least she wouldn't have to worry about that young fool.

Helen's ordeal was almost over. Once she had her hands on Laredo's computer disk, her job was done. She'd turn it over to Phil. He'd give it to the authorities. Helen would be free.

All she had to do was find the disk.

Helen saw something else now in the wavering light. A naked man was fingering the undead corpse's lily bouquet.

The dandelion blonde regarded him with absolute ennui. The man had to be dead to miss it. But he did. He also didn't see Helen. The blonde didn't care.

Helen reached into her pocket for Fred and Ethel's metal slivers. She moved her hand along the edge of the casket and left a trail of metal bits.

"Excuse me," she said. "I need to check this casket. Routine maintenance."

"What?" the guy said. "Beat it. We're busy."

"You're going to be on the floor at the crucial moment, buddy, if you don't let me fix this. See the problem?" Helen pointed to the metal. "This coffin's coming apart. I can fix it with a simple adjustment." She showed him the toolbox.

The blonde looked frightened—the first emotion Helen had seen on that dead-white face. Her lipstick was a bloody slash. Maybe she saw herself in a casket for real.

"Come on, sweetie, it will just take a minute." The blonde sounded like a nanny with a balky toddler. "Help me out of here." She thrust her lacy bosom against his bare chest. It was too much for him to resist. He did the manly thing and helped her out of the casket. The blonde rolled her eyes at Helen when his back was turned.

"Thank you," Helen said. "I'll just be a minute."

"Nice set of tools, Billy," leered the corpse-lover, eyeing Helen's khaki chest. In this crowd, clothes were a perversion.

The dandelion blonde led her man into the blackness. She was having trouble keeping her dress on with that slit up the back.

Helen checked the coffin mattress first. It felt thin as a sofa bed. Helen hoped it was comfortable for the corpse. It would be hell to spend eternity in the guest room. She found no disk in the mattress. There were no slits in it, either.

The sides of the coffin were lined with pleated white satin. Helen wondered if she'd be able to feel the disk through the thick fabric. She kneaded it like bread dough. She massaged the coffin innards all the way down the long side and didn't find anything. She was about halfway around the head end when she felt something flat and square. Helen leaned over for a closer look. In the dim candlelight, she saw a slit along a pleat. She stuck her hand in and slid out a red plastic computer disk.

She had it.

Helen took a deep breath. The worst was over.

"What are you doing? What's that in your hand?" The voice cut like a knife.

Helen slowly turned. She recognized the face from the society pages. But the outfit was new.

It was Mindy Mowbry. In skin-tight black vinyl. With a wicked whip.

Chapter 27

Mindy's whip was black leather, slender and flexible. Her heels were cruelly high.

She wore a catsuit like Diana Rigg in *The Avengers*. Except Mindy's nipples were showing. And they were pierced with needles.

The black vinyl cat suit clung like slick, synthetic skin. A spotted scarf floated around her neck like a fashionable disease.

This can't be real, Helen thought. I'm with the Wicked Whip of the West.

But she could smell the burning candle wax, the funereal flowers and her own fear. Pale, naked lovers crawled out of the shadows like resurrected corpses. They surrounded the black casket, watching Helen with dark, feral eyes. The room was a black cave. It was a long way to those demon-studded doors.

"What are you doing here?" Mindy had the clothes of a porn queen and the languid lockjaw voice of a rich woman.

"I said, 'What are you doing?'" Mindy's eyes shone with crazy light. Helen thought if she looked into them, they would steal her soul.

"Maintenance." Helen's voice sounded surprisingly normal. She hoped the bluff would buy her a few seconds.

"Liar. You found something in that coffin. Hand it over. Now." Mindy's whip tore through Helen's shirt and left welts on her neck. No hesitation. No warning. No change in those crazy eyes. She lashed out, and the disk spun out of Helen's hand.

The pain stunned Helen. Then it enraged her.

This house and all its kinky riches came from the Mowbrys' telemarketing sweatshop. Helen spent her days in that filthy boiler room, so Mindy could spend her nights in extravagant depravity. She thought of her coworkers, cheated and abused in the boiler room. The money they needed to live decent lives cost less than Mindy's twisted flowers.

Now this vinyl-coated scum had slashed her with a whip. It was too much.

Helen swung her metal toolbox and caught Mindy in the face. She went down like a sack of cement. Her whip flew from her hand and hit a serpentine flower vase standing by the casket. The vase toppled and took down a tall candle. The ebony casket rocked backward, but righted itself.

Helen flung herself on top of Mindy, throwing punches wildly. Some slid off uselessly. Some landed. One caught Mindy in the mouth. Her teeth cut Helen's knuckles.

"You miserable, greedy, no good——" Words failed Helen, so she hit Mindy again. She saw with satisfaction that Mindy's face was bloody.

The women rolled around on the carpet, trying to bite, scratch and kick each other. Mindy's razor-sharp heels cut Helen's leg. She bit Helen's hand and scratched her face. Helen landed a good jab in Mindy's gut and pulled out a hunk of sprayed hair. Hah! Try wearing that hairdo to the Langley School PTA.

Some orgy goers thought the wrestling match was staged for their entertainment. They shouted advice and encouragement.

"Get her eyes."

"Hit her in the boobs."

"Kick her in the crotch."

"Five on Mindy."

"Fifty on the big brunette, Billy."

"A hundred on Billy."

The major money is on me, Helen thought, and couldn't help being pleased. Then she heard why: "That Billy babe's got a good thirty pounds on Mindy."

I do not! Helen wanted to shout. It was ten pounds. OK, fifteen—max. She'd stopped pummeling the porn queen a second for this weighty issue. Mindy took advantage of her hesitation. She punched Helen hard in the right breast. The pain was so bad, Helen fell backward on the floor, gasping.

Mindy got to her knees. Then, wobbly as a newborn colt, she stood. The crowd cheered. Mindy accepted their applause with a regal incline of her head.

Too soon to be taking your bows, Helen thought. This fight isn't over yet. She dragged herself upright and kneed Mindy in the groin. She'd read that maneuver had the same effect on a woman as a man. The article was right. Mindy doubled over, clutching herself.

This time, there were no cheers. The crowd was ominously silent. Helen felt something cold and hard at the base of her skull. The rage drained out of her, replaced by freezing fear.

"Move and you're dead," a man said. "Now, down on your knees."

He's got a gun, Helen thought. He's going to blow my head off. No one will help me. These ghouls will watch me die—and enjoy it. I won't whimper. I won't beg. And I won't lay down and die. I thought my way in here and I can think my way out.

"Darling." Mindy's voice was silky as her scarf. "You've saved me. It's so delightfully old-fashioned."

"You can take care of yourself, babe. But this farce has gone on long enough. You women look stupid when you fight, all that hair pulling and rolling around and shit. You can't throw a decent punch."

That voice, Helen thought. I've heard it before. But

where? Mindy's husband, Dr. Melton? No, Melton Mowbry came from money. This guy sure didn't have a private-school accent. Helen couldn't turn around and look at him with the gun barrel jammed in her head. Her mind was working so slowly.

"We girls are lovers," Mindy cooed, "not fighters."

"Get the disk, Mindy, and let's get out of here." The man sounded impatient. And frustratingly familiar.

"You're so masterful," Mindy mocked. "Whatever you say, Hank."

Hank? Of course. It was Hank Asporth. How could Helen forget his voice? He was Mindy's lover? She had a husband and little twin girls. And I am such a Midwesterner, Helen thought. Melton and Mindy were hardly Ozzie and Harriet.

Then Helen heard someone shout, "Hey! The curtains are on fire."

The candles. One had been knocked over during the fight. No one had seen the fire start. They were too busy watching the women wrestle. Now the dry black velvet curtains behind the coffin were in flames. The fire was small and energetic. It seemed an acre away in the huge room.

But Helen saw little flames, like malignant sprites, running along the silk rug toward the ebony casket. It burst into flames. The satin lining caught fire. A crazy giggle rose up inside her. Shouldn't a casket be fireproof—especially for this crowd?

Smoke from the finest ebony smelled like the world's best autumn bonfire. Helen also smelled raw panic. Naked people were screaming and pushing one another as they ran for the double doors. The doors were closed, the demons dancing insolently in the fiery haze.

A skinny woman rushed by, her waist-length hair on fire. A muscular middle-aged man was knocked sideways against the double doors. His black toupee came loose and slid along the floor like a hairy hockey puck, until it hit the blaze and burst into flames. But the newly bald man was strong. He pushed and punched his way back to the doors. Then he tore them open and escaped.

An older, flabbier man was not so lucky. He was trampled by panicked people rushing toward the doors. He tried to rise to his knees, but someone kicked him in the head. His body was pushed back toward the flames, and he did not move again.

Helen hoped the man was unconscious when the fire engulfed him. She felt oddly numb, as if she were watching a movie.

Hank and Mindy stayed cool in the chaos. Flames did not frighten them. Hell was their home.

"Get the disk, Mindy, and I'll put a bullet through her head," Hank said.

"Can't I strangle her?" Mindy twisted her long filmy scarf.

"There's no time," Hank said.

"I'll be quick. I always am."

Her eyes were savage. Helen saw one thing clearly in the smoky darkness: Mindy liked to murder.

"You killed her," Helen said. "You strangled Debbie."

"Of course, you idiot. And that stupid piece of trailer trash."

"Laredo? You killed Laredo? Hank strangled her. I heard him."

"You heard *me,*" Mindy said. "Hank watched. Hank likes to watch. This time, he saw more than he wanted. Scared the poor baby."

"I wasn't scared," Hank snapped. "I was angry. You shut her up too soon."

"And now you want to rush." Mindy slowly drew the scarf through her fingers.

The air was electric with heat and black with smoke. Helen could see the disk on the floor, next to her abandoned toolbox. Soon, the only link to Laredo's murder would be a lump of melted plastic. Little fires burned along the floor only a few yards away.

"Mindy, move," Hank said. "The place is on fire."

"I know it is, lover, and it's glorious." Mindy seemed to delight in the destruction of her home. She threw out her arms and shouted, "Welcome to hell!"

There was an odd *whump* and Mindy's sheer scarf ignited. Flames ran down her vinyl catsuit and up into her hair. Mindy shrieked and beat at the fire with her hands, but the vinyl melted into her skin. Her screams turned to hellish howls. She collapsed on the floor, rolling frantically to smother the flames. Her blazing body tossed and tumbled dangerously close to the computer disk.

"Make it stop!" she shrieked. "Make it stop!"

Hank was paralyzed. Helen could feel the gun pressing harder into her skull, but Hank's hand was shaking. Mindy gave another inhuman cry and the gun barrel lurched upward, digging a trench in Helen's scalp.

The pain made Helen look away from the madly screaming Mindy.

"Help meeeee!" But no one could help her now.

Helen had to run for it or she'd burn, too. The way Hank's hands were trembling, he might miss if he tried to shoot her. Helen had a chance if she moved fast. But she wasn't leaving without that disk.

She hit the hot floor and felt around for the disk. She found the toolbox. It was warm. The oven cleaner! Savannah's oven cleaner was inside. Mindy, burning and screaming, was inches away. If the oven-cleaner can exploded in the fire, the metal toolbox would disintegrate into deadly shrapnel.

Helen heard Hank take quick strides toward her, as she frantically searched for the disk in the smoke. Now he was right behind her.

"Pleeeeeeease," Mindy pleaded.

Helen started to crawl forward, but Hank's huge hand grabbed her around the neck. She couldn't move. She couldn't breathe. She heard him draw back the trigger. He was so close, Hank couldn't miss if he tried.

This is it, Helen thought. I'm dead.

Chapter 28

I can't hear, Helen thought. He shot me in the head.

The silence was frightening. She could see people screaming, but there was no sound. She didn't feel any pain. Helen knew that was shock. The pain would come later.

Hank had let go of her. She sat up.

Helen felt her face for the sticky spurt of heart-pumped blood. Nothing. She checked the back of her head for leaking brains. No squishy mass. Both ears were still attached. There were no gaping gunshot wounds on her arms, legs or gut.

He didn't kill me, she realized with dazed wonder. Unless I'm dead and don't know it. I could be in hell.

Smoke swirled around her. Helen smelled roasting meat, but her mind skittered away from that. A million miles away at the far end of the room, the black velvet curtains flared into yellow sheets of fire. The coffin was a brimstone baptismal font.

A small fireball ran along the floor like a mouse. Helen gawked, then gulped like a goldfish. That cleared her ears. They opened to unearthly sounds: infernal shrieks of panic, squeals of pain.

Helen heard another shot, and hit the floor. A bullet zinged past her and buried itself in the floor three feet away. Hank wasn't aiming at her. He was shooting at Mindy.

"Aahhhhgh!" Mindy's burned lips could no longer make human sounds. Her body bucked and tossed in the flames.

Hank fired two more shots. Both went wild. One hit near Mindy's smoking shoulder, the other by her fiery hair.

Another shot, and Mindy's lost-soul wails stopped.

Mindy lay deathly still, tiny flames crackling quietly on her vinyl catsuit. Helen saw the bullet wound in her forehead, a red hole like a third eye.

Even in hell, I will never see anything this horrible, Helen thought.

Hank Asporth had shot his lover. Four of his bullets had gone wild. But the fifth hit the mark. He had one shot left.

Helen could see Hank lurching through the smoke. His big body was hunched like a cave creature. His jaw was slack with shock. His eyes were white and wild in his smoke-smeared face.

Now he pointed the gun straight at Helen. It was a revolver. It looked small in his huge hand, like Det. Lennie Brisco's little revolver in *Law & Order*. Helen looked down the short barrel for a long eternity.

"You made me kill her," Hank said. "I loved her. She's dead and it's your fault."

"No," Helen said. "No, you don't—"

Hank pulled the trigger. I'm never going to sleep with Phil, she thought. I'll burn in hell because my last thought was about boffing the hunk next door. She braced herself for the impact. She heard a loud snap.

Snap? What kind of noise was that?

The gun was empty. Of course. The *Law & Order* gun was a five-shot snub-nosed .38, not a six-shot at all. Helen nearly collapsed with relief.

Hank threw the useless gun into the smoke, then scooped up Laredo's disk and began a clumsy splay-legged run for the door.

She couldn't let him get away. Helen started after Hank,

her own gait wobbly and erratic. She coughed and choked on the smoke. Her lungs were dead sponges. They wouldn't take in any air. She pulled her shirt up over her nose and mouth to help her breathe. That was a little better, but she still couldn't move with any speed. She could hardly see. The demon doors were in another dimension. She'd never reach them.

You can't let Hank escape with that disk, she told herself. Laredo bought it with her life. Helen kept slogging through the smoke-thick air. The demon doors never seemed to get any closer. A short, furry man ran past her. His hairy back was on fire.

Then, just like that, she was out and into the long corridor. She looked for Hank, but he was too far ahead. The air was better in the hall, but the panicked crowd was more dangerous. People pushed her forward. She could not stop. She'd be trampled if she tried. Helen struggled to stay upright.

Suddenly, she felt a stream of deliciously cool air. Was she near the entrance? No, the fresh air was coming from the tall window. Ten minutes ago, she'd stood there looking down at a lavish party. Now the portable bars were overturned, and the food and flowers were trampled. A naked woman floated face-down in the pool.

A French-rolled brunette shoved Helen so hard her forehead hit the wall. I'm going to die if I don't get out of here, she thought. The open window was her quickest way out. She climbed over the sill and nearly lost her balance. It was a fifteen-foot drop to the ground. If she was lucky, she'd land in the soft garden. If she wasn't, she'd hit the concrete like a watermelon dropped off a roof. She sat on the sill, hoping someone would come along below and help her down.

With a *whoosh*, a fireball exploded down the hall, turning the panicked pushers and shovers into living torches. The heat scorched Helen's back. She didn't hesitate any longer. She dropped straight down.

Helen landed in the mulch-cushioned flower bed and rolled onto the concrete, knocking her head against a teak chaise longue. She saw stars. Then she saw feet. A man's feet in neat black Bally loafers.

"I see you fell for me again." Phil said.

"This is no time for jokes." Helen brushed the major mulch bits out of her eyes. "Hank Asporth just killed Mindy Mowbry. He shot her in the head. He has Laredo's disk and he's headed that way."

Helen pointed toward the hall entrance. Phil didn't ask what disk. He took off after Hank. Helen ran after him, but Phil was faster. She could hear sirens in the distance as they ran in the cool night air. The cops could chase Hank better than she could. But she kept running.

Phil raced around the building, Helen trailing after him. She saw Hank running across the wide lawn toward the dock.

"Phil! He's heading for the boat!"

Hellfire, the Cigarette boat, was still at the Mowbrys' dock. The painted flames licking its hull no longer seemed childish. They were a prophecy.

Phil poured on the speed. Helen tried to run faster, but she was panting like an old dog on a hot day. She hadn't exercised much while she worked in the boiler room. All those salt-and-vinegar chips slowed her down.

Hank jumped aboard the boat.

"He's untying the ropes! He's getting away," Helen said.

The five-hundred-horsepower twin engines started up. They sounded like an explosion and Helen was nearly deafened again. She could feel their rumble. Blue-white gasoline smoke poured from the exhaust. Just before the boat shot forward like a rocket, Phil sprang onto the deck with a corsair's leap.

Helen made a leap, too. She missed the boat, nearly landing in the water. She grabbed a piling to keep from winding up in the drink, and scraped her arm.

"Shit!" Helen said.

The Cigarette boat was gone in a roar of smoke. Helen hauled herself back on the dock and stood there, trying to catch her breath. She was surprised to see that she was still holding her toolbox. She ran to the water-taxi stand.

She was in luck. There was a taxi waiting. It was empty, too. The captain was young and blond and looked like a Coast Guard recruiting poster. He was wearing a white captain's shirt with four gold bars. His air of authority was undermined by his peach-fuzz cheeks.

Helen jumped on the water taxi. It rocked rudely under her weight, reminding her of that thirty-pound remark.

"Follow that boat!" She pointed at the Cigarette boat disappearing in the distance.

"Sorry, lady. I don't leave for another four minutes."

"You're following that boat." Helen pulled Savannah's can of oven cleaner out of the toolbox. "Do what I say or I'll shoot."

The captain did not look frightened. "Is that pepper spray?"

"Oven cleaner. Do you know what this can do?"

"No. My oven's self-cleaning," the captain said.

"It contains lye. It can blind you. Now get going."

"Aww, Jesus, lady. Can't you just carry a gun like everyone else in South Florida?"

"Hurry! They're getting away."

"Of course they're getting away. That's a Cigarette boat. This is a tub."

Helen shook the can. "Try," she snarled.

"I can't go fast. It's a no-wake zone," the captain said.

"I'll pay the fine. Now floor it, or whatever you do with boats." She put her finger on the nozzle. He still didn't look scared, but at least he got the boat moving. They chugged through a wide, mansion-lined section of the Intracoastal Waterway. The channel was broad, flat and black.

Even a landlubber like Helen could see the captain was right. Their lumbering craft was no match for the sleek Cigarette boat. It seemed to be miles ahead. It barely touched the water, racing through the channel with great leaping belly flops. *Whump! Whump! Whump!* The Cigarette boat walloped along at what looked like a hundred miles an hour. Water shot up behind it in a curving arc. The powerful engines roared like an army of leaf blowers.

The tubby taxi wallowed along, rolling and shifting. Cold, dirty water splashed through its open sides. The water taxi was doing one thing really fast—falling behind. Helen could barely see the Cigarette boat.

"We've got to stop them," Helen cried. "Call the Coast Guard."

"I've radioed twice, lady. They're on their way."

Then, in the distance, they saw a little dinghy crossing in front of the Cigarette boat. It was small, slow and headed for disaster.

"Don't look," the captain said. "It's going to be ugly."

The Cigarette boat tried to avoid the dinghy. It went into a frantic spin, plowing the water on its side. The passengers in the dinghy took one look at what was heading their way and jumped into the water. The Cigarette boat missed them and hit a dock with a tremendous *crack!*

"Jesus," the captain said, as bodies tumbled into the water. The single word sounded like a prayer.

Helen kicked off her shoes and dove into the churning canal. It was nearly twenty-five years since her Red Cross lifeguard course at the Webster Groves pool. She hoped she remembered what to do.

The water was cold, oily and oddly thick, but Helen felt revived. It cooled the burn on her scorched back. Now she was glad for all those salt-and-vinegar chips. A little extra body fat would keep her buoyant.

The first person she spotted was Hank, floundering in the water. He was still clutching the disk in his hand. Helen grabbed him by his hair.

"Ow!" he yelled. "Those are plugs. Cost a frigging fortune. They've just taken root. Don't pull them out!"

"Give me that." Helen reached for the disk.

"No way." Hank would rather be snatched bald than give up that disk. On land, Helen had no chance of defeating him.

But the big man was desperately afraid of the water. She pushed his hair-plugged head under again. Hank came up spluttering and choking.

"Help me. I can't swim." Hank grabbed Helen's arm in a death grip and nearly pulled her under. She could drown with the desperate Hank. She chopped at Hank's grasping hand until he let go of her arm.

Helen pushed his newly sodded head under once more. That did it. She pried the disk out of Hank's hand and stuck it in her pants pocket. Then she let go of Hank.

"Please, don't let me drown." Hank kept sinking and swallowing water. Helen grabbed his collar. She started to tow Hank to the water taxi when she saw another body in the canal.

It was Phil, floating face-down.

Helen let go of Hank. When he tried to cling to her, she kicked him hard in the gut. She reached Phil in two strokes and pulled his head out of the water.

"Phil," she said. "Phil, please talk to me."

He was unconscious. The back of his shirt was dry. Helen hoped that meant he'd just gone into the water. She tried to turn him over on his back, but his body was too heavy and slippery. All she could do was keep his head clear of the water and try to drag him to the taxi. She forced herself not to think about the things brushing against her legs.

Helen was so exhausted, she was afraid she wouldn't be able to hold onto him. To keep her concentration, she talked as she towed Phil toward the water taxi.

"All this time, I thought you were invisible," she said. "Do you know how hard I tried to see what you looked like? I'd get up at six in the morning. I'd stay up until three A.M. I didn't get a glimpse. I called you Phil the invisible pothead.

"When you saved me from that fire, I tried to thank you in person. I even left Cherry Garcia ice cream on your doorstep. You took it and said nothing. Didn't even give me a peek at your face. What was that all about?"

Phil's face was like something carved on a sarcophagus.

If she kissed his cold marble lips, would he come back to life? That happened only in fairy tales, not in dirty canals. Helen kept paddling toward the water taxi, splashing and floundering, but moving forward.

"I even envied your pot-smoking because you could summon your dreams whenever you wanted. I was involved with a couple of jerks. Those guys were real nightmares. It was much harder to make them go away."

Phil's eyes stayed closed.

"Please don't die," she pleaded. "You're the only decent guy I've met in Florida."

The man had to be made of stone. Phil was growing heavier. Her fingers were cramping. She was afraid she'd lose him. Helen kept stroking toward the taxi, babbling to distract herself.

"Actually, I'm glad you're out cold and can't hear this. I can talk to you better that way. When you rescued me that time from the fire, I still remember how your hands felt. So strong and soft and hard at the same time. I figured a man with hands like that had to be good in bed."

Helen's own hands felt like lead. Her arms were logs of dead flesh. Her legs were lumps of rubber. She bumped into something hard. The boat. She'd reached it at last.

Strong hands lifted Phil into the water taxi while she treaded water. When Phil was safely aboard, she was lifted in. She saw flashing lights and knew the Coast Guard was on its way. She was vaguely aware of three wet-haired women and a sneezing young man huddled under blankets. They must have been in the dinghy.

I'm going to spend the rest of my life in jail for hijacking a water taxi, Helen thought. But at least I saved Phil.

He was stretched out on a bench, covered in blankets. His head was pillowed on a life jacket. She sat down beside him. Phil's eyelashes fluttered. They were longer than hers. It wasn't fair to waste lashes like that on a man. Then his eyes opened.

"Phil, you're OK."

"Better than OK. Who hauled me out of the water?"

"I did. Now we're even."

"Not yet." Phil pulled her down and kissed her hard. This was no marble man. His lips were warm and deliciously wet.

The boat rocked as the Coast Guard arrived to take her away.

I'll remember this kiss, no matter how many years I spend in prison, Helen thought.

Chapter 29

That kiss saved Helen.

She was still in a lip-lock with Phil when the Coast Guard arrived, flashing blue lights bouncing off the night-black water. The water taxi was flooded with pulsing color.

Helen didn't stop kissing Phil. This memory had to last a long time. She was going to jail.

Helen took a peek. She saw two small Coast Guard boats, about the size of Boston Whalers. She counted six men in dark blue uniforms.

Helen heard a soft, cultured voice say, "Are you the Coast Guard?"

That must be one of the rescued women huddled under blankets on the water taxi.

Helen had seen enough. Once the captain started talking, it would be all over for her. Was boat-jacking a capital crime? She went back to kissing Phil.

"This is Capt. Jack Klobnak," the rescued woman said, as if she was at a party. She'd bothered to learn his name. Helen had just threatened him.

"I'm Jan Kurtz. The captain saved us. He tried to head off that speedboat. It was running straight for our dinghy. The driver had to be drunk. That boat was going so fast. There's no way the captain could have caught up with it. But he was there when we overturned. We would have drowned without him."

Helen came up for air and sneaked another peek. Jan was about forty and would have been pretty if she hadn't been dunked in a dirty canal. Her brown hair was plastered to her head and her eyeliner left muddy streaks.

"I think Capt. Klobnak saved the man over there, too," Jan said. "That woman is giving him mouth-to-mouth resuscitation."

"That will explain the lipstick all over your face," Helen whispered in Phil's ear. It felt like a fuzzy peach. She longed to nibble it.

"Ow. Don't make me laugh. I've been kicked in the ribs," Phil said. "You better stop resuscitating me, before they see you've revived another body part."

Helen pulled herself away while Phil bunched the blankets strategically around his middle.

"Are you OK, sir?" The Coast Guard officer was twenty-something with a shaved head and a lobster-pink sunburn. "Do you need medical assistance?"

"I'm fine."

He's better than fine, Helen thought. The man kisses like a dream. She'd finally met her dream lover and she was going to jail for kidnaping a water taxi captain—if she didn't die of pneumonia first. Her wet clothes weighed four thousand pounds. Her teeth were chattering.

"You're cold." Phil pulled off a blanket and wrapped it around her shivering shoulders. "Ouch. My ribs. Take this."

Helen, bundled in coarse wool and wet khaki, felt a *zing* when she looked at Phil. Even soaking wet, that man was something. Especially wet. His shirt clung to his chest in interesting ways.

Helen jumped at a faint scraping sound. She saw the captain scooting her toolbox under a bench with his heroic foot, as if he didn't want anyone to know he'd been hijacked by a woman wielding oven cleaner.

Maybe I won't go to jail for water-taxi piracy after all, Helen thought.

The rescued Jan was still praising Capt. Klobnak and giving party introductions. "He saved my nephew, Christian Muys, and my friends Megan Kellner and Elaine Naiman. And me, too. He's a hero."

The captain blushed deep red, even in the flashing blue lights. But Jan was right. The man was a hero. And if Helen was going to save herself, he'd better stay one. She slathered on praise while covering her waterlogged rear end.

"That's right, officers," she said. "The captain was supposed to take me to Las Olas, way in the other direction. But he saw that speedboat go flying by, and he knew something was wrong. He went after it. I'm glad he did. When I saw that boat heading for those poor people, I thought they were goners."

"Capt. Klobnak saved us all," Jan said. "Well, not all. I saw the Cigarette boat driver go into the water, but I don't know what happened to him. I was too busy jumping out of the way."

There was a *flap-flap* of helicopter rotors and bright white lights blazed on the water.

"What's that?" Helen said.

"The Coast Guard chopper is looking for bodies," Phil said.

Helen shivered, and this time it wasn't from the cold. The helicopter searchlights over the flashing blue lights were disorienting. Everyone seemed to be talking at once. Helen couldn't take in any more. She stared at the wrecked Cigarette boat and abandoned dinghy.

Debris fanned out from the swamped boats: suntan-lotion bottles, beer cans, beach toys. She saw a beer cooler bob by, a canvas seat cushion and a bloody head.

A head?

Helen shook off her lethargy. The head belonged to the half-drowned Hank Asporth. He was doing a pathetic one-armed dog paddle while he clung desperately to a boat bumper. Hank paddled mostly in circles, although an occasional wild sweep of his arm would move him forward. Another sweep would splash water in his face and set off convulsive gasping and choking.

Helen saw a round red wound in his scalp. I must have pulled out one of his precious hair plugs, she thought.

"That's the maniac who was driving the Cigarette boat!" Jan said.

The dripping, snuffling Hank was pulled into the closest Coast Guard boat. Phil threw off his blankets and produced his ID. "I'm a private investigator. This man is Henry Asporth. He was running from the scene of a homicide. He shot and killed Mindy Mowbry."

Capt. Klobnak whistled. "He killed the rich lady in that waterfront mansion?"

"I did not!" It was the first time Hank said anything. He looked like a walking dead man, the red hole in his scalp echoing the bullet wound in Mindy's head. "There was a terrible fire. Mindy's clothes were melting into her skin. She was screaming in pain. You've never heard a sound like that. She wasn't going to survive those burns. I loved her. I couldn't stand to see her suffer."

Hank started to weep. His sobs sounded like someone opening a rusty grate. Helen almost felt sorry for him, until she remembered how he'd stepped over Mindy's dead body to get the disk. Was he in shock or a stone-cold killer? She didn't know. But she patted her pocket. Laredo's disk was still there.

"And this woman here . . ." Phil smiled at Helen.

Oh, no, she thought. I can't be mixed up in this. She elbowed Phil hard in his injured ribs.

"Urf!" he said.

"Are you OK, sir?" the sunburned Coast Guard officer said.

"My ribs." Phil clutched his side.

"You were saying about this woman?"

Helen shook her head slightly and hoped Phil got the signal.

"She was in the water taxi when Capt. Klobnak saved me," Phil said. "Hank Asporth tried to kill me."

"I didn't see any of that," Helen said. "I closed my eyes when it looked like the boats were going to collide. I didn't want to see those people die."

"We'll get a statement from you later, Billy," the Coast Guardsman said.

Billy? Who's Billy? Helen almost blurted, then realized she was still wearing Margery's work shirt with BILLY on the pocket.

The Coast Guard boat took Hank Asporth away, blue lights flashing ominously.

"What's going to happen to Hank?" Helen asked. "Will they arrest him?"

"No, the Coast Guard are federal law enforcement," Phil said. "They'll turn Hank over to the local police department. He was speeding in state waters, so I suspect the Florida Marine Patrol will also get involved. Hank will have a long list of charges, starting with gross negligence and ending with Mindy's murder."

"And what about Laredo? Mindy killed her, but Hank didn't stop her. He helped hide the body. He knows where Savannah's sister is buried."

Phil sighed. "I don't know if we have anything to connect him to Laredo."

Helen gave Phil the disk. "Will this help?"

"You saved it?" he said. "Helen, this is important. I can get you a reward. That list you gave me was a good start. But this could wrap up the case."

"No!" Helen was desperate to make him understand. "I can't be in any computers."

"Are you in trouble with the law? I've got connections. I can help you."

"I'm on the run from my ex-husband. He'll do anything to find me. If I'm in a computer, he can track me down." That was true—mostly. "I don't want the money. If you nail Hank Asporth and find Laredo, that's reward enough."

"I'll do my damnedest." Phil's eyes were such a sincere blue, she had to believe him.

"Are you going to give that disk to the Feds?" Helen said.

"Yes. But I don't want to tip off Hank that I have it. I need a few hours. Once he calls his lawyer, the shredders will start working in the boiler room. We'll try to get a search warrant and raid the place first thing in the morning. You might as well stay home and read the want ads."

"Oh, no," Helen said. "I'll be there. I wouldn't miss it. What's going to happen to us now?"

"The Coast Guard will escort the water taxi to the closest marina. You can see it—that patch of lights over there. Then they'll take statements from everyone."

"They think I'm Billy," Helen said.

"Good. Let them keep thinking that," Phil said. "I need to get away now. I'll say I have to go to the hospital, and they'll airlift me out. Then I'll set the computer experts to work on your disk."

"I guess those broken ribs will come in handy."

"They're not broken," he said. "I know what broken ribs feel like. Besides, that's not the excuse I'm using."

"What are you going to say?"

"I have a slipped disk."

Phil grinned. Then he kissed her once more and was gone.

Chapter 30

Helen came home in a sheriff's car at five in the morning. She sat in the screened-off back seat like a felon. She'd had no sleep. Her chest and neck throbbed from Mindy's whip slash. Her scorched back pulsed like a superheated sunburn.

She'd never felt better.

All the lights were out at the Coronado. She crunched her way across the parking lot. Something hissed at her in the dark.

A cat? A snake?

It was Margery. She was on her doorstep, her purple chenille robe tied crookedly, her red curlers askew. Her toenail polish looked like ten drops of blood.

"Where the hell have you been? Your cat was howling all night. I finally fed it to shut it up. Now the cops bring you home. What's going on?"

"I'm in love." Helen knew she had a big, sappy grin on her face. She didn't care.

"Love? You look like you've been mauled by bears. Who is this goon?"

"Phil the invisible pothead."

"Oh, my God. Let me put on some coffee. Go change out of those wet clothes. I'll wake up Peggy."

Helen floated back to her apartment, feet barely touching

the concrete sidewalk. When she unlocked the front door, she was met by a ticked-off Thumbs. His big paws were planted firmly on the floor. His yellow eyes were angry. He punished her with the cat cold shoulder for about thirty seconds. Then he demanded an ear scratch. Helen scratched him contritely until he flopped on the floor and allowed her to rub his belly, the sign of feline forgiveness.

Helen showered, dried her hair and dressed for work. Thirty minutes later, she was back at Margery's.

Her landlady's kitchen smelled of hot coffee and warm chocolate. Margery was heating chocolate croissants in her microwave. A sleepy Peggy, wearing jeans and an inside out T-shirt, was huddled over a fat mug of coffee.

"Where's Pete?" Peggy always looked incomplete without her parrot.

"At home asleep," Peggy said with a yawn.

"Where we all would be, if you weren't blundering around, falling in canals and falling in love. Spill. Now," Margery commanded.

Helen did. She told them about the disk in the coffin, the fire in the mansion and Mindy's death. She told them about the boat chase and how she saved Phil.

"Then he saved me. With a kiss," Helen said. "Just like in the fairy tales."

"He's a real prince." Margery's sarcasm was like honeyed acid. Helen sat in silence, sipping coffee and waiting for their verdict.

"What do you think?" Margery asked Peggy, as if they were two doctors on a consultation.

They're heart specialists, Helen thought, and nearly giggled. She was punch-drunk after the long night.

"This romance shows promise," Peggy said. "But I should talk, considering my track record with men."

"If Phil hurts her, I swear I'll evict him." Margery's mouth went into a hard line and little cracks appeared around her lips.

"He won't," Helen said.

"How would you know?" Margery said.

"I don't know. But I feel it," Helen said.

Margery snorted like a Clydesdale. "What you ought to feel is tired. It's time for you to go to bed."

"It's seven thirty," Helen said. "It's time for me to go to work."

"You're not going back to that boiler room," Margery said.

"Try and stop me." Helen took a final gulp of caffeine. "Look, I really appreciate this. But I have to be there."

She put her coffee mug in Margery's sink, then stepped outside into the new morning. It was clear and clean. Helen's fatigue disappeared. She felt hopeful for the first time in ages.

The boiler-room shift started like every other. The two bikers, Bob and Panhead Pete, clocked in, looking hungover. Zelda was already at her desk, wrapped in her big sweater. Taniqua was spray-cleaning the nicotine stink off her phone. She looked like a modern version of those fifties commercials where housewives wore fancy dresses to clean floors. Taniqua wore purple satin heels, purple pants cut way south of the border and a purple top that barely covered the subject.

The night shift had left a gutted sub sandwich on Helen's desk. Cheese and chopped lettuce were piled on her phone.

"Haven't those slobs ever heard of a trash can?" Helen said.

"No room." Taniqua handed Helen the spray cleaner and waved at the overflowing cans.

At seven fifty-eight, Marina teetered in on black high heels, carrying a drowsy Ramon. He was drooling on her black spandex top, and clutching one of her black bra straps. She spread a quilt underneath her desk. The little boy curled up at her feet and slept. His brown curls were heartbreaking.

No child should have to sleep on that filthy floor, Helen thought sadly. The overfilled trash cans were only a foot away.

The computers flipped on at eight oh-two and started

dialing. With the calls came the rustle and crunch of sixty telemarketers staving off the nation's abuse with junk food.

Helen checked her computer. It was dialing Maine. A staid state, she thought. Folks in Livermore Falls wouldn't waste their breath cussing her out. They'd just hang up.

"Hi, Burt. This is Helen with Tank Titan Septic System Cleaner. We make a septic tank cleaner for your home system that is guaranteed to help reduce large chunks, odors and wet spots—"

"Get stuffed, bitch," Burt said. So much for her theory about Maine.

At eight oh-six, federal agents burst into the boiler room. Someone barked out an agency name, but Helen didn't catch it. She was being cussed out by an irate homeowner in Skowhegan.

When the agents roared through the door, both bikers dove under their desks. The telemarketers were ordered to stay where they were.

Two agents had Vito on the floor with a gun to his head. Vito seemed smaller, his egocentric energy gone, his round pink body deflated. Two more agents came out of the office with the elegant lizard, Mr. Cavarelli. His face twisted into a grimace when he was ordered to the floor.

"He don't like putting that fancy suit on that raggedy-ass floor," Taniqua said.

"Floor's good enough for my little boy, it's good enough for him," Marina said. Ramon slept near the trash pile, oblivious.

"Shh," Zelda said. "I'm trying to hear. The Feds are talking about money laundering. But I can't tell if they said there were drugs or rugs here."

"I see more police running up the stairs to Girdner Surveys," Taniqua said. "They got the elevator and the exits covered. Penelope gonna shit when they break into her office."

"I think Tank Titan is in the toilet," Marina giggled. Helen had never seen her smile before. She realized the tired single mother was just a girl.

The computers were frantically dialing Connecticut and the Carolinas, but nobody was selling septic-tank cleaner.

"Hello? Hello!"

Helen jumped. The voice was coming from her abandoned phone receiver. Her response was automatic: "Hi, this is Helen with Tank Titan Septic System Cleaner."

"You're the septic-tank-cleaner people?" The woman was so old and frail, her voice sounded like tearing tissue paper. It had the sweet, trusting quality that made her a prime boiler-room victim.

"Yes, ma'am," Helen said.

"I'm Mrs. Gertrude Carter. A nice young man from your company called here last week. My son hung up on him. Roger can be rude, I'm afraid. He doesn't mean it—he's just protecting me. Roger said your product was overpriced junk. But I've been thinking about what that young man said. Two hundred ninety-nine dollars seems a good price for a seven-year supply. I'd like to buy it."

"Your son is right, Mrs. Carter," Helen said. "Tank Titan is outrageously overpriced. Save your money."

"Well! You're an honest young woman."

"I just started this week," Helen said.

Loud cheers drowned out Mrs. Carter's reply.

"Helen, you be missing it," Taniqua said. "The police got that tight-ass Penelope in handcuffs. I'd give all my money to see that bitch in jail. Vito and the New York guy be with them."

As the boiler-room bosses were led away, Taniqua stood up and applauded. She was joined by the other inmates. Even the bikers, Bob and Panhead Pete, crawled out from under their desks. All sixty telemarketers gave the Feds a standing ovation. They didn't seem to care that their jobs were gone.

Then a half-full drink cup went flying through the air and splattered on Penelope's beige-suited back. Suddenly, all the trash in the room was pelting the three bosses. Helen found herself throwing a handful of left-behind lettuce. It made a greasy splash on Mr. Cavarelli's elegant suit.

If they'd cleaned the boiler room, this wouldn't be happening, she thought, and hurled a stale cheese slice like a Frisbee. It stuck to Penelope's back like a starfish.

The telemarketers threw with furious precision. No trash touched the agents. The agents were stone-faced, but Helen thought she caught an occasional lip flick that might have been a suppressed smile as they hustled the three forward. When the boiler-room doors closed on the bosses, the trash-pelting stopped.

A swarm of agents started carrying out boxes of files. There was an electric *pop* and the computer screens went blank.

"The phones stopped," Taniqua said.

"Tank Titan just hung it up," Helen said. "I'm out of work. And you know what? I've never been happier."

Epilogue

It was over. But it wasn't a happy ending.

Helen walked home from the busted boiler room feeling oddly empty. A wild vengeance had surged through her as she'd pelted her bosses with trash, but its hot satisfaction did not last.

She knew Hank Asporth was in jail, charged with everything from boating under the influence to money laundering—everything but Laredo's death.

Laredo. She was the problem. Helen had never met the woman, but she'd heard her die. Now Laredo seemed more alive than ever, standing in front of Helen in her mock pinup pose. Helen could see her long blond hair, short-shorts and saucy red shoes. Laredo laughed at Helen, taunting her. And she haunted her.

Helen didn't believe in ghosts. But she did believe in guilt.

Helen felt bad about Laredo. Yes, she was a blackmailer, and that was wrong. But Helen understood why Laredo did it. She'd worked those awful jobs, too. They killed your soul for six dollars an hour. Laredo was murdered trying to escape her hopeless past and dreary future. Helen knew she'd died in Asporth's house. So why wouldn't Laredo go away?

"I'm not going to live with you," Helen said to her.

A woman loaded with shopping bags stared at Helen, then hurried past her. Helen realized she'd been talking out loud on Las Olas Boulevard—without a cell phone.

I'll call Savannah, Helen thought. Maybe if I give her the news about Hank's arrest, she'll feel better. Maybe that will get Laredo out of my head.

She found a pay phone and got Savannah on the first ring. "I can take a break," Savannah said. "Meet you in ten by the café. But I don't feel like eating. Let's go for a walk."

Savannah was easy to spot in the crowd. She was wearing one of her fussy frilled dresses. This one was a bright cerise that drained the color from her face. She had grown scrawnier since the last time Helen had seen her. Savannah was hungry for justice.

"So Hank's in jail?" she said.

"Right," Helen said.

"But not for my little sister's death. He's dropped her somewhere like a sack of trash. She'll never be found unless he talks."

"He won't talk," Helen said. "He'd incriminate himself."

The situation was hopeless, and they both knew it. They walked wordlessly for awhile down Las Olas, but neither one liked the crowds. They turned off on a side street and found a canal. It was a peaceful scene: low-hanging trees, bright flowers and a mother duck paddling in the water with her babies. Helen knew the fluffy little creatures would grow up to be ungainly Muscovy ducks with black feathers and ugly red wattles.

"I wish I could find Laredo," Savannah said. "What do you think Hank did with her? How could he hide a whole car?"

"I don't know," Helen said. They'd had this conversation a hundred times. They'd probably have it a hundred more.

They watched two boys, about ten years old, fishing from the canal bridge. Their musical accents marked them as natives of the Caribbean.

"I've caught a whale," one kid said. Small and wiry, he was reeling frantically. His fishing pole was bent almost double. Whatever he caught, it had to be huge. Then Helen heard his friend laughing. The young fisherman pulled out a Michelin tire.

"Keep fishing, and maybe you'll catch the whole car," his friend jeered.

That's when something clicked for Helen. "Laredo's car is in the water," she said. "That's deep water behind Hank Asporth's house. I bet anything he put the body inside the car and dumped it in the canal."

"And how will you prove that?"

"Let's go look at Hank's house," Helen said. "I think I can show you."

They rode over in Savannah's rattletrap Tank and parked in the empty driveway. Hank Asporth's house had a neglected look. Newspapers were piled on the porch, the lawn needed mowing and plastic bags had blown into the ornamental plants.

"Anybody watching us?" Helen said.

"Don't think so. There are no cars at the next-door neighbor's and the old man on the other side has his TV blaring."

"Good," Helen said. "Let's go around to the backyard."

There was no fence. They slipped around a bird-of-paradise bush. Helen had never seen the spiky orange blooms outside a florist's bouquet. The backyard was expensive waterfront real estate. The lawn near the house was covered with pink paving blocks. When they ended, there was grass to the water's edge.

"There's your proof," Helen said. "I should have seen this before. It was right there all the time. That grass is going to trip up Hank Asporth."

"Why?" Savannah said.

"That's new sod. Look." Helen pointed to a broad swath of lighter grass running through the yard. "It's covering the tire tracks through the yard to the water's edge."

"I see it," Savannah said. "But how will we get the police to see it? They think you're a nut and I'm a nuisance."

"I know someone who'll get their attention," Helen said.

Helen waited the rest of the day for Phil to come back to the Coronado, but he remained invisible. She didn't have a number to reach him or a phone to call him if she had. About five o'clock, she knocked on Margery's door. Her landlady came out in heliotrope shorts, holding a tall screwdriver garnished with lime.

"Do you know how to get hold of Phil?" Helen said.

"Which part do you want to hold?" Margery had obviously been getting her liquid vitamin C.

Helen was irritated because she'd spent a lot of time speculating on exactly that subject. "This is serious. I need to reach him for business. Can you get a message to him?"

"Of course I can. Keep your pants on," Margery said.

Helen wondered why everything sounded suggestive.

"Go on back home," Margery said. "I'll handle it."

Margery worked her magic. She found Phil, and he found the authorities.

At seven the next morning, Savannah and Helen were standing at the dock in Hank's backyard, like mourners at a grave. Savannah stared into the dark water. Helen looked for Phil, but he wasn't there. It was an achingly beautiful day.

Helen didn't know how long it took the police dive team to find Laredo's little yellow car. Time seemed to stretch, then fall away. When the battered Honda was pulled from the canal, Savannah did not say a word. Helen was afraid to offer any comfort, even a hug. If she touched Savannah, she would shatter, and they'd never put the pieces back together.

When the grim business of resurrecting the dead car was complete, the police opened the trunk. There was a body inside. The police would not let Savannah see it, but they said it was a small blond woman wearing short-shorts and one red high heel.

Laredo had been found.

"It's over," Savannah said. For a brief moment, she looked like her old self. "I can bury my little sister. And she won't wear a dress slit up the back."

•   •   •

At sunset, Helen was sitting by the Coronado pool with Margery and Peggy. Pete sat on Peggy's shoulder, munching an asparagus spear. The chubby parrot was on a diet.

Helen brought out a box of white wine. Peggy found a can of cashews. Margery added a plate of chocolate-dipped strawberries. The evening breeze sent bougainvillea blossoms sailing across the pool. It was just like old times.

"So tell us what happened this morning," Margery said, "after they pulled out the body."

"The police got a search warrant for the house," Helen said. "They were looking for evidence to link Laredo to Hank Asporth."

"You think they'll nail the bastard?" Margery took a big bite of her strawberry. It dripped on her purple shirt.

"I hope so. He can say Laredo's fingerprints were in his house because he dated her. But he'll have a harder time explaining away her purse. It was in the same closet where I found her red shoe. They found other stuff, too. He's been charged with the murder of Laredo Manson."

"I thought Mindy killed Laredo." Peggy picked up a cashew. Pete eyed it.

"I heard her say it, right before she went up in flames— and off to hell. Once the car was found, Hank started babbling and his lawyer couldn't shut him up. He swears Mindy strangled Laredo and he was only a terrified bystander."

"But that's true, isn't it? Aren't you going to tell them about Mindy's confession?" Peggy ate her cashew and picked up another. Pete watched with beady-eyed interest.

"Hank could have stopped her from killing Laredo. He hid the body and nearly worried Savannah into her own grave. I'm not testifying on his behalf," Helen said. "He kept his silence—I'll keep mine."

"What happened the night Laredo was killed?" Margery took a healthy gulp of wine.

"I think I've pieced it together from random remarks by the police, some stuff Savannah said and educated guesses. I know Laredo got some damning information from Hank's home computer the night he'd abandoned her to talk on his cell phone."

"Served him right," Margery said. "I hate people who ignore you to yak on their cell phones. So she put it all on that red disk and tried to blackmail him?"

"Yep. Hank offered Laredo twenty thousand dollars for the disk, then doubled his offer. I think the cops found some uncashed checks in her name. But Laredo didn't want money. She wanted Hank to marry her. Savannah told me that. The confirmation was in the Girdner Surveys files."

"Where?" Peggy finally popped the cashew in her mouth. A disappointed Pete bit his asparagus.

"Laredo told the survey taker that she lived at Hank's house. I saw that information in the Girdner files. Laredo wanted to be Hank's wife and have the big house and a place in Lauderdale society. I think that's why she was at his house the night she died: Laredo threatened to go public with the information if he didn't set a wedding date.

"Hank was not going to marry her. Laredo was definitely going to talk. It would have brought down the whole money-laundering operation. That's when Mindy strangled Laredo."

"With the same scarf that caught on fire?" Margery liked the gruesome details.

"I don't know," Helen said.

"How'd they get rid of the body so quick?" Margery said.

"The cops think Hank and Mindy carried the body to Laredo's car, which was parked in Hank's garage, and put it in the trunk. Mindy removed the drink glasses and other signs of Laredo. Hank stuck a murder mystery in the VCR.

"He was congratulating himself when he noticed one red heel and her purse by the couch. He tossed them in the guest-room closet as the police rang the doorbell."

"And where was Mindy?" Peggy listened spellbound, yet another cashew in her hand. Pete moved stealthily toward it.

"She drove the car with Laredo's body in it to the driveway next door. Then she went for a walk until the police left. When the cops were gone, Hank and Mindy dumped the car in the canal. They had some trouble with it. We'd had a lot of rain that week, and the car sank into the mud and tore up Hank's backyard when the wheels spun.

"His lawn service told the police he wanted them to replace the damaged grass. They have the order. Hank called them the day after Laredo was strangled. Hank still owes them money, so they'll be happy to testify against him."

"How come no one saw the car go into the canal?" Margery said. "It's bigger than a bread box and bright yellow."

"Hank's next-door neighbor wasn't home. The other neighbor was almost deaf. The house across the canal was shuttered and the snowbird owner wasn't in Florida until January."

"And what about Mindy's car? There's no parking on those private streets." Peggy's cashew was suspended in midair. Pete leaned forward, watching it.

"On Las Olas, where she'd been drinking before she showed up at Hank's house. Mindy took a cab over to Hank's because she was afraid of a DWI. The police found the cab records. Hank drove Mindy to her car afterward. Pushing a car into a canal must be a sobering experience. She drove home—but a parking ticket placed her on Las Olas that evening."

"Ow!" Peggy said, as Pete grabbed her cashew and ate it.

The newspapers reported that sixteen people died in the fire at the Mowbry mansion. Uncounted careers went up in smoke that night. Two city council members and a state senator announced that they wanted to spend more time with their families. They would not be running for reelection. There were twelve early retirements in corporate Lauderdale.

The assistant United States attorney general in the Southern District of Florida refused to prosecute Hank Asporth for the murder of Mindy Mowbry. But the prosecutor did want him for killing a witness—and Laredo's murder carried a death sentence. Hank sang to save his skin. He got life without possibility of parole, but he won't be sunning himself in some federal country club.

Thanks to Hank's testimony, Dr. Melton Mowbry and his partner, Dr. Damian Putnam, along with his funeral director wife, Patricia Wellneck, and the boiler-room bosses Vito, Penelope and Carlo Xavier Cavarelli, were indicted by a federal grand jury for Medicare fraud, money laundering and conspiracy to commit wire fraud. All those coast-to-coast calls were interstate wire communications. They were each sentenced to twenty years.

The burned-out Mowbry mansion was leveled and the property sold to pay Dr. Mowbry's legal bills. A sixty-something Dallas car dealer bought the land. He plans to build a newer, bigger mansion on the site. It will have three swimming pools, including one with a swim-up bar for his twenty-year-old trophy wife.

But that was in the future . . .

"I start my new job on Monday," Helen said.

"Isn't it a little soon to go back to work? The boiler room has only been closed three days." Margery was in her yard, whacking off dead palm fronds with a long-handled cutter.

Whack! Chop! Thud!

A branch hit the sidewalk, and Helen backed away.

"What are you getting yourself into this time?" Margery said. "I'm not sure I can take much more excitement at my age. Please tell me it's not another dirty boiler-room operation."

Whack! Chop! Thud!

"Absolutely not," Helen said. "I'll be surrounded by chiffon and flowers. I'll be with the richest people in Lauderdale on the happiest day of their lives."

"You're working at a funeral home with the loved one's heirs."

"Wrong. I'm working at an exclusive bridal shop. We're talking ten-thousand-dollar dresses."

Whack! Chop! Thud!

"Well, that's a relief. How much trouble can you get into

zipping women into wedding gowns? Maybe you can get a good deal on a dress for yourself."

"Not with my luck with men," Helen said. "The only aisle I'll walk down is at the supermarket. I think I'll go sit by the pool."

Whack! Chop! Thud!

Margery attacked the palm with renewed fury, cutting off its coconuts. "Men!" she muttered, as she de-nutted the palm.

Helen hadn't heard from Phil since the night she'd rescued him. He'd kissed her good-bye and vanished. She sat by the pool in the noonday sun and pretended to page through the paper. She was really watching Phil's door.

Margery said nothing, but Helen could hear her thinking, "I told you so."

She'd been stupid again. She knew it. Phil was another handsome jerk. He was never coming back.

She was dozing in the chaise longue when Margery woke her up. "Why don't you take a nap inside?" she said. "You're going to get sunburned. I'll bring you some food later."

"Thanks, but I'm not hungry." Helen stood up stiffly. Her scorched back and whip-slashed chest and neck still hurt. She went inside, spread aloe vera lotion on her burns, and fell asleep on her bed with her arm around her cat.

She was awakened two hours later by a knock on her door.

Margery, Helen thought. She was such a mother hen, fussing over Helen and bringing sandwiches, chocolate and wine.

"I'm fine." Helen opened the door. "I don't need any—Phil!"

He was standing on her doorstep, impossibly tanned and handsome. His ponytailed hair was silver-white. His broken nose went off in an interesting direction.

"I wanted to thank you," he said. "I'm about finished here. I'll have to go back to Washington. But I thought I'd take a few days to kick back and see Fort Lauderdale. Want to go with me?"

Helen studied the soft hollow at his throat. It looked vulnerable. She remembered his hands when they pulled her out of the fire last year. They were strong.

"I'd love it. I can show you places the tourists never see," Helen said.

"Where?"

"Right here." She opened the door to her apartment. "How do you feel about cheap champagne for breakfast?"

Please read on for an excerpt from

the next Dead-End Job mystery

JUST
MURDERED

Coming from Signet in May 2005

It was the morning of the lost men.

They sat on Millicent's gray husband couch like sailors stranded on a desert isle, dazed and bleak. Helen thought the couch cast a spell on men, sucking out their money and their hope.

One couch castaway was in his late twenties. Mark was a lawyer who looked like he was wearing a tie even when he had on a Polo shirt. His bride, Courtney, was in butt-sprung shorts and broken-down mules. Helen wouldn't wear that outfit to take out the trash.

The bloom is off that rose, she thought. Helen saw the couple in twenty years, gone to seed and planted in matching recliners.

"I haven't given Courtney the ring yet," Mark said. "She's picking out the dress. I guess we have to get engaged."

He sounded so hopeless, Helen said, "You don't have to. It's not too late."

"I don't have any choice," he said.

The bride marched out of the dressing room, flushed with triumph. Millicent carried a plastic-shrouded gown. Courtney paid for the dress, then dragged her not-yet-fiance with her like a newly captured slave.

"How do you pick out the dress before you get the ring?"

Helen said when the couple left. Courtney's quick-march through the store had left a gaggle of gowns tangled on their hangers. Helen pried them apart carefully, protecting the delicate fabrics.

Millicent was rehanging rejected gowns. "Are you kidding? I get brides in here who don't have the groom yet. If a woman wants to marry, she will. She goes out and gets herself a man. Don't believe that stuff about women waiting for the right man to pop the question. In my experience, women do the picking. The smart ones let the guys think it was their idea."

"That groom sounded awfully trapped."

"He trapped himself," Millicent said. "Mark wants to make partner at a big Lauderdale law firm. He's marrying the boss's daughter."

"How do you know this?"

"Courtney told me."

"She doesn't care?" Helen dropped a heavy duchesse satin in surprise. Good thing Millicent had her back turned and didn't see it hit the floor.

Millicent's white hair disappeared into the snowy gowns, making her look headless. Now she faced Helen, using a blood-red nail to emphasize her words. "Listen. Courtney is getting what she wants—an ambitious husband. Mark is getting what he wants—a partnership in a big firm. People always get what they want, Helen. They just don't realize it."

Millicent looked out the shop's front window. "And I'm getting what I want. Kiki's back. That's her Rolls. She's ready to spend more to spite her ex. She's going to bleed Brendan dry with this wedding. I swear, the only way he'll stop her spending is to kill her."

Millicent put the last dress on the rack. "His loss is my gain. Helen, run upstairs and get Desiree's dress from the seamstress. I'll take some veils to the fitting room."

Helen stopped to peek at the Rod and Kiki show. This time, it was disappointing. Kiki's exit from the Rolls was decorous. She wore a black pantsuit, so there was no southern exposure. She didn't molest the chauffeur. Desiree crept out behind her mother, wearing something rumpled.

Helen ran up the steps to the seamstress's room. Desiree's heavy Hapsburg princess dress hung on a rack, bristling with colored dressmaker's pins and encrusted with crystal. Helen carried it carefully as she would an irritated porcupine.

In the fitting room, she helped Desiree into the gown. The bride was annoyingly limp, like a protestor who'd collapsed on police lines.

"Straighten your shoulders," her mother commanded. "And smile. You're a bride, not a corpse."

The bride did look more dead than alive. Desiree failed to smile, but she dutifully tried on veils. Some went to her fingertips. Others fell to the floor. Desiree could have been in a coma for all the reaction she showed.

"Which do you like?" Millicent asked, hoping for some response.

Desiree shrugged.

Of course, Kiki had an opinion. "That long veil has the same beading as the dress. I like it."

"It's a bit heavy, don't you think?" Millicent said, tactfully.

Desiree looked like a ghost haunting her own wedding.

"It needs a crown," Kiki said. "Something to brighten it up."

Millicent saw a chance to make Kiki's bill bigger. "Helen, go get that crystal crown off the display."

The crown was five hundred bucks, more than Helen made in a week. Perhaps it was worker's sympathy that made her glance out the window and see Rod the chauffeur standing next to the car, mopping sweat off his brow with a white handkerchief.

Helen came back with the crown and said, "Kiki, your chauffeur looks hot. You want to let him come in and cool off?"

"My chauffeur is hot," Kiki said suggestively. "Let him sweat. He's well paid."

"Helen," Millicent said. "Can you help me with a delivery in the back room?"

She dragged Helen into her office, shut the door, and said in a whisper, "Listen, Helen, Kiki wants her chauffeur to stand by that car. That's his job. He's not a husband, although God knows he has some of the same duties."

"At least he's well-paid," Helen said.

"He thinks he is, the fool," Millicent said. "Kiki's had many chauffeurs. She pays them minimum wage and puts them in her will for a million bucks. When she bounces them, she writes them out. Gets herself cheap help that way. It must be a shock for those young men to go from millionaire dreams to minimum-wage reality. I can't imagine what it's like."

I can, Helen thought. I used to make six figures and live in a mansion before I caught Rob with my next-door neighbor. I'd kill Kiki if she pulled that on me.

"How do you know these things?" Helen whispered.

"It's the talk of the town," Millicent said.

Which town? Helen wondered. No one at the Coronado discussed it.

"This chauffeur is about to get his walking papers," Millicent said. "Kiki didn't grope him when she got out of the car."

The doorbell chimed. "I'll get that," Millicent said. "You go back to Desiree."

Desiree was wearing the veil with the five-hundred-dollar crown. She looked like it gave her a headache.

"Do you like it?" Helen asked.

Desiree shrugged. Helen wanted to shake her. Why didn't she stand up for herself?

Helen was grateful when Millicent stuck her head in the dressing room and said, "The groom's here. Should I send him back?"

"Isn't it bad luck for the groom to see the dress?" Helen said.

"Join the twenty-first century," Kiki said. "These days, the groom may pick out the dress."

"Luke might as well see it," Desiree said, as if he was viewing a fatal accident. "I'll be out in a minute. Just leave me alone."

Helen tiptoed out front for a quick look at the groom. Luke was definitely scenic. He wasn't tall, probably about the same size as Millicent. But he was perfectly made from his cleft chin to his well-shod feet. His deep-brown hair was so thick, Helen wanted to run her fingers through it. Luke's lightweight blue sweater and gray pants were nothing special. Yet Helen noticed them, because they seemed so absolutely right.

Luke was with a skinny man about sixty dressed in black. His clothes and goatee screamed, "I am an artiste."

"I'm Luke Praine," the groom said to Helen and Millicent. "This is my director, the owner of the Sunnysea Shakespeare Playhouse, Chauncey Burnham."

"Kiki, darling, so glad to see you." Chauncey had a sycophant's smile. His lips were unpleasantly red and flexible. Helen wondered if that was from smooching patrons' posteriors.

"Really, Chauncey, can't I have any peace?" Kiki said.

"I saw your car and I had to come over and say hello." Chauncey's smile slipped slightly.

"You've said it. Now go." Kiki started to turn away.

"Er, could we have a moment alone?"

"Anything you have to say, Chauncey, you can say right here." Kiki was daring him.

The director took a deep breath, rubbed his goatee and pursed his rubbery red lips. "Alright, I will. Kiki, you promised my company five thousand dollars so we could get through December. Now you say you can't give us any money until January first."

"I can't, Chauncey. The wedding has been expensive."

"The landlord says he'll close us down next week in the middle of the run. We haven't been reviewed yet, Kiki. The critic for the *Herald* is coming tonight. I know we'll get a big crowd when we get a favorable review." Chauncey was pleading now, like a mother begging for the life of her child.

"*If* you get a favorable review. He called your last production 'uninspired and derivative.'" Kiki's face was a frozen mask of meanness.

Chauncey showed a brief flash of anger. Then he puckered properly. "Kiki, please. You know Luke is marvelous in this production. I beg of you, help us. We won't make it to January without your support. We'll die."

Kiki's smile was cruel. "Only the strong survive. And don't beg, Chauncey. It's weak."

Chauncey hung his head. Helen pretended to check a price tag. Millicent moved away. Humiliation might be catching.

Desiree appeared in her frumpy wedding dress and veil, an expensive specter. "You could pray for her to die, Chauncey," she said in a dead voice. "She's left you a hundred thousand in her will."

There was a shocked silence. Chauncey turned white, down to those mobile lips. "I'd better go," he said. "You look lovely, Desiree."

"I look like shit," Desiree said. "But rich shit."

"Mind your manners, dear," Kiki said. "Or I'll write you out of the will."

Shop till You Drop

A DEAD-END JOB MYSTERY

Working for a living
can be murder....

"Dead-on funny."
—Jerrilyn Farmer

"Irresistible."—Jane Heller

Elaine Viets

0-451-20855-2
www.penguin.com